Pawns of the Wall

A Love Story

Derrik Woodbury

Coming soon from Derrik Woodbury

The second edition of:

Deception

For

Carson and Rex

Chapter 1

I never meant to be complicit in the death of my only, real friend in Patagonia. I certainly didn't want the possible father of my child to suffer untold agonies by torturous nerve toxin poisoning. After all, I'm a physician, a healer. And then to be accepted into the community as a leader, a stalwart citizen afterwards, well, it's a little hard to comprehend.

This all came about because I thought I had the moral high ground. Which perhaps shows there is ignorance in experience and innocence in knowledge. But this holier than thou attitude doesn't keep anyone from suffering.

Chapter 2

I looked through the screen door and out past the porch. The Arizona night was in total darkness from where I stood in the cabin. In the distance, I saw headlights. Then, as if an afterthought, the sound of an engine became audible.

"Someone's coming," I said.

"Finally," Mary said. "Dylan has no sense of time." As the vehicle grew closer I could tell it was a truck.

"It's not Dylan," I said. With that, Mary threw her blunt into the fireplace. Sparks jumped up the flue. Outside the taillights of the truck illuminated a plume of red dust in the wake of the vehicle as it drew closer. The driver was riding the brakes. On the driver's door, large block letters said "Santa Cruz" above a fluorescent six-sided star on the modified Ram 2500.

"Then who …" Mary began.

"It's the sheriff."

*   *   *

It wasn't the Sheriff, though. It was his deputy, Bill Sturgill. The Sheriff was wily. This minion, not so much.

"Evening, Bill," I said as the deputy approached.

"Hello, Harper," the deputy nodded, pausing on the first step. "Can I come in?"

I thought of the lingering smoke in the cabin. It was illegal to possess recreational marijuana in Arizona. "I've got company, Bill."

"Is it Mary Durant?"

"Why would you say that?"

"Isn't that her car right there?" he said, pointing to Mary's Prius parked at the side of the cabin.

"Ahh … yes. Yes, it is," I said, somewhat chastened. Maybe I wasn't very wily either. Still, Sturgill made no attempt to enter the cabin.

"Sheriff wants to see both of you at the office. Tell her to get dressed."

"She is dressed. What's this about?"

"That's all he said."

Bill wasn't the type of person who would admit he didn't know something. "Give us a minute."

"I'll wait for you in the truck and you can follow me into town." His radio squawked from the truck and he turned to go back to his vehicle. Then he paused. "Sorry about the hour," he said over his shoulder.

When we came out of the cabin, Sturgill was leaning against the sheriff decal. "Change of plans. We're going to meet the sheriff at the coroner's office. It's next door to the Sheriff Department building, but the parking lot is different so pay attention when I turn in."

"Why are we meeting the sheriff at the coroner's office in the middle of the night?" I asked.

"Looks like we have a dead body."

Mary looked at me with a bewildered expression. "Do you want to drive in with me?" I asked. She hesitated.

"No," Mary finally decided. "I'll follow you."

"Don't fall too far behind," the deputy said as he pulled himself into the truck. The big engine roared with ignition.

I walked Mary to her Prius and winced as I bent forward to open the door for her. My ribs were sore on my right side and I was sure there was a big bruise developing. The adrenaline was still surging through my body so the pain was not obvious to others. Sturgill led us back into town.

*   *   *

As I hypnotically trailed the deputy's truck lights on the deserted road and checked my rearview mirror to make sure Mary was still behind me, my thoughts drifted back to our last hour at the cabin. We both had been restless waiting for Dylan to arrive. To give Mary some space, I opened the screen door and walked out onto the porch to stare at the night. The gloaming hour had passed and the high mountain wildlife south of Patagonia was coming alive. The wind had died down and the earth was cooling off. An early chill in the air portended a cold night.

Despite the clear sky abundant with stars, it was very dark where the porch light faded twenty yards from the front step. In the distance to the right, I could see the flickering light of a campfire on the beach of Lake Patagonia. Left of the campfire, I could barely make out the communication tower lights on the top of Red Mountain. I knew the desert was alive and deadly out there, whether by man or beast, but it looked innocent in the darkness. I idly wondered if Mary would stay with me tonight if Dylan didn't show.

"Dylan could be late for any number of good reasons," Mary had said. "But he should have called."

"This is a very busy time for me," Dylan had told me earlier. That he hadn't called was commonplace with Dylan. Thinking of others was not his strong suit. Looking through the screen door I could see Mary sitting on the couch. Her bare feet and legs were tucked underneath her. The rich curve of her calves compressed together. I had come home to her sitting in that position while waiting for me many times in the past. I stopped peering through the screen's scattered light and closed my eyes. For a moment, I was back with her a few months ago when we were a couple. I shook that memory off and opened my eyes. Mary's face was silhouetted by the forty-watt end table lamp. I couldn't see the deep blue iris of her eyes, but I could make out the gentle contours of her mouth. She seemed far away, deep in thought. I shuddered. The night was growing cooler but the biting breeze that sliced through me was made of melancholy, not wind. I went back inside.

The shadows inside the cabin flickered with the light of the dying fire. "I tried to call you earlier, but it went right to voicemail," I said.

"I had a doctor's appointment in Tucson."

"Again?" She didn't answer. "Is everything okay?"

"I'm fine. I've just been having some stomach troubles."

I was going to ask what she meant by 'stomach troubles,' but this didn't seem like the right time. "You might as well get some sleep," I said and went to the stone fireplace and poked the spent wood with the fire iron. Sparks flew up and a brief burst of flames resulted. I replaced the fire-screen.

"I'm going to give him a little more time. He tries so hard," Mary said.

I wondered how she knew that with such conviction. What did they even have in common to talk about? I had suffered Dylan's discourses on all things political. Mary was very intelligent but she was young enough to be a blank canvas. Was it naiveté or enthrallment that prompted her to embrace his diatribes, let alone his conclusions?

"It's getting cold. Let me get you a blanket," I said, walking into the back room.

A gust of wind whistled through the trees. It blew the tall ocotillo shrub on the east side of the cabin hard enough to bend it into the wall and strafe the house repeatedly with its slender branches like fingernails scratching a blackboard. As if the desert was flogging the cabin. The wind died down and the green whip of the ocotillo scraped more tenderly against the log siding. The cabin creaked. I came back with the worn, thin, Pendleton blanket Mary liked so much. I unfolded it and placed it around her shoulders.

"He's never *this* late," she repeated, more to herself than to me.

"I'll be in here," I said gesturing to the inner room. The curtains were still open in the small room I used as a study so I closed them to keep the warmth from leaking out the warped window. The desert sun spares nothing during the day but creates a vacuum when it descends at dusk. The room seemed smaller than I remembered. I stretched out on the couch. Although exhausted, I knew I couldn't sleep let alone rest as multiple mental images of the night bombarded my brain. Mary had said she and Dylan went to breakfast at her favorite diner in Patagonia early this morning. She told me Dylan had criticized her shoes. "Too clunky," he had said. She told him this was Arizona, not Paris. But what else had they talked about?

I shut my eyes and she was my Mary again. Her body draped along the inside crease of the couch and folded around mine. My left arm up and around her neck resting along her spine. My hand ending in the hollow of the small of her back. Her head on my chest. My reverie was broken by the persistent cold draft coming from the window leaking through the curtains. The spell extinguished, I twisted and turned on the couch. I was restless and couldn't get comfortable. I went back out to the front room.

"Do you love him, Mary?"

"Let's wait until he gets here before going into that." She wrapped the blanket securely around her.

There had been a time when I thought her love would save me. I had never felt a peace as pure as her head on the pillow next to me. I gently touched the blanket covering her shoulder.

She had started rolling a joint. "Would you like one?" she asked. "This helps settle my stomach."

"No."

"It will make the waiting easier."

"Does Dylan smoke weed?"

"Oh no. He says it's against the law."

The lamplight hit her face more fully now as she bent over and intently twisted the two ends of the reefer. The clean, strong lines of her high cheekbones arched down in their heart shape to her pressed lips. The dim light infused her soft skin giving the unblemished cheeks a faint yellow hue. She straightened up to draw deeply on her bulbous creation and her face disappeared out of the light and into the shadow.

"He probably thinks we fell asleep and he'll pop by in the morning," I said, although I didn't believe a word of it.

"No. He wanted to see us." She exhaled, holding the joint away from her body and looking at it. "I haven't had one of these for a while. I can feel it helping already."

I wondered again if she would stay if Dylan scrubbed this strange meeting. It was going to be a cold night. Up this high in the Santa Rita Mountains winter was slower to vacate the land close to the

Mexico/United States border. If she stayed, I could feel her warmth against me again. I would not wake up alone. We could have coffee together as dawn eased over the eastern peaks. Then I came back to my senses.

"He's not coming," I said. "If he was coming he'd be here by now."

"Why isn't he here?" she asked with innocent confusion.

I hesitated. "I'm not sure."

"Didn't you two have dinner tonight?"

"He said he couldn't make dinner and wanted to meet back here around 10:00PM."

I walked over to the door. A coyote howled in the distance. The brooding outline of the mountains north of the Sonoita Valley was now visible in the early light of moonrise. The Patagonia mountains loomed south of me. As my eyes adjusted I could make out the final curve of Mt. Washington's peak. The Sierra San Antonio mountain range could be seen winding its way south to Mexico. The mountains tapered gently in their journey to the horizon as if the effort exhausted them.

That's when I saw the headlights.

*   *   *

When we arrived, the sheriff was smoking a cigarette under a faded, unilluminated sign that said "Coroner's Office." Only the light from the doorway made it readable. Mary and I followed a few steps behind Sturgill to the building's entrance where the sheriff stood next to a brick wall that provided shelter from the quickening late night breeze. The sheriff threw his cigarette butt onto the asphalt and ground it down with the heel of a hefty cowboy boot. Mary knew the sheriff from her years in town, but I had only seen him from a distance. He made a gesture of tipping his hat to Mary as we approached.

"Good evening Miss Durant. Sorry to drag you down here this late in the evening," he said. Turning to me, "I know who you are, Doc, but we haven't met. My name is Lorence and I'm the sheriff." He did not extend his hand. I nodded in recognition.

For a long moment, Lorence gazed intensely at Mary, then shifted his attention back to me. "I have some bad news. Dylan Kermer is dead." Mary gasped. "Why don't we come in out of the chill for a moment?" He turned and opened the door to the building. Mary slumped against my shoulder. I put my arm around her and led her through the entrance. Sturgill trailed in behind us.

We walked into a typical county anteroom. Plastic chairs welded together were set against the outer window and I guided Mary to one of them. I could feel her shallow quick breathing beside me. I squeezed her shoulder and whispered to her, "Deep breaths, Mary, deep breaths." Lorence looked at us dispassionately.

"I need someone to identify the body," he said with a trace of impatience. "Then we can go next door and chat a bit."

I looked at Mary. "I'm feeling queasy again," she said.

"I can do it," I said quietly to her. "Is that okay?" She nodded yes. "Will you be alright?" Again, she nodded yes. I turned to the silent deputy-in-waiting. "Bill, could you get her a glass of water and stay with her until I get back?" His sigh implied consent.

I followed the sheriff to a set of automatic double doors. He pulled out an ID card on a retractable zip line attached to his pocket and palmed it against the keypad. The doors creaked open.

Lorence hadn't been waiting at the morgue to comfort me. He watched me closely. I met his gaze unflinchingly. Then he led me to the basement. There was total silence as we walked to the storage area. The absence of background music itself was unnerving. Every public place has at least elevator music filtering about. We tune it out so effectively that when we're faced with quiet, it's unsettling. There were no religious artifacts in this area of the building. Even in this predominantly Catholic community, no crosses were on any of the walls. Leave your religion at the door, this basement was saying. This is the real thing.

The sheriff paused at an oversized entryway. "Normally the next-of-kin is here to identify the deceased and we show them photos of distinguishing features carefully screened to minimize upsetting the relative or friend. We don't have one of those fancy video hook-ups that the big city budgets allow. Heck, we can barely get funding for elementary school down here in Santa Cruz County. With a murder, we like to have the body observed and identified. We've found it can be very helpful in our investigation."

"I didn't kill him," I told him.

11

"Didn't say you did," Lorence said opening the door. "Right this way." A body was already in the room. It was naked on a medical examiner's steel table. The table had troughs around the entire periphery for fluids to drain. The table looked cold, hard and uncomfortable. Lorence put on a pair of latex gloves and I moved closer, the steel gleaming from the harsh lights. At first glance, I was stunned and time slowed to a crawl for me. Dylan's skin was an off-white, bluish pale. He had no hue. His body was an achromatic gloom. His eyes were open, vacant and unblinking. Everything he ever knew, gone. All intelligence extinguished. Whatever made Dylan unique was nonexistent. What always struck me the hardest in viewing the dead body of someone I had known, was the total absence of their life force. Gone was that ineffable energy in us when we're alive. What is left is mere flesh beginning to rot. Good for replenishing the fields. Food for some creature to create energy to be recycled into the universe.

Then my mind recovered from the shock and my experience in clinical observation began to take over. Dylan's eyes were protruded and his face was swollen as if he had been choked, but there were no bruises about his neck. Blisters had formed around his mouth. Dried saliva trails led from his nose down his cheeks and chin. There were two long caked rivers of green snaking down from the corners of his mouth ending at his collarbones. His left arm was at an unsightly angle above his elbow and bruising had pooled along his triceps posteriorly. His right shoulder was swollen. He had soiled himself and the stench was overwhelming.

"Well?" Lorence asked. He was still watching me closely.

"Yes. That is Dylan Kermer."

"It's a weird presentation. Ever seen anything like this before?"

"I'm not a pathologist."

"I'm not asking you to dissect him," the sheriff said sarcastically. "What do you think killed him?"

"I suppose it could have been a heart attack."

"Oh, come on! At his age?" Lorence said with a dismissive wave of his hand. "Any other thoughts?"

"It looks like he choked on his saliva and vomited. He also lost bowel and bladder control."

"How about this broken arm?" Lorence pointed to the angulated limb. "Do you think he was tortured?"

"I can't say. His right shoulder looks dislocated. He might have had a violent seizure."

Lorence acted like he was giving a lesson to a fifth grader. He reached his gloved hands under Dylan's left shoulder and rolled the upper body to the right. With his right hand holding the body in this position he roughly grabbed Dylan's hair and twisted his head to expose the back of his head. "Even you can see the bullet entrance wound in the back of his skull if you looked for it," the sheriff said triumphantly. Like all bullies, he relished the upper hand. "You have to learn to turn the body over. He was shot in the back of the head. That's what happened. It must have been a small caliber weapon because it didn't come out of the brain." He let Dylan fall back on to the table and for a moment I thought the body's momentum might carry it off the table and onto the floor. The left side of Dylan hung out over the edge but stabilized there. Lorence paid it no attention. He saw me looking at something else.

I was surprised to see a small tattoo etched into Dylan's left groin. I moved closer to examine it. It was a cat. Actually, two small cats. One black and one red cat. Their tails were up and ears perked. They looked about to pounce although their visage was more curious than predatory.

"What do you make of that? "the sheriff asked.

"No clue. Didn't know he had a tattoo."

"I probably should have had Ms. Durant identify the body," he smirked. "She might have had more knowledge of this clue." I remained stone-faced, trying not to give him any satisfaction from his crass innuendo. "Do you think he was in a gang?" he added, as the thought came to him. Not too much of a filter there.

I was getting tired of his posturing. I turned to him. "A small tattoo of cats on his groin? I don't think so Sheriff, unless the gangs in your county are a little cuddlier than those out east. Kermer was straight as an arrow. The darkest connection I can make of this 'finding' is a potential school fraternity hazing pledge. The body is Kermer. If you need me to sign something, I will. Let's get on with it." In my mind, I saw Dylan in the Wild Horse animatedly making his political arguments. Then a brief image of him dancing with Mary and grinning like Lewis Carroll's

Cheshire Cat. I shook my head to lose the images of the dance and the tattoo.

"You're not going to toss your lunch, are you?" Lorence said with a mean twinkle in his eye, mistaking my head shake.

"I'm fine. I've identified him. Don't you have other people to do the forensic autopsy?"

Lorence shrugged. "Thought you might be interested. You being a hotshot Eastern doctor and all. They'll get to the autopsy tomorrow. He's not going anywhere." I turned and walked to the door. Lorence made a gesture to a window that must have been a reciprocal two-way mirror and then turned to follow me. I resisted the urge to make my own gesture to the mirror and walked out.

We walked back up the stairs in silence. What was gnawing at me and what I hadn't told the sheriff was that Dylan's body exhibited all the signs of being poisoned. Was the gunshot before or after he died? Was Dylan shot to cover up another means of death? Was he tortured? It would be harder to answer those questions if they waited a day to perform the autopsy. I gathered up Mary from the waiting room. She appeared vapid and spiritless, having withdrawn into a safe place inside herself. She let me take her elbow and the four of us trekked across the parking lot to the sheriff's office.

Chapter 3

Even well into the 21st century, in Santa Cruz County the Sheriff was a person to be reckoned with. If you wanted to be left alone you went along with the man who wore the star. Veterans of many happy hours at the Wild Horse Saloon recounted stories of people without longstanding roots to the community disappearing from the county after some skirmish with the Sheriff Department. There were always the open legal methods of enforcing the law, but rumor had it there were more expedient methods employed by the Department to keep the sheriff's peace. Townspeople whispered of agitators vanishing from the area. Even with social media and the Internet, they were never heard from again.

Frank Lorence had held his job as the elected Sheriff of Santa Cruz County for almost thirty years. He ran unopposed for two-thirds of that time and was a formidable local force. A pilot in the Vietnam War, he had spent much of his early adult life at Davis Monthan Air Force Base on the southern edge of Tucson. Like many of the men at Davis Monthan he remembered fondly the health, adventure and good times of his youth and drifted back to the Tucson area when his days of service on the Air Force's dime ended. He bought a small place outside of Rio Rico. He wasn't a farmer or a horse person, so when the sheriff position opened up after an untimely heart attack felled the post's previous occupant, Lorence campaigned hard on law and order while highlighting his military service. Over the years, Lorence had used his lawman influence to prosper through holdings in a medley of small businesses: a beer franchise out of South Tucson, a bustling artist's warehouse in Tubac, storage facilities in Rio Rico and cash opportunities here and there no one could trace. As often happens with the seductive power of elected officials, Lorence now felt entitled to such financial abuses. He slowly built his fiefdom and the citizens became comfortable with the status quo. He had proved fair if you were a voter and mean if you were not. This was still the wild west to Lorence, where bulls weren't challenged and neither was the sheriff. The end justified the means and might meant right. He lived by one credo: do whatever was necessary to keep his job and the privileges that went with the position.

Lorence's office was cold. The sheriff sat in a lush, dark brown leather swivel chair behind a large intricately carved mesquite desk of Mexican origin. The other furnishings were of county issue: institutional file cabinets and uncomfortable chairs for visitors. I helped Mary into her seat and sat down in the chair beside her. Lorence absentmindedly swiveled right and left in front of us. Even more so than in the morgue, I sensed this man was not my friend. He wouldn't like the uncertainty I brought to his office. He didn't know enough about me to predict my behavior and I wasn't a Santa Cruz voter.

I declined a cigarette and scrutinized Lorence. Forty years of whiskey had broken too many veins in his face. His leathered complexion couldn't mask the damage. The harsh Arizona sun had been ruthless to this man's skin. Crevasses deeper than the Everest Khumbu Icefall crisscrossed his visage. When he forced his obsequious smile as he turned to Mary, those crevasses folded like a cheap accordion. The sheriff appeared tired and old by the fluorescent light overhead but he visibly straightened gazing at his female visitor. I had heard the sheriff liked the ladies.

"If you prefer, Miss Durant, I could interview you in private," Lorence said with a drop of his chin and a squint of his eyes meant to exude charming politeness. His leer had the confidence of an experienced predator.

"I don't prefer," Mary said flatly.

Lorence's face hardened and his eyes narrowed.

I interjected. "What's this about Sheriff?"

Lorence slowly took his glare off Mary and turned to me.

"How long have you known Dylan Kermer?"

"A few months."

The sheriff turned to Mary. "You live with Kermer, is that right?"

"We spend time together."

Lorence sneered. He turned back to me. "And I understand she used to be with you."

"Why are we here Sheriff?"

"Kermer's dead," Lorence said. "You two seemed to know him best." He shrugged his shoulders. "It makes you, what we call 'people of interest.'" I maintained eye contact with Lorence and with effort, held my bland expression.

"You don't seem surprised at his death," Lorence said. I felt like he was poking me with a cattle prod.

"I knew something bad had happened or you wouldn't have called us down here in the middle of the night," I offered. I sneaked a glance at Mary. She still looked devastated. Her face was expressionless and pale. Her posture limp in the chair. She was still stunned; as if she was still processing the sheriff's words from outside the morgue. I felt bad because at this moment, I couldn't feel anything. "We didn't have anything to do with his death if that's what you're driving at," I added, turning back to Lorence. I thought of Mary. I didn't know what she might know, but she was in no condition to be questioned by law enforcement. I had to get her out of here.

"Wasn't he your friend?" Lorence said.

I answered quickly so Mary didn't have to. "I suppose so … yes, he was my friend," I answered. "He went his own way. But I knew him." Did I really?

"How do …" the sheriff stumbled for the right words. "How did you know him?"

What should I tell him? What could I tell him? Why should I explain how I met Dylan? I thought back to that night five months ago.

*   *   *

I had been sitting at the new bar the Wild Horse Saloon had just finished renovating and gazing out the large picture window when Dylan walked down the sidewalk of McKeown Avenue. He turned into the watering hole with a defiance straight out of a John Ford movie. The aura was immediately broken when he slipped and fell on the freshly polished floor. I jumped off my stool and helped him up. Only his pride was hurt. He mumbled something vulgar to the floor and quickly collected himself. The bottoms of his contemporary cowboy boots were as shiny as the new varnish on the bar top. Composing himself anew - a trait I would soon see in other situations - he introduced himself and ordered a beer.

"Mind if I join you," he asked.

"Not at all." He pulled out the stool next to me and sat down.

Seeing his handsome, cherubic face up close made me feel old. It was a feeling I had been having more and more of late. This counterpoint didn't help. Despite the ignominious entrance, Dylan was serious and mildly irritating from the start.

"Do locals hang out here or is this a tourist trap?" he asked.

I looked around. The place was empty except for us.

"Hard to tell."

Dylan lit up a cigarette. The bartender immediately came over. "There's no smokin' in here, son. You can go outside, away from the door, if you gotta smoke." Dylan snubbed out his cigarette on his drink napkin.

"I thought out West you could do whatever you want," he grumbled. "What happened to personal freedoms out here?" He said this a little too loud to the departing barkeep who did not take the bait. Dylan looked at me for validation.

"Nothing's constant but change," I said diplomatically.

"Change can be good, or it can be bad," he harrumphed. Dylan looked down at my running shoes. "You look more like a tourist," he decided. The comment was mildly annoying, but offered without malice. Another trait I would observe too frequently. "What brings you to this neck of the woods?" he added.

I normally don't talk to people about my life. Just because they ask, I don't believe they deserve to know all the personal details that go into my story. None of their business really. I'm not hungry for their approval, blame, sympathy, advice or criticism. Usually vague generalizations suffice and allow them to move on to what they really want to talk about: themselves. But something about Dylan piqued my interest.

*　　*　　*

"It's very late. Are we being charged with anything?" I asked the sheriff. "Do we need lawyers?"

"Not right this minute," Lorence said with a sigh, looking at his watch. It was well after midnight. I knew he was thinking foremost of his own fatigue rather the grinding gears of justice. "But I'm going to want to talk again - probably later today. Make sure Sturgill has your cell numbers." I looked at Mary. She had her cell phone cupped in her palm. It was on her lap below the level of the desk. I could see the red light on between her fingers. Lorence nodded to Mary. "This next time I'm going to talk to you separately. There'll be no need for lawyers but there are procedures that need to be followed. You can go." Then he added ominously, "For now." Despite her paleness, Mary faced Lorence implacably. How could she hold it together, I wondered? Her world was rocked. She had cared deeply for Dylan and now he was dead. All that promise: for him, for her, for both of them together … gone.

Our chairs squeaked as we both got up to leave.

"Not you Harper," the sheriff said. "You stay."

Mary began to protest which Lorence halted with one beefy palm raised.

"Not negotiable," he said.

"I'll be alright," I said to her. "Wait for me out there." I nodded to the lobby we had passed on arrival. "I won't be long." I looked at the sheriff to emphasize this point.

Lorence stood up and opened the door for Mary. I sat back down. If I got this out of the way maybe I could spare her the hassle. This was no place anyone wanted to come back to.

When the door closed, Lorence returned to his desk but he did not sit down.

"What do you want to know?" I said to Lorence. He remained standing behind his desk. Then he leaned forward resting on his outstretched arms, elbows locked. He was in full intimidation mode.

"Where were you tonight?"

"I had dinner at the Wild Horse. A lot of people could tell you that. The bartender and the waitress, for starters."

"Who did you have dinner with?"

"Just myself. I was supposed to have dinner with Kermer but he cancelled. Said he'd stop by my cabin later." I left it that. No reason to get chatty with this man.

"Why did he cancel?"

"He didn't say."

"What did you do after dinner?"

"It was already 9:00PM. I went home. It's about a fifteen-minute drive."

"Anybody see you?"

"I don't know. They might have seen my jeep. It was already dark."

Lorence looked down at me. He didn't like me and he didn't care if I knew it. I tried to show him I didn't care either with my poker face. I loved poker but was not the best bluffer.

"Did you stop anywhere?"

"No. Drove to my cabin."

"Then what?"

"Shortly after I got home, Mary showed up."

"Were you expecting her?"

"No. She said that Dylan had left her a message to meet him at my place."

"Didn't you find that strange?"

"A little," I admitted. "But I thought he was going to come clean about him and Mary."

He leaned even more forward on his hands. Trying to get into my face. Thankfully, it was a big desk. "And that didn't upset you?"

"No," I said. "I already knew. The only person in town who probably wasn't sure I knew about them was Dylan. It had been going on for a while."

"Pretty good reason for you to kill a man," Lorence said scornfully.

"Maybe in your world," I replied. Lorence bristled. I went on. "I didn't do it. I was jealous, of course, but I wouldn't have harmed him."

"Why not?" he spat out derisively.

"Because I think Mary loved him."

"So, she did it, you're saying?"

"No," I said, shaking my head. "You're missing the point. I think she loved him … and he probably loved her."

"People kill in the name of love all the time," Lorence said.

After a moment I asked, "Where did this happen?"

"I don't know where he was killed," Lorence said. He looked peeved. "His body was found off Highway 82 - halfway to Nogales. No attempt to hide the body. Truck driver who found him thought he saw a hurt deer off to the side of the road and pulled over. There was still some snow on the verge from that spitting we got this morning. The trucker thought the deer might have been hit by a car because he saw blood tracked on the snow. He came up on

Kermer's body and got sick. He contaminated the whole damn crime scene. Finally, he pulled himself together and called us."

"I don't know what Dylan was doing. Maybe he got into something. Maybe over his head."

"It never does any good to stick your nose where it doesn't belong," the sheriff said, staring hard at me. "You should remember that." The veiled warning was not lost on me.

"He was a believer," I said.

"What's that supposed to mean?"

"Just that he believed strongly in his ideals and convictions. He talked about them openly and would debate anyone, anywhere."

"Even if they didn't make an acorn's bit of sense?"

"They did to him."

Lorence hesitated. Then he continued. "His wallet was on him. Driver's license. Cash in it too. The truck driver was blubbering to everyone about that." Lorence shook his head like he was surrounded by idiots. "That will bring on a lot of attention. Pretty much rules out robbery. Too many people can see that."

"Can I go now?"

"One more thing. Do you know where Dave Nance is?"

Surprised, I stammered, "Why would I know where Dave Nance is?" Nance was the popular owner of The Writer's Feast – the busiest coffee house in town.

Lorence frowned. "We can't seem to locate his whereabouts." I was silent. The stillness aggravated the sheriff. "We received a tip early today," he continued, looking at his watch. "Early yesterday," he corrected himself. "It was a solid source regarding the tower explosion, so I had Sturgill follow Nance. He followed Nance to Phoenix where Nance met with a guy at a donut shop. Sturgill said they appeared to be arguing when some exchange was made. They must have gone out the back because Sturgill lost Nance at that point. Eventually Sturgill drove back here with his tail between his legs." Lorence looked disgusted with his deputy. I didn't say anything. "I thought you and Nance were close?"

"I enjoy talking to him – like everyone else who goes into the Feast." I stood up. "Can we call it a night?"

The sheriff looked exasperated. "Yeah," he finally said, grudgingly. He was allowing this only because he was tired. "Write your number down here." Lorence passed me a legal pad. "I'll want to talk to you again."

*   *   *

I walked out with Mary. We were both quiet. I did feel something. I felt hollow. Dylan was dead. All his loves, his passions, gone. All that could have been in his life had been taken away. If life was hope, then death was the absence of hope. The bluster that sustained me in the sheriff's office had evaporated.

Mary didn't say anything as we walked to our cars. The streets were wet. My mind rambled. I could hear water running in the bed of a small tributary of the Sonoita Creek. No doubt the creek was topped off by the passing shower while we were inside. Dylan had been found in some roadside snow. More precipitation at the higher elevations was always good for the desert. This creek might run for another month with a good snow dumping in the mountains. Eventually, though, it would revert back to the sandy ditch that belied its name. Death brought the Sonoran Desert into sharp relief. It was fairly wet for a desert, but without water it was a forbidding place. I could make out the ominous silhouette of saguaro cacti by the starlight, but I knew they were merely a sentinel for the ferocious flora I could not see. Bushes, plants and trees with an arsenal of sharp, spiny weapons were ready to prey on interlopers with fierce indifference and without forgiveness. Mary continued to walk robotically and in silence next to me. Unseen in the darkness of the desert, the detritus of love in Patagonia was scattered here as it was everywhere. Bodies and broken hearts in quiet homes just out of sight. Casualties of ego, possession, pride, ignorance, self-loathing, desperation, innocence and loneliness.

Mary shook her head when I offered a ride to her apartment. She shook her head no again when I offered to follow and make sure she got home safely. We reached her car. Her eyes wouldn't meet mine. She was still numb, I thought. She fixed her gaze on the lock. Then the door handle and finally the road ahead. I watched her drive off and I thought: people throw that word 'friend' around very loosely.

Chapter 4

The next morning, I called Mary to check on her. She sounded listless and her replies to my inquiries were disjointed. She sounded hollow. Distractedly she said she had to go get her things from Dylan's room. I was worried for her and offered to drive her. In her preoccupied state, she surprised me by accepting.

In the car, she kneaded a small Ziploc bag filled with kibble. "Embers has gone missing," was all she said when I picked her up. She loved her cat.

Dylan had been renting a corner suite in the Stage Stop Inn since his arrival. It made for a good home base. I had been in his place and it was expansive, yet cozy. The Inn was on the main street of town in the center of Patagonia and Dylan's rental was a sizable suite with a kitchenette. There was a door next to the flat screen in the bedroom which led to a balcony with two chairs. The spot overlooked McKeown Ave, the city park and the Creative Arts Center. The Wild Horse restaurant was on the ground floor, west of the lobby. A common wall and two independent entrances separated the restaurant from the bar.

The deputy sheriff's truck was parked outside the lobby entrance on McKeown. Mary and I climbed the winding inside stairs to the second floor. We walked through the mezzanine which had a small lending library, a few plush reading chairs, its own flat screen television and a computer desk with a printer for guest use. I followed her as she turned left at the hallway and walked towards the entrance to Dylan's suite. As we approached, we could see that his door was open. As we drew closer, Bill Sturgill stepped out of the doorway, simultaneously snapping off his latex gloves. The sight of Mary directly in front of the deputy startled him.

"Morning Miss Durant," Sturgill said straightening.

"Morning Bill," Mary said. Sturgill nodded at me. Mary made to go past Sturgill into the room. Sturgill stepped quickly into the doorway. "Can't go in there, Ma'am."

"I just want to get my things," Mary said.

"I can't let anyone in," Sturgill said uncomfortably. "Sheriff's orders. He says it's a crime scene."

"Surely you don't need my night clothes and underwear," Mary said. But Sturgill had recovered and was back on firm footing.

"Nobody goes in, and nothing goes out. Sheriff's orders. I was just going to put the tape on the door," he said, pointing to a yellow roll of police tape. We all stood motionless for a long moment.

"Any updates since last night?" I asked.

"We found his rental car in the hotel lot." Sturgill was happy to have something to say. "The gas tank was full," he added with some excitement.

"So, he went out in somebody else's car?" I asked.

"That's the way I read it," he said. "There are only a couple of cabs around town. I checked and Kermer didn't call either of them. Sheriff said it must be someone he knew," Sturgill added proudly.

"He could've walked," Mary mumbled.

"But he would need a car to meet us at my cabin," I said.

"Maybe he had an errand to run and he was going to come back to get his car," she said.

"Do you have any ideas?" I asked Sturgill.

"Probably illegals wanting his ID or money," Sturgill said.

"But the sheriff said his wallet was untouched," I said. Sturgill pondered that.

"Then a drug deal gone bad or …" he stopped.

"Were you going to say jealousy?"

"I was just thinking out loud," Sturgill said.

Probably not a good habit for this deputy, I thought. "Well if it was jealousy, it wasn't us," I said. "He didn't want to be a deputy sheriff, did he?"

Sturgill's nostrils flared slightly. "He never said anything about wanting my job. Or my wife." He turned to Mary. "Maybe after you have that talk with the sheriff, he'll let you come get your stuff," he said. "Under supervision of course." We heard lumbering steps on the stairway. Turning at the mezzanine exit and heading towards us was the sheriff.

"What are you doing here?" Lorence asked me gruffly.

"I didn't let them in," Sturgill interjected nervously.

"I've come for my things," Mary answered.

"Let's go find them," Lorence said, passing Sturgill in the doorway.

We walked into the suite. The coatroom and bathroom were straight ahead. We turned right into the kitchenette/sitting area. The separate bedroom was through a door on the far wall. We went directly to the bedroom. Lorence stood in the doorway as Mary went to the closet and took out her spare clothes. She draped them on the king bed. Two nylon stockings were knotted around the bedposts. Mary disinterestedly untied them and threw them on the clothes. When she went to the dresser she stopped and looked around to Lorence. Pointing to an empty cardboard box against the wall she asked, "Do you mind if I use that box?"

Lorence said she could and Mary started putting her more intimate items from the dresser into the box. I noticed a framed photo on the nightstand. In the photo, Mary was sitting on a picnic blanket. There was a body of water and rolling hills behind her. Dylan must have taken the picture since I could see a bare foot creeping into the foreground at the base of the image. From the background, it looked like they were at Parker Canyon Lake. I put the photograph in the box. Mary paused, looked at the photo and then threw the rest of her undergarments on top. She did not look up at me.

I went through to the sitting area. It dawned on me that Dylan and I had only ever sat on his balcony. A wave of melancholy washed over me because in truth, I had a lot of people I thought of as friends yet I had never been to where they live. The thought seemed to undermine the substance of my world. Dylan had a small bookcase in the sitting area. I noticed the two books he had mentioned to me: Unknown Strangers and Go Back to Where You Came From. He had studied them in a political science seminar at Davidson. They had made an indelible impression on him. He repeatedly referenced these books when debating current politic strategy. There were some business binders but also Chernow's book on Ulysses S. Grant and Rather's The Palace Guard. I was surprised to see The Great Gatsby on the lower shelf and bent down to get a better look. Tucked away in the corner was The Modern Kama Sutra: The Ultimate Guide to the Secrets of Erotic Pleasure. I stood and backed away. Too much information.

The top of the bookcase caught my eye and I stopped. It was strewn with mineral rocks, gems and crystals. On the floor, between the bookcase and the window was a box with more rocks in it. On the side of the box a label read "Tucson Gem and Mineral Show."

"He liked the stones," Mary said in a flat voice from behind me. "He believed they harnessed energy and spirituality."

"I think we're done here," Lorence said. Mary was holding the box and her clothes were draped over the top. Mary walked out first. Lorence stopped me at the door.

"How about a beer at the Wild Horse?" he asked.

"It's too early for me, Sheriff."

"Are you sure he didn't tell you anything last night?"

"Only the message that he couldn't make dinner and we'd meet later."

"You know he was not just a security consultant."

"I seem to be the last person he would have confided in."

Lorence looked out through the doorjamb watching Mary's retreating figure. "Remind your former girlfriend, I want to talk to her today." He turned back to me, tucked his thumbs behind his belt buckle and leaned against the wall. He intended that comment to smart, but I tried not to give him any satisfaction as I walked past him out into the hallway. Mary and I went through the inside courtyard and then exited the building through the Wild Horse Saloon entrance. The bar was deserted. I drove Mary to her car. She said she was going to tend to a couple of things and then go get that interview with the sheriff out of the way. I drove home. When I arrived at my cabin I made a cup of coffee and took it out to the rocking chair on my porch. I mulled over the recent events and thought of Mary being grilled by Lorence. It was several months later when Mary finally told me about her interview with the sheriff.

* * *

The deputy led Mary into the sheriff's office, nodded at Lorence and shut the door behind him when he exited. Lorence motioned for Mary to be seated as he hung up the telephone and made a note on a piece of paper before sliding the paper to one side of his desk. Then he looked up at Mary.

"Hello again, Ms. Durant," he said ingratiatingly. "What a pleasure it is to see you on a recurrent basis."

"Your deputy said you were busy. I hope this doesn't take too long," Mary said evenly. Lorence waited for the expected genuflection to his title, but it was not forthcoming. A flicker of annoyance crossed his eyes, but then he continued.

"Thank you for coming back in."

"Did I have a choice?"

Now Lorence was irked. Like any browbeater, he craved respect. "This can go easy or it can go hard. Entirely up to you," he snarled.

"I have no idea what you're talking about, Sheriff. I can't believe you even talk like that. You're a cliché." Lorence's face began to flush.

"I can lock you and your old boyfriend up for murder, you little wench!"

"On what proof?" Mary said defiantly. "Neither of us did it. You know that. You lock us up and you'll be driven right out of your plush chair. Dr. Harper's more beloved in this community after a few months than you'll ever be." Mary looked down at her lap. Her phone video record button was bright red.

"Why don't you tell me your whereabouts last night. "

"I'm sure you heard this already. I was at home in the early evening and then went over to Dr. Harper's. I was there until your deputy came and fetched us."

"Do you have anyone who can vouch for that story?"

"Dr. Harper."

The sheriff sneered. "That is pretty convenient. If you two were plotting to get rid of the third lover in your triangle, it would be very likely you'd meet up and cover each other with an alibi. Where were you before you pranced out to Harper's cabin?"

Mary bristled at the 'pranced' characterization, but let it go. "I told you. I was at home. I made myself a little pasta for dinner and watched some television."

"Can anyone corroborate that?"

"I live in a small apartment building. Someone probably saw me come in and someone probably saw me leave. With all the nosy people in that building, if you checked around I'm sure you'd find people who could tell you what sauce I put on the pasta and which show I was watching on the TV."

Lorence stood up and casually came around the desk and stopped in front of Mary's chair. He leaned back against his desk. His tone changed to a friendly, cajoling person just trying to be reasonable. "Look, Mary. May I call you Mary?" He didn't wait for a response and continued. Mary stared up at him looming over her. They locked eyes. His eyes were boring into hers. "I don't think you murdered this Kermer guy, but I'm not so sure about your saintly doctor friend. Now, I have a job to do. I'm sure we could work something out and make all this unpleasantness go away."

Mary broke eye contact and glanced down. When she looked up, the sheriff had a leer on his face and his right index finger was pointing to the zipper on his pants. Mary pulled her phone up to her cheek, but Lorence had already awkwardly bent over and was attempting to kiss her. Mary stood abruptly and the crown of her forehead smashed into the sheriff's nose. He backed his head away as his eyes filled with water. Mary snapped one flash photo of Lorence, his finger frozen at his waist and then drew her knee back before planting it with as much force as she could muster right into his groin. Lorence bent in two, moaning in agony. He took a step backwards, but tripped over the edge of his desk sprawling onto the carpet on his back

Mary stood over him for a moment flashing her cell phone in his face. "You stay away from me, you vile creature! If you bother me one whit, this photo goes viral!" Then, another wave of stomach nausea hit her and unceremoniously, she vomited all over his waist. She stood up, wiped her face with the back of her hand and left the office. She left the sheriff's door wide open as she walked out.

Chapter 5

This all started several months ago. In my mid-forties, I was already a victim of burnout. Success had been killing me in the Northeast. My New England practice was depleting my love for medicine. Having become a doctor at the age of 24, I hadn't fully realized that hospitals are where people go who have had terrible things happen to them. Those terrible things – people shot or stabbed, trauma, infection, cancer, disease – leave behind a wake of suffering, injustice and loss for those individuals and the people who love them. Caring for such devastation was draining my spirit as surely as opening a major artery would drain my vascular tree. My brakes were thin; my tires bald. I needed a change and started looking for places to take a sabbatical. I wanted somewhere I could get back to the basics - lead a simple life, re-group and recharge my personal batteries. For a lot of people, a disappointment in love might have been a factor, but that was another of my problems – there was no one. It seemed I was always meeting the wrong person. If you don't believe me you could ask them and they would agree. I was in a rut. I needed change.

In a medical journal, I saw an ad for a Patagonia, Arizona Indian Health Clinic physician provider. The position required a local interview. I asked for some information on the position and was referred to their website.

I learned the Patagonia job was at a satellite clinic owned by the Tucson Indian Center. The organization was put together just after World War II when leaders from the Archaic, Hohokam, Tohono O'odham and Pascua Yaqui tribes decided they needed an institution of their own to provide housing, education and health services for their people. They formed the Native American Club in 1957 and eventually morphed into the Tucson Indian Center.

The clinic was only two days a week and as medical director there would be no salary, but I would be given a housing stipend. It was a six-month agreement and except for the nurse, medical assistant and receptionist, almost everyone else who worked at the clinic volunteered their services as well. I called back and arranged an interview. I took a long weekend off of work and bought a ticket from Southwest Airlines. The Tucson Indian Services Health Manager met me at Tucson International Airport's newly renovated west terminal.

Mrs. Dorothy Graham said they were looking for a doctor to provide general medical care in one of their satellite clinics. She sketched with broad strokes the history of the clinic as we drove the sixty miles to Patagonia. Maneuvering the country roads with ease, Graham said the clinic serviced the people living among the Santa Rita and Patagonia mountains as well as the villages along the Harshaw and Sonoita creeks.

"We really don't turn away anyone in Santa Cruz County," Graham added. "Many of the people are quite poor and living off the land." Although the word "Indian" figured prominently in the sign, the clinic cared for all comers. Indian Services obtained most of its operating budget from the Tribal coalition, but also received some federal funds. No state money was allocated, but the clinic did participate in the Arizona Medicaid program.

We pulled into a dirt parking lot on the edge of town. The clinic was the last of several one-story commercial buildings built a long time ago. The parking area was adjacent to the clinic entrance and bounded by the last intersection in Patagonia before leaving town. Ms. Graham took me in to meet the doctor I would be replacing: a general surgeon from Chicago. He seemed to be on a similar quest to mine.

"The waiting room is too small and it's crowded," Dr. Weiskoff said by way of introduction. "We are understaffed and the paper work is onerous. But the problems are real, the people are grateful and I think we make a difference." He thought for a moment, then added, "It's also beautiful country."

I accepted the position on the spot. Mrs. Graham gave me information about housing and I spent the rest of that weekend exploring the area and looking for a place to live. I found a log cabin that was a twelve-minute drive from town and signed a lease for six months. The cabin was northwest of

Patagonia along the Sonoita Creek. I felt fortunate to get the rental. The owner of the cabin spent most of her time in Seattle, but continued to nurture a soft spot in her heart for the Patagonia Indian Clinic. There was a working fireplace but the main source of heat came from a wood burning stove. A functioning well and a generator were the highlighted amenities. No landline phone, but there was good mobile service thanks to the cell tower in the Sonoita preserve. The phone tower was topped off with a plastic evergreen tree that somewhat matched the tree line. Its presence was grudgingly accepted by the townspeople because the bird watchers who came from all over the world to this area had to report their observations in real time. The birdwatchers were undeniably good for the local economy.

My cabin was isolated and cozy. Off the northwest side of the porch, you could see the Mt. Wrightson wilderness. Southeast of the porch was the Coronado National Forest. Straight South of the porch steps you could hear the Sonoita Creek as its water drained from the Santa Rita mountains making its journey southwest to join the Santa Cruz River a few miles north of Nogales. The creek itself was down a short path from the cabin. At the end of the path one could usually find a great Blue Heron. The Heron was most commonly near the base of a 100-foot tall eucalyptus tree serving as the sentinel of the path. The tree was magnificent with its salmon colored bark. Its glistening green leaves provided a good amount of shade when needed. Those leaves shed easily during a wind storm, fluttering down to act as a nicely cushioned carpet for people making their way creekside. Standing on the porch of the cabin I felt like I was renting the stage of the Hollywood Bowl. I was looking out at a vibrant natural amphitheater where the flora and fauna could take your breath away.

After signing the lease, I flew back to New England and started reading anything I could get my hands on about Arizona. I had moved many times in my life for medical training, but never without a calculating preparation that left little to chance. The change from New England to Arizona would be jarring - a jolt I was looking forward to. My roots had always been too much like the Arizona saguaro: shallow, sprawling and fragile. I was hoping to cultivate roots more like the native mesquite tree: deep enough to find peace and maybe even that ultimate prospector's lodestone ... love. In retrospect, some force - a constellation of dreams, movies and romanticism - must have made me choose Patagonia. But I didn't realize it at the time.

Chapter 6

My first few days on the job overlapped with Dr. Weiskopf and he acclimated me to expectations, procedures and traditions. I had met Rachel, the clinic receptionist and Becky, the Medical Assistant during my interview visit, but I was pleasantly surprised to meet Mary Durant. She was a Registered Nurse and had been working at the Indian Clinic for eighteen months. She was not present when Mrs. Graham showed me around several weeks earlier. Her degree from Northern Arizona University hung in the waiting room and from her graduation date I placed her at about 32 to 33 years old. She was very pretty and vivacious. My spirits picked up just being in her presence. I sensed it would be fun working together.

As Dr. Weiskopf packed up the last of his personal things in the tiny office reserved for the clinic's physician, he shared some history with me.

"It's not required or written down anywhere, but for as long as the clinic has been operating, the attending physician here has been asked intermittently to make house calls across the border." He waited for me to register the implications and then continued.

"We have no license to practice in Mexico and, of course, no malpractice insurance. We don't go often and when we do, we don't cross at the ports of entry. We don't accept money for these visits."

"I'm expected to illegally cross the border and practice medicine?"

"You might be asked. You don't have to go. Usually, it will be for a sick child in a very poor family." He saw me wrestling with this news. "If you do decide to go when asked, you will feel more like the doctor you wanted to be when you applied to medical school then anytime since," he added.

"But, how . . ."

"We're almost finished here. When we leave I'll show you the route we have all used to hike across the border and help those in need. Do you own hiking boots?"

I nodded.

"Good. I'll show you the way. We'll stop at the border. We won't cross. Then, when the time comes, you can make your own decision."

Weiskopf was true to his word and that's how we spent the rest of the afternoon. He dropped me back off at the clinic in the late afternoon.

"Good luck," the surgeon said. "I'm sure this experience will be one of the highlights of your life." We shook hands and he was off to the airport.

The next day would be my official first day as physician of the Indian Clinic. I was on my own.

Chapter 7

The day I met Dylan for the first time in the bar of the Wild Horse Saloon, I had spent the morning and early afternoon at the clinic. We were about an hour into our morning and the waiting room was full, as it always was, when there was a sharp rap at the side door of the building which served as our main entrance.

"Border Patrol! Coming in!" The door flew open and in streamed Border Patrol agents in full body armor and weapons out. Other men in dark Immigration and Customs Enforcement jackets with handguns drawn were interspersed among the agents.

There was no room in the overcrowded waiting area. Agents stood towering over our patients with AR-15 assault rifles held inches from the patients' petrified faces. My tiny office had a door exiting to the back alley and this burst open in a splintering crash as the meager lock pulled out of the door frame. More agents hustled in.

Mary came out from behind the reception window where Rachel was cowering fearfully. "What's the meaning of this?"

The lead officer ignored her. Swinging his rifle as he spoke, "Everyone show some proof of citizenship! Let's see your passports! Get out your papers." He repeated this in Spanish. The agents bulletproof vests were rubbing against each other as they repeatedly turned and rotated over the patients. It made an ominous low, muffled scratching sound.

The agent in charge turned back to Mary. "You too, ma'am."

By this time, I was out of the patient examining room and had overheard the exchange.

"You can't do this!" I said. "We're American citizens. Do you have a warrant?"

The I.C.E. agent stepped forward. "We can do this and we are. Statute 8 U.S. code 1357 says we can conduct searches without a warrant if we have reason to suspect that an individual may be deportable."

"And what reasonable cause do you expect to find in a doctor's office?" I demanded.

"We have reason to believe a person on these premises was ordered removed from the United States pursuant to the Immigration and Nationality Act."

"This is not a 'show me your papers' country," I said heatedly.

"The President has issued an Executive Order mandating expedited removal," the lead agent replied and tilted his head sharply to his men. They responded to this order by moving even closer towards the seated patients and motioning for them to open their purses and pockets.

Mary interrupted. "I want a lawyer."

"You can get a lawyer, ma'am," the agent replied calmly. "This is not an interrogation. If you or anyone else is denying that you are in the United States illegally, the burden is on you to prove you are not an alien."

"Nobody in their right mind carries their passport around with them everywhere they go!" I said.

"A voter I.D. or birth certificate will be sufficient."

I rolled my eyes. "Two things I never leave home without." The agent ignored me and back turned to my patients.

"Show your documents or start walking to the bus outside," he said gesturing with his combat weapon.

An elderly woman with diabetes opened her purse. "Will a driver's license do?" she asked. The agent shook his head no and repeated: "Voter I.D. card, birth certificate or passport." The agents worked the room and in the absence of proper documents appeared to resort to racial profiling. Eventually six people were led outside. The agents began to leave.

"What about us?" Mary asked. No one had checked our credentials.

"You have a good day, ma'am," the agent said, tipping his helmet and shutting the door behind him.

Chapter 8

Needing a beer to recover from my first encounter with ICE was how I happened to be in the Wild Horse just before Happy Hour when Dylan ventured in. The beginning of our conversation started out with Dylan reserved, but intensely serious.

"You're a physician?" Dylan said with disbelief, looking down again at my running shoes.

"Is it really that inconceivable?" I replied, feeling somewhat amused and faintly peeved.

"I suppose you believe in vaccines and all that stuff?"

"I do. I believe immunizations and penicillin have saved more lives than probably anything else in the last one hundred years."

"I think it's better children develop their own immunity through illness rather than vaccinations," Dylan said offhandedly. Before I could respond, he plowed onward. "Do you only read medical journals?"

"No. I like picture books as well."

Undeterred, he shed his reserve like an ill-fitting coat and asked excitedly, "Have you read <u>Unwelcome Strangers</u> by Professor David Riemers - he's a serious academic. How about <u>Go Back to Where You Came From</u> by Polansky?

"Are those really books?"

"Oh yes! Very fascinating reads. You'd like them."

I looked dubiously into my drink.

"Good parts in those books," he continued, "about what happens to countries - especially western democracies - that don't secure their borders." He voiced his concern about Mexican gangs and drugs.

"Who's not concerned about gang violence and drug abuse?" I asked. Statistics show immigrants commit crimes at a lower rate than citizens."

"Statistics are for losers. Whose side are you on?"

"Decency," I said. "But I didn't know it was a side."

"You're a dreamer," he said into his drink.

"No, I was born here. But I do support Dreamers." I meant to lighten the conversation. He didn't get it. "DACA," I added helpfully.

"What does the capital of Bangladesh have to do with anything? This is war," Dylan said simply, looking up from his beer.

"Not if you retain your humanity. Then it's just life. What brings you to this small town?" I asked.

"I'm a consultant."

"That could cover any manner of sins." He remained quiet. I persisted. "What do you consult in?"

Dylan's eyes drifted to the blinking Coors sign. He pursed his lips and his left index finger and thumb erased the condensation ring at the base of his glass. After a pause. "Security," he said. He took a sip of his beer. "I'm with a firm out of California. Clients all over. Specialize in tech stuff." He took another swallow. "It's good to meet a local. Get the lay of the land and all."

"Local might be a bit of a stretch. I haven't really been here very long," I said, feeling I had just scratched the surface of getting to know the people, the politics and the magic of the geography. "I can tell you where the post office is, but not much more." I was finding Dylan's discussion of immigration a little refreshing after all my time spent with East Coast colleagues. Medicare and Medicaid payment inadequacies and frustration with electronic medical record documentation were the main topics of conversation with my peers in New England. Canada was our border country and everyone loved Canadians. The Southern U.S. border issues were abstract problems to most of my friends, patients and co-workers. They were happy to espouse solutions, but only as passing intellectual concepts. The Southwest was so far away it was hard for their stories to find traction in the day-to-day struggles of life in the Northeast. The more we talked, the more Dylan began to open up and his arguments became more confident and assertive.

Dylan snapped his fingers and it startled me. "HELLO! Where did you go in your head? I asked you a question."

"Sorry. I spaced out for a second. What was your question?"

"Do you do that often? Wait! That's not my question. Doesn't seem like a commendable habit in a doctor to space out every once in a while. It's a good thing you're not a surgeon . . . or a pilot." I smiled ruefully. He continued. "I was asking you: Where do the illegals come through around here?" Dylan asked casually.

I raised an eyebrow. "You mean the immigrants?"

"Yes. The illegal immigrants."

I shrugged. "Probably along the washes."

"Which washes?"

"Near Lochiel. Maybe by the Santa Cruz River. I really don't know."

"They cause a lot of trouble?"

"Not that I can see. They cross mainly to go to work. They do housekeeping, farming, construction, landscaping."

"What about all the drug smugglers?"

"They cross with the rapists. They have their own wash," I said.

He frowned. "I know you're making fun, but these are serious matters. Our country's security is at stake."

"I'm a physician," I said. "I see what drugs do to people. I despise drug smugglers as much as any human being. I just haven't seen any problems like that here. Maybe because I haven't been here long enough," I shrugged.

"You don't even know what's going on in your own backyard," he said with a dismissive shake of his head. "These immigrants are taking jobs that should go to Americans."

"This seems very personal to you. Is it part of your job?"

He looked at his drink for a long moment. "I'm supposed to help out on the SBI-Net Tucson West Tower project."

"I have no idea what that is. Sounds like you should be in Tucson if that's where the project is," I said. "What are you doing in Patagonia? What's 'SBI-Net'?" I asked.

"The Secure Border Initiative," he answered. "It's set up to help US Customs and Border Protection - the CBP – get effective control of our borders. When we're through we will have a tactical infrastructure with proven technology and response platforms integrated into a single comprehensive border system to protect the United States. The tower acts like a communication satellite, radar, sonar and infra-red sensor all rolled up into one tech platform. It's going up right here in Santa Cruz County."

"I haven't heard of that. Do people around here know?"

"The agency is going to release that information soon."

"I see," I said. "After building is completed and it's up and running they'll announce it. Better to ask forgiveness later than permission now."

"Less hassle that way," Dylan nodded.

"You mean fewer environmental protests and no bad local publicity."

Dylan shrugged. "What's an owl or two."

"What about the impact on other imperiled species around here – like jaguars?"

"A small price to pay for the safety and future of our country," he said.

"But shouldn't you still look at the environmental impacts of these actions first? Then you could at least temper the damage."

"We don't have time to waste getting bogged down in those details. Besides, it's just a tower," he said coldly.

"It's reconstructing the wilderness. You are talking of a trickledown effect of roads and fences . . ."

"The times change and we have to change with them, Harper. Nostalgia won't protect the security of our country."

"Can't we be secure and still not interfere with streams and forests? These things support human life down here and everywhere. Security is important, but these other consequences need to be considered as well."

"I bet you are a climate control nut, too," Dylan said contemptuously with a half-wave of his hand.

I sighed. I had lost him. He was looking out the window thinking of other things. It was now Happy Hour and the bar was filling up with people he might find more interesting.

"And right here - in this area – you're building this tower?" I asked.

"Yes."

"Where will it go?"

"I can't tell you the exact location. The local people don't want it. The information I did tell you is not classified, it's just not widely known. The tower location is classified. In fact, you should probably just forget I said Santa Cruz County."

I left him with his SBI-Net tower plans swirling in his beer. It would be up to him to discover what had held people to this area for centuries: the blue-green cast of moonlight on these mountains, night skies so dense with stars that you could imagine nebulae elbowing each other over dark matter. Then in the morning, a cobalt blue atmosphere that could burn your retina. The day slowly easing into a pinkish-gold sunset until finally you could hear the coyotes, hummingbirds, wood warblers, crickets, owls, cicadas, and doves intensifying their calls to a crescendo. The ensuing din covering the stealth of the cougar, bobcat, deer, quail, and hawk. The cattle and horses sensing their vulnerability, nervously pawing the earth as the distant lightning heralded an imminent monsoon strike. An arroyo swelling quickly with water, turning a small creek into a muddy rampage. The next dawn giving way to wet, ripening grapes and endless rows of green vines, pecan trees and blooming cacti. The fresh air filled with the wafting smell of beans cooking next to huevos rancheros at a road-side stand. In my New England home, right now the weather would be a beautiful snow scene resembling a Currier and Ives painting, but at this moment I was happy to be here. I headed home to my cabin.

Chapter 9

Trish became my first real friend in Patagonia. Tonight, she is the bartender at the Wild Horse and is serving me a beer. It's only four o'clock in the afternoon and so I have about an hour to decompress from my duties at the clinic before the place starts getting busy. Tomorrow Trish could be your waitress in the restaurant or the hostess who escorts you to your table. She does everything at the Wild Horse and it is immediately obvious she has a lot energy and a big heart. I like her. She is pretty, bubbly and smart. She's also not shy. I already know she has four children by three different husbands at the tender age of thirty-three. Sandwiched as she is between the army base to the east of us at Fort Huachuca and Davis Monthan Air Force base to the west, her husbands have all been servicemen. She is separated from the third husband, but I have never seen even a trace in her attitude that life has been a disappointment. She's trim, fit and about 5 feet two inches tall. If she hadn't told me her age, I would have guessed she was 25 years old.

"How are things at the clinic?" she asks, as she plunks down my beer.

"Good," I answer. "How are things with you?"

Trish ignores my question. "You ask that Mary Durant out yet?"

Surprised, I manage a "No," without choking on my first sip. I say it as if the thought is ridiculous. Trish wipes down the counter with her bar rag, although it doesn't need cleaning.

"You should. You aren't getting any younger."

"I'm well aware of that, but thank you for the friendly reminder."

She smiles. "Heck, forget about asking her out. You should ask her to marry you."

I harrumph. "And why's that?"

"Even a fool like you – who probably has early cataracts - can see she's beautiful. But that ain't why. She's probably the only girl around here who's smarter than you." Trish finishes the bar wipe down with a flourish at this statement.

"How would you know?"

"Because I went to school with her forever, that's how."

That's worth a big sip of my beer. "Where?"

"I went to high school with her in Tucson. She was miles smarter than anyone else. She ran track and cross-country and even started the school's first women's hockey team. Pretty bold, us being in the desert and all. But that fell apart after Mary went off to college. She got full-ride scholarships to all three Arizona state schools, but wanted to live in a more rural place, so she picked Northern Arizona University. I guess I just wanted to be like her, so I followed her up there for school. I only lasted a year and a half though. School was not my thing. I got pregnant, dropped out and got married. Lived on the base for as long as that lasted. Mary and I fell out of touch around then."

"School is not for everyone," I said.

"It was perfect for Mary. She was pre-med at NAU. All A's, just like high school. Then she switched to nursing."

"Why did she switch?"

"I heard she spent the summer between sophomore and junior year working at a hospital in Phoenix and didn't like the hours the doctors had to work." Trish leaned in and in a more confidential tone, added, "There was talk of her falling real hard for an intern. He foolishly put medicine before Mary and it broke her heart when he ended it just as she was going back to school."

I didn't know what to say to that. Trish didn't notice. She continued. "I think that's why she left University Hospital in Tucson to come down here. She was tired of all the doctors asking her out. She thought, in the end, medicine would always be the winning jealous mistress and she would get hurt time and again."

"So, you want to throw me into that situation?"

"You're different," Trish said, with an all-knowing, worldly air, put on for my benefit, "you're here because you know medicine is important, but not the most important thing in your life."

"And what might that be, all-wise-one?"

"That's for me to know and you to find out," she said with a little pirouette, as she went down the bar to attend to another customer.

Chapter 10

Trish's comments correlated with my observations of Mary at work. During a brief coffee break, we stepped outside on the backdoor stoop to savor the pretty morning.

"What brought you down to Patagonia from Tucson and your job at the University Hospital in Tucson?" I asked.

The breeze blew her hair around and with her free hand she pulled the hair from in front of her face. "I enjoy the freedom of this clinic setting versus the rigid constraints of a teaching hospital." She thought for a moment. "The pace is slower and I can spend time with the patients. The gratitude of the clinic patients makes the hard work and relatively low pay worthwhile. I can hike and bike while it's still light on." She looked at me and eyes smiled a bit "And I have time to take Italian lessons. I don't know why, but I've always wanted to learn how to speak Italian."

It was time to go back in and I held the door for her. She entered the building with an athlete's grace. I knew she wasn't looking for a relationship with a physician, but it was impossible not to be attracted to Mary. Her unfailing good cheer, high energy and piquant appearance were too endearing. She had high cheekbones and a strong jawline. Her hair was a bright copper that counterpointed eyes clear and blue. She had a bold mouth and a radiance about her. Effortlessly she exuded an air of mystery about her that was undiminished by the frequent impudent twinkle in her eye. The combination was very alluring. When you had a conversation with her you could feel her total attention focused entirely on you. The first time she asked me an innocuous clinical question about a patient, my mouth went dry. Her voice was light and pleasant. As I listened, the thought of being close to her made my stomach flip. Decades of hard earned and studiously collected medical knowledge evaporated in an instant. I couldn't process a response to her simple inquiry. I felt small beads of perspiration moistening my upper lip.

I worked hard to stay professional. Quietly trying to prove to myself and to her that not all doctors were bad personal risks. One afternoon in my third week at the clinic Mary handed me an MRI report. She was close enough that I could smell her. It wasn't a perfume but rather a clean freshness. Maybe it was pheromones, but it was sexy. Her hand touched mine ever so lightly and lingered for an extra second when she gave me the report. She turned, left the room and the memory of the softness of her skin lingered until the end of the day. We walked out together and I locked the office door to the sound of our last patient pulling his car out of our gravel parking lot. We started walking to our respective cars. Mary paused, "Would you like to get a drink and watch the sunset?" she asked. "I know a good place."

I was stunned. Foreshadowing my great conversational skills, after a beat I answered, "Sure." She was non-plussed.

"Follow me since you don't know the area that well," she said.

And I did.

Mary took me to her favorite coffee place in town. Called The Writer's Feast, it had a large color poster of the movie *Doctor Zhivago* in the anteroom entry. Pasternak's Lara featuring Julie Christie is gazing up longingly at Zhivago, played by Omar Sharif. They are framed by the Ice Palace in the background and a Russian Revolution battle on the periphery.

"That's the owner's favorite movie," Mary said. We walked in and took a table for two against a far wall. I pointed to the wall.

"That would be my favorite," I said. This poster of *Casablanca* showed a serious Ingrid Bergman in profile searching for something in Humphrey Bogart's eyes. A somber Bogart cannot meet that penetrating gaze and focuses on Bergman's lips. A twin-engine Lockheed Electra Junior Air France plane is at the ready behind them and the Spanish architecture of the Casablanca skyline looms in the background. The poster had been colorized. "Although I might prefer the black and white version," I added.

There was one more poster framed next to *Casablanca*. This one was in black and white.

"Another reference to Russia," I noted curiously. It was *Ninotchka*, where Melvyn Douglas makes a no-nonsense Russian woman played by Greta Garbo laugh for the first time on film.

Mary looked up from her brief glance at the menu and followed my gaze. "The owner talks about that movie a lot," Mary said.

"Interesting."

The coffee shop was crowded and all the bustle gave Mary and me a unique privacy. Two men at a table nearby spoke harshly to each other in a language I didn't understand, but soon I was lost in conversation with Mary. We talked effortlessly in a gentle dance of getting to know one another. When we finally stood up to pay our bill, I noticed the table with the foreign strangers was empty. I had not seen them leave. Being with Mary had made everything else in the coffee shop fade out of focus to the background.

Chapter 11

After Mary introduced me to The Writer's Feast, I found it to be the best hangout in town if you weren't looking for alcohol. I had become friendly with the owner, a man named Dave Nance. A widower with three grown children scattered over the United States, Nance had moved to Patagonia seventeen years earlier to escape his own work demons. Dave's goblins were of a corporate nature and his transition to Arizona life was eased by selling vast holdings of dot.com stock before the crash at the turn of the century. He sought a simpler life and opened a coffee shop in town and added a bookstore. Hence, "The Writer's Feast." Nance was a good conversationalist on all subjects. We enjoyed each other's company. Plus, he knew everything about everyone in the area. A naturally quiet man, people gathering in his popular meeting place would often forget he was present in the establishment and talk in their groups without inhibition. As the soul of discretion, he never shared gossip or rumors. Nance astutely knew that would be the death knell of his business, but it was also not his style. He didn't say much, but Dave was acknowledged to be intelligent, accomplished, and was a well-respected member of the community. He exuded competence. He became one of the people I looked forward to seeing whenever I was in town.

I saw Nance sitting at a back table near the courtyard when I entered the Wild Horse Saloon and he waved me over to join him. As I sat down, he cocked his head in the direction of loud arguing just below the big screen television over the fireplace. "They're at it again," he said.

The United States Attorney General was speaking from San Diego on the evening news. Two groups had formed on either side of the large flat screen in an ironic parody of a Western stand-off. Both sides argued with each other and with the image of the Attorney General.

"What's this?" I asked Dave, gesturing to the television.

"The AG is talking about the "Zero Tolerance" border enforcement policy," Dave explained. "It's getting these people riled up."

". . . parents who attempt to come into this Country," the Attorney General drawled in a sing-song cadence, "with their families, will be separated from their children. The children will be sent to juvenile shelters while the parents face charges and do their time in jail . . ."

"You are cruel and heartless!" one female Wild Horse patron shouted at the television screen, which invited a large boo from the other side of the television.

Another official took the podium on the news feed. "If you don't want your families broken apart, don't come into the country illegally."

"Message seems clear to me," said a man on the opposite side of the television. The Wild Horse debate picked up there and drowned out the voices on the television. I turned back to Nance.

"They used to just bus the families back to Mexico," Nance recalled. "Especially if the parents had no previous criminal record. Now it looks like the Administration wants to use children as pawns in their strategy to end immigration."

I was surprised. This was the first comment I'd heard Nance utter about the Border problem. His understated confidence and soft spoken wry humor were usually directed at less divisive issues. He never voiced any political opinions. Nance registered my surprise and quickly switched gears.

"Enough of that," he said. "How's Mary?"

"Good. It's still early days, but I like her a lot."

"So, do I," Nance said approvingly. "She's special. Make any other new friends?"

"A new guy in the area joined me for a beer recently. "He says he's working on a 'Tower Project', I jerked my thumb to the two groups still arguing around the television. "To help control immigration.

Nance's eyes narrowed. "What's his name?"

"Dylan Kermer. Do you know him?"

Nance grimaced. "He's been in the Feast quite a few times, but I can't say I know him." He looked around the Saloon searching for something, but evidently, he didn't find it.

"Come with me. I have something I'd like you to see. I'm tired of having no one to talk to about things," he said, backing his chair out and standing up.

"Where're we going?"

"Not here. We'll talk away from here."

I followed his second gaze appraising the Wild Horse crowd, but had no idea what or who Nance had been looking for. I looked for something Dave might have been attuned to and saw nothing out of the ordinary. Perplexed, but curious, I trailed Nance out into the street.

We drove out of town in Dave's 2500 Ram truck. "There's something strange going on out here," he said, pointing at the hills to our south. "How well do you know Dylan Kermer?"

"Not well." I told him what I knew. Consultant and all that.

"I heard him talking in the coffee shop last week with some men I didn't recognize." Nance glanced over at me. "I have a more elaborate bistro security system than the average coffee bar."

I raised an eyebrow to him. "What's that entail?"

"I have the CCTV on a two week save, but I also have a biometric artificial intelligence application programmed into my computer."

"You mean a facial recognition system?"

"Yes. It can take the digital image of a person and analyze their unique facial features and shape. Using a comprehensive database, it can then identify that person with a greater accuracy than either fingerprints or eyeball iris recognition systems."

"I know your coffee is expensive, but that sounds a little over the top," I said. Nance gave me a rueful smile. "Why would a coffee shop owner have a set-up like that?" I continued with mild astonishment. "Where would you find the computer program, let alone the database?"

"It's readily available to download on the Dark Web."

"The database is?"

"Yes."

"But that doesn't answer why a barista needs this. How do you even know about these things?"

"I was in the computer business before I came to Patagonia. Many people have several lives before settling in a small town," he said, dryly. "I'd appreciate it if you kept my enhanced security system to yourself."

"Easy to do, since I don't understand it."

"The thing is," he continued. "I applied it to the two men Kermer was meeting with and I got a hit on one of them." Nance looked at me, expecting a response. I waited. He went on. "Turns out one of the men works for the American Photography Restoration Society in Washington, D.C."

"He refurbishes old photographs? Like of the Grand Canyon, for instance. Is that what you're saying?"

"Hardly. The APRS is a known fictitious company often used for off-the-books government intelligence operations."

"Whoa! That's a leap."

"Maybe not. What prompted me to check this guy out was I overheard Kermer talking about a launching site down here. Above Patagonia Lake. I was so curious I followed him that afternoon."

"Launching site?" I repeated. "You mean as in missiles?"

"I didn't know. It crossed my mind. Anything's possible. We have people living around here in old underground Intercontinental Ballistic Missile silos that the Government sold off after the SALT Treaty in 1980. Without the missiles, of course."

"I would hope so."

Nance smiled. "There is one site the government preserved and now it's a popular museum off I-19 just west of here. The 'Titan Missile Museum.' You should check it out some lazy afternoon. It's a pretty chilling tour. Anyway, I think Kermer was talking about a place to launch an operation, not a missile"

"Did you use your facial recognition on Dylan?"

"I did. Nothing. He's not in the database - and the database I use was hacked straight from the NSA."

Nance turned down the mouth of a narrow dirt road. The truck bounced us around through the scrub and cacti amid the rolling hills of Southeastern Arizona. After about ten minutes, he cut the engine. We were just below the top of a ridge overlooking a small valley.

Nance put his fingers up to his lips and climbed out of the truck. He shut his door softly. I followed suit. The daylight was still good. He opened the rear of the truck and pulled forward a small duffel bag. From the bag, he extracted a powerful pair of binoculars and we walked to the edge of the ridge. Nance rested his elbows on a tree stump and scanned the valley. "There," he said and offered me the binoculars.

It took me a minute, but then I saw a small, branch road emerging from the other side of the ravine and leading to a clearing. A black Hummer was parked at the edge of a clearing. I focused the binoculars on the General Motors H2 and the shadow of a structure lurked behind it in the trees. It was a Quonset hut and I could make out a couple of four-wheel all-terrain backroad vehicles tucked in the trees as well. It was a good location. Essentially a box canyon with steep walls of tree and brush on three sides. I could not make out any windows in the building. I saw something move on the periphery of my viewing field and swung the binoculars to my right.

"They have security," I said quietly.

"Really?" Nance replied. He gestured for the field glasses. I handed them over and he did a skilled, measured scan. "I see two of them in the woods at the last turn of the access road before the clearing." He gave me back the glasses. "They're armed." We looked at each other.

"This is over my pay grade," I said. "What's going on down there?"

"Something shady. That's all I can tell from here," Nance said.

I looked back down with the binoculars and saw the door of the Quonset hut open. Dylan stood in the threshold talking to someone inside. My stomach flipped. "It's him. Kermer," I said, giving Nance back the glasses.

With my naked eye, I could see the distant figure walking to the Hummer. He stopped and inexplicably looked up our way and I rudely pushed the binoculars down from Nance's face.

"He sees us," I said. Nance was patient with me.

"No, I could see his face. He was just stretching."

I wasn't convinced. We saw Dylan turn the H2 around and begin to pull out. He stopped to say something to one of the security guards and then accelerated forward and up around the bend. Nance said to me, "I think Kermer hides the Hummer in the woods before he gets to the main road. He then transfers to his Buick."

"We should get out of here," I said.

"I agree."

On the drive back into town we tried to make sense of what we had just observed.

"What could you launch from there?" I asked.

"Maybe he's making something in there," Nance offered.

"Drugs?" I thought for a moment. "That just doesn't seem his style. He's so strait-laced."

"Not to ingest. To sell. Maybe meth."

"But why?"

"Why does anyone sell drugs? To make money."

It didn't feel right. But I didn't have instincts for this line of work. There were forces operating in Patagonia foreign to my experience. My gut told me nothing. My sixth sense was worthless.

"You seem to know something about this sort of thing," I said, after a few minutes.

Nance sighed. "Thirty years ago, I did some work for the government. Not in the U.S., but on the other side of the world." He looked at me expectantly. I said nothing. He took a deep breath and continued. "It was in the U.S.S.R. A fascinating country. Majestic lands, wonderful people and a mean, ruthless government. Gorbachev, however, was a visionary. He wanted a better life for the Russian people and a group of us helped him. When the country collapsed, I had to leave Moscow quickly. I miss the people, but I will never be able to go back."

There was a long pause while I digested this information. Then Nance broke the silence with another bombshell. "Earlier today I misled you about Kermer's face not showing up on my facial recognition system. It's true, he's not part of the American Photography Restoration Society."

"So, he's not CIA," I interjected.

"No, he's not," Nance answered. "His face did come up in the system, however."

I waited expectantly.

"He's an aide to the White house based office of the National Security Council."

Chapter 12

I invited Mary to come out to see the cabin the following Friday night. I told I would make dinner for her.

"Should I bring something, just in case?" she teased.

"Probably a good idea," I agreed.

She brought a lovely Merlot. She opened the wine while I cooked and then she surprised me.

"I have two tickets to the Kitt Peak National Observatory for evening and I wondered if you would like to go with me?" Earlier in the week, I had asked her during a rare lull at work what she liked best about living in Patagonia. She had answered without any hesitation. "The night sky. We live in one of the best places on Earth to watch and study the stars . . . I feel so lucky."

Reading my mind, she said, "After our brief talk about the stars, I'd like to show them to you."

I told I would love to go with her. She told me the plan: we were to arrive an hour before sunset. We could use the waning light of day to explore the exhibits and interactive displays before the staff served us a light dinner and presented an introduction to astronomy and to the National Observatory.

"Sounds like fun," I said, throwing a little pasta at my wall to see if it was ready to eat. The pasta didn't stick, but I thought it might be the logs. Plastered walls are much more reliable for discerning when the pasta has been cooked just right. Log cabins are okay if you want the pasta al dente.

Mary tossed the salad, but fortunately, not at the wall, and gave me my briefing. She told me that Kitt Peak was almost 7000 feet high and the observatory sat on leased land from the Tohono O'odham Reservation. "At sunset, you can see 100 miles in any direction because of the thin air and scarcity of light pollution," she said. "The program is four hours long and we need to dress warmly because it can get cold and windy up there."

We sat down to eat. "This marinara sauce is excellent," Mary said. "What did you put in it?"

For a fleeting second, I thought of taking the credit but couldn't do it. "We really have to thank Mr. Newman for the sauce," I said, weakly.

Mary's eyes widened. "Really? 'Newman's Own?'" My mouth was full and I nodded yes.

"Well done!" Mary took a big bite of her pasta and washed it down with a gulp of the merlot. "I hope you like the observatory as much I'm enjoying this spaghetti," she said, reaching for the garlic bread.

The next day driving up to Kitt Peak, Mary was so keyed up to show me this new world she was squirming in her seat. "Did you know that Kitt Peak's work provided the first indication of dark matter in the universe," she said at one point.

"Is that the same thing as the Dark Web?" I asked, with feigned innocence, immediately thinking of Nance's security system.

Mary frowned. "Very funny. Dark matter may dominate everything we see in regulating the dynamics of the entire universe."

"Even more than Fake News?" I said, but this went too far.

"You're not taking this seriously."

"I am. Honestly," I said. "I'm fascinated by this stuff. It's just that you are so darn cute that I can't help teasing you a little." In truth, I loved her passion. She looked slightly mollified.

I decided to change tack. "Tell me about your family," I asked

Mary adjusted in her seat to face me at a 45-degree angle. "My father is an astronomer."

"That makes sense. Now I see where you get your knowledge of the stars."

"It's not quite as obvious as it looks. His training is actually in astrophysics, but he veered off and wrote a couple of books on astronomy and now he teaches."

It took me a second to digest that information. "Are you and your dad close?"

Mary put her knees together and hiked her legs up underneath her. She leaned toward me. "I love my dad, but he makes it difficult. He's so smart he's often tough to reach. He's always thinking of something else. It's easier to love the stars."

"Is he at Kitt Peak?" I asked.

She put on her sunglasses. We were heading west and the setting sun was dipping below the visor. "No, he teaches at UCSD."

"Do you see him very often?" Mary settled back against the passenger door and thought for a moment.

"No. He left my mom. I stayed with her. He basically left me too. Now that I'm older, I can see it wasn't as personal as I took it. His first and only love will always be his work. Being rejected for the universe isn't the worst slight, but it still hurt. It was just my mom and me for about fourteen years until last year when my mom remarried. I have a few cousins scattered about that we see on special occasions."

I had to put my hand up over the top of my sunglasses. The sun was bleeding through under the visor right at my eyebrow level. "Do you like your stepfather?"

Mary rearranged her body to face the road. "We're very different, but he's a good man and I'm happy my mom is not alone."

"If you don't see your father, do the two of you talk very often?" The road took a curve, blessedly taking the sun out of my eyes and onto my left cheek. The light was now leaking through the side of my glasses.

Mary's eyes were on the road ahead. "Not often. We always end up arguing." She looked over at me. "He's very conservative. He like rules and order. Checklists. He thinks life should fit into one of his equations. Because we're family I can get him riled up with any offhand comment. Of course, he can push my buttons without much effort. I sometimes feel I'm an old push button phone when I'm talking to him: 'to get your daughter to cry, press 9.'"

I looked over at her. She shrugged. "Which buttons are those?" I asked.

She had her sparkle back. "You'll have to learn that in class, Doc."

The two-hour drive from Patagonia went by quickly with all the information Mary was throwing my way. "It's a faster drive from Tucson," she said. "That's where most of the tourists come from. These night viewings are almost always sold out."

I told her I was suitably honored. We entered the Quinlan Mountains and weaved our way up the corkscrew access road to Kitt Peak until we reached the summit. We were then parked in a caravan formation. We quickly scampered up to the Visitor Center, not wanting to miss any part of the sunset and views.

The stunning mountain desert vistas sprawled out below us and we joined the others taking photographs. Mary ran over to say hello to someone she recognized from the University Hospital. I glanced about me and did a double-take. About thirty yards away, Dylan Kermer was earnestly talking to a man in a sport coat wearing an official-looking lanyard around his neck. Dylan made a wide, sweeping gesture out over the retaining wall to the south and abruptly dropped his hand when he saw me. He looked just as surprised as I was. Turning back to the official, I could see Dylan's right index finger go up in the universal language of "hold on, I'll be right back." Soon, he was at my side.

"Harper! What are you doing here?" he asked, a little breathlessly.

"I was just about to take the tour. What about you?"

Dylan looked around carefully, then leaned in close to me and spoke in a low voice. "I'm trying to talk this administrator into letting me put a SBI-Net tower up here." He made that sweeping gesture again. "Look at the range we would have. This site would be perfect."

"What does he think?" I asked, waving at the official who appeared to be losing his patience with the interruption.

"He's a bureaucrat. He has no vision. I'm having trouble reaching him." Dylan turned to the official and put his index finger up again. This served to rankle the man further.

"I better go," Dylan said, turning back to me. "Let's get together again soon. That dinner was fun." He thumped me on the back. "Wish me luck!" he said, hurrying away.

I saw Mary beckoning to me at the building entrance and caught up with her.

"Who was that?" she asked, as we made our way to an open table and sat down.

"A guy I met at the Wild Horse. Dylan Kermer."

"What's he doing here?"

The crowd hushed as the man at the podium started our first lesson on how to use a star chart to find specific stars and constellations in the sky using binoculars.

"Protecting our country," I whispered. Mary looked at me skeptically, then slowly turned back to the speaker. Soon the telescopes were made available to us.

"This is the largest solar telescope in the world," the guide said.

As we looked through the eyepiece, Mary said it was famous for searching for near-Earth asteroids and calculating the probability of an impact with our planet. "Perhaps our greatest risk of extinction," she added.

We learned about the two National Optical Astronomy Observatory sister sites in New Mexico and Chile. We were able to see planets, multiple star systems, planetary nebulae, star clusters and other galaxies. It was beautiful, educational, fascinating and overwhelming. On the ride back to Patagonia we were quiet driving down the mountain. The vastness of the cosmos and the unadulterated beauty had subdued us.

"What was your favorite part?" Mary asked softly. "Other than being with me, of course."

"That goes without saying," I smiled. After some consideration, I replied. "I think it was actually seeing another galaxy. Trying to wrap my head around how there are billions of stars in this galaxy alone . . . and then looking through a telescope and seeing other galaxies that have billions of stars as well . . . it's unfathomable and I felt incredible small and humbled. Thank you so much for showing me this."

"I wanted to share this with you," Mary said. "Stephen Hawking said, since we can understand it, that makes us special."

I learned over and gave Mary a kiss. "What was that for?" she asked.

"Professor Hawking also said that if you are lucky enough to find love in this universe, remember it is there and don't throw it away," I said, returning my eyes to the road.

"I like that," Mary said, curling up

Chapter 13

The first time Dylan met Mary was at the Wild Horse a few days after our Kitt Peak road trip. Mary and I were eating dinner outside. It was early evening and the earth was almost done releasing the heat absorbed from the day's sun. The air was getting chilly and heat lamps had been brought out to the deck area. The street was busy with people making their way home from work and running last minute errands. A group of bicycle riders pedaled past, all wearing the same colorful jerseys and speaking animatedly in what sounded like Italian and I saw Mary perk up in interest. As the bicyclist rounded a far corner, I noticed Dylan looking at us from the patio entrance. I waved him over. He hesitated, then made his way around the tightly arranged tables. The candle on our table flickered when Dylan awkwardly approached us. Mary was pouring a glass of the chardonnay we had brought to dinner with us. She spilled a small amount over the side of her glass looking up as Dylan introduced himself. He took the proffered chair that I tilted towards him. He stared at Mary a second or two longer than was comfortable.

"Dylan and I met a few weeks ago, just after he arrived in town," I explained to Mary. She raised her eyebrows and was about to say something.

"Did you hear about the skirmish?" Dylan interjected with excitement after he had spread his napkin on his lap with precision.

I looked at Mary. She shook her head. "No, we haven't," I said.

"A couple of our guys got into a scrap with two mules carrying backpacks near Kino Springs."

"Our guys?" I asked.

"Border Patrol. We might have missed them completely if the National Guard spotters hadn't picked them up on their heat and motion sensors."

"We have National Guardsman working around here?" I asked in disbelief.

"Oh yes," Dylan said, warming up to the subject and his audience. "Regular army coming soon as well. All part of the "Secure the Border" initiative."

"I thought in this country it was against the law to use active-duty service members for law enforcement inside the United States?" I said.

"Funding hasn't quite cleared Congress yet," Dylan's voice lowered, "but the Executive Order was given two weeks ago. National Security."

"That excuse is a Presidential get-out-of-jail card, isn't it?" I said. "It's right up there with 'consultant.'" Dylan scowled. Mary was still preoccupied with the incident.

"What happened in Kino Spring?" Mary asked. It was the first time she'd spoken. "Two mules with backpacks? What is that?" she added, puzzled.

"Smugglers," Dylan clarified. "'Mules' refers to people hired to carry something – in this case, illegals are paid money to carry drugs across the border." Dylan added, "Boy, were they surprised! Shots were fired. They dropped their loads."

"Anyone hurt?" Mary asked, worry in her voice.

"Did they catch them?" I asked simultaneously.

"No one hurt," Dylan said, nodding at Mary. "They scampered back across the border. We got the loads though. Weighing the marijuana now. Some photos taken, thanks to the Guardsmen. Those illegals won't be using that route into our country again any time soon!" he said triumphantly.

"How do you know they were illegals?" I asked.

"Why would they try to sneak into our country if they weren't?" Dylan said triumphantly.

"Americans sell drugs too," Mary said casually. "Since it's illegal, if you were carrying a back pack with marijuana you wouldn't just stroll through Nogales Customs. And if you were caught illegally crossing in a wash with it, wouldn't you scamper back to Mexico instead of being arrested here?"

Dylan flushed. "You're obscuring the obvious," he said.

"She doesn't know any better," I said. I didn't like him picking on Mary, but I immediately regretted saying it. Mary didn't need protecting. She evidently didn't care if there was a potential slight. Why should I be offended?

"These were bad guys breaking the law and our men stopped them," Dylan countered.

"Fair point," Mary said, rising. "Excuse me, I'm going to wash my hands before dinner. Be right back." She left the patio and entered the restaurant.

"Who's the girl?" Dylan asked once she was inside. "She's a spitfire." He was energized by the conversation.

"Mary Durant. She is an independent sort. She's the nurse at the medical clinic."

"The one you work at?"

"The same."

"You guys married?"

"We've been on a couple of dates."

"She's a looker."

"I'll tell her when she returns."

Dylan looked stricken. "Don't tell her I said that."

Mary returned, sat down and adjusted her napkin. We continued with our dinner. Dylan was a strident conversationalist and it put me off from the very beginning. He liked to lecture on complex subjects and plumbing the depth of his platitudes was like watching a flat stone skip across a pond. Immigration, drugs, guns, health care - he had naive and clichéd views of policy and how certain decisions would change the world. He was extremely confident of his beliefs and his plans. I felt slightly diminished because my rebuttals were couched by possibility and probability. I had lived long enough and learned the modicum necessary to be humbled by the capriciousness of life. Too many times in my past I had absolutely known a thing to be true and it had turned out to be false. But, I could tell immediately that Mary was intrigued by his zeal. This seemed to overwhelm the flimsy content of his arguments. Her idealistic youth seemed smitten.

We were just finishing our meals and about to leave when two men approached our table. They were locals and I'd seen them in town often enough to nod at them when we passed in the street. They had not been to the clinic, but it was a small town and I knew they worked highway maintenance for the State of Arizona. Usually the tall one was accompanied by his mean-looking German Shepherd when he was in town running errands. Tonight, the two men were on their own and had been drowning the frustrations of their week in some of the microbrew available at the bar.

"Hey Doc," the tall one said. "Joe and me were having a bet over there," he waived his arm in the general direction of the bar. "He says you are some sort of Clinton-loving liberal from the East sent to spy on us deplorables. Is that true?" Joe stood there smiling a sloppy grin. He was stout with big shoulders and arms. He could have been a fullback or a linebacker.

I could feel Mary tense up. "I am from the East," I said. "You've got me there."

Joe could speak after all. "Mike disagrees and says you're here to sabotage the President's new 'zero tolerance' policy to those people who shouldn't be here anyway."

"No more 'catch and release' school yard games," Mike chimed in with a malevolent grin.

"This country is playing hardball now." Mike and Joe looked at each other, laughed and high fived.

Looking at Mary, Dylan frowned. I could see he wasn't worried about me or the rhetoric, but he didn't like rudeness in front of the lady. Mary started to say something, but I interjected. "Where are you going to hold all those women and children?" I asked with my best impersonation of respectful curiosity. "More taxes to build more jails? The courts will be so jammed up you'll have to feed them for two to three years before their cases are heard. That will cost even more in taxes." I paused. "Even people from the East hate taxes."

"When all the National Guard soldiers get here, they'll just shoot them," Mike retorted.

"Shoot the immigrants?" I said. "We don't need military protection around here. School shootings in America are much more violent and deadly than anything along the Arizona border."

Dylan spoke up. He could be very literal. "The National Guard won't be allowed to shoot anyone," he said in all seriousness. "They'll be here in an advisory, helpful role."

"Like we were in Vietnam," Joe sneered.

"The Guard is also supposed to assist with road construction," I offered helpfully. "Hopefully, save some Arizona state dollars by enabling some job cuts in the highway department." Mike and Joe looked at each other slightly confused.

"I hadn't heard that," Mike mumbled.

Mary stood up. Even in the clinic she was always a peacemaker. "Mike and Joe." She knew everyone in town. "I can tell you're both thirsty as hell. Please let me buy you a round." She flashed a ten-dollar bill and her smile. "Come with me." She hooked her arm inside their elbows affectionately and, not sure exactly what had just happened, Mike and Joe allowed Mary to herd them back to the bar.

"I was going to ask that new guy if he wanted to join us," I heard Mike say as they walked away.

"He's with us tonight," Mary said soothingly.

When we left the restaurant, Mike and Joe were still at the bar, loudly rolling for their drinks with three other friends. The bartender had provided a nice leather mug to hold the dice. The sight brought me back to my college days. We used to play the game to see who would buy the next round of beer. It was a primitive poker game that demanded no skill whatsoever. Five dice were shaken in a cup and then cast on the bar top like it was a Vegas craps table. Only pairs, three of a kind, full house, four of a kind, etc., mattered. Five sixes were unbeatable, but three deuces would probably keep you from having to pay the bar bill.

After saying good night to Dylan, Mary and I walked down McKeown Street and picked up a couple of ice cream cones to enjoy as we sauntered through town. The full moon was so bright, for a moment I thought there had been a light dusting of snow while we were preoccupied with dinner. The whole town was bathed in moonglow. I looked at the old wooden buildings and the sweeping wilderness beyond. The lurking mountains blocked sections of the flickering stars. This land had been supporting rebellious humans for centuries. What was the National Guard doing here? Were American citizens really going to allow the military to establish a presence inside our borders to "protect us?" This is how repressive regimes started. Or had the politics of fear reached a religious fervor? Fear of people with different ideas, different gods or most of all, people who looked different from us? Who was going to protect us from this contrived malice?

"I like that guy Dylan," Mary said. I could see the appeal. Up till now, life had not disappointed Dylan. He had yet to disappoint himself. He was ambitious and enthusiastic instead of cynical. His juvenescence was endearing to Mary. He was unsullied and as fresh as the air after a morning rain.

"He annoys me a little," I said.

"He's harmless," she said, grabbing my hand with hers.

"I'm not sure he's harmless, but I see what you mean. He looks out of place for whatever it is he's doing in this town."

"He looks lonely," Mary said. "That's what it is."

"He's a little intimidated by you, but soon he'll feel more comfortable," I said with a wry smile. "Then, watch out."

Mary removed her hand and put her arm in mine. "That's a practiced move," I said. "I saw that move in the restaurant and noticed it worked well on Mike and Joe. Thanks for that, by the way." She smiled by way of response.

"What was that 'National Guard highway construction assistance' about anyway?" she asked.

"Misdirection," I smiled. "Two can play that game." She laughed.

The night was getting quiet. The odd pickup truck rumbled by. Some laughter and shouts could be heard in the distance. A pack of coyotes howled just outside town. Backyard dogs started barking from every direction. Slowly the cacophony died down, our ice cream disappeared and I walked Mary back to her car.

Chapter 14

The Saturday night after our chance dinner with Dylan, there was a dance at the Patagonia Union High School gymnasium. It was a benefit for the Indian Clinic with a small price for admission. The high school students - the Lobos - had decorated the gym very nicely. Plastic pine trees with white lights, no doubt taken from Christmas decoration boxes in home garages and attics throughout town, lined the perimeter of the basketball court and enclosed the tables and dance floor. Colorful bunting connected the trees and reflected the soft single camping light placed on the dining tables which were covered with white tablecloths. Local restaurants had constructed small, makeshift booths to show off their food. Some local artists donated their works and a mini-auction was held. The big attraction was a regional up-and-coming country western band. The elevated stage at the north end of the gymnasium was set up with their instruments, amplifiers and speakers. The band was coming off a popular performance the year before at the Country Thunder Weekend Festival in Florence, Arizona. Fortunately, the town had booked them before their big breakthrough and to their credit, the band was honoring this commitment. It was an exciting night for the clinic and the town.

I wasn't the only one stealing a glance at Mary. She looked beautiful wearing red cowboy boots that stopped half-way between her ankle and knee, a white blouse that exposed her bare shoulders and a short, black, flowing skirt. The skirt had small, mauve wildflowers sewn into it. My heart fell out of my chest when I first saw her. When she noticed me watching her she gave me a sassy smile and did a little sashay. I was hooked. Right through the cheek. No way to shake that hook or spit the bit.

The auditorium was very crowded and I saw the Fire Marshall had a look of consternation on his face. Mary and I walked to our table. As representatives of the clinic we had a choice position on the edge of the small dance floor. We found our name tags and sat down. A moment later, to my surprise, Dylan came to our table, picked up a name tag and sat down on the other side of Mary.

"Good evening," he said. "My company made a sizable donation to your clinic and offered me a ticket for tonight. I hope you don't mind, but I asked to sit with you both because I don't know anyone else." Introductions were made around the table and I heard Dylan tell Mary, "You look very pretty tonight." She murmured a thank you.

The acoustics in the hall were awful and it was difficult for the three of us to carry on a conversation. When Mary turned her head to Dylan I couldn't make out what they were saying at all. For Dylan to talk to me he had to shout across Mary. Even then it was difficult for me to hear him. The gestalt of their conversation was all superficial pleasantries but I was feeling left out. It appeared they could hear each other fine.

"I forgot to ask you: were you able to convince the Kitt's Peak administrator to let you put a tower up?" I managed to shout at Dylan over the din.

He immediately looked crestfallen and shook his head. "No, like I told you, I could tell the guy has no vision."

"I saw you talking to that man," Mary said. "It looked like you were making a strong case."

Dylan brightened immediately at the idea Mary had been watching him. Practically beaming, he said, "It was a strong argument for our country's security. He should have said yes."

An announcement was made and our table stood and led the way through the crowd to the food stations. As we moved from among the various restaurant groups, different cuisine began to pile up on my plate. The variety of flavors was always welcome, the superficial small talk to the people in attendance, somewhat onerous. When we sat back at our table I felt sheepish. I could never eat all the food on my plate.

Dylan leaned over to Mary, "What is that food you picked out?" he asked, pointing to a flour-fried buttery fillet on the side of her plate.

"The caligraphied sign at the Kingfisher stall said 'Sole Meunière,'" Mary answered, gently separating a piece with a flick of her fork.

"Translation, por favor," Dylan said to both of us.

"White fish with vertigo," I offered. Mary's eyes crinkled as she chewed, but my answer didn't register with Dylan. She told him it was a French fish dish and he vigorously started in on his own selections. The three of us worked on our multiple courses until we finally reached the elaborate desserts. Coffee was brought around.

Dylan pulled out a pack of cigarettes and lit one.

I leaned over. "The fire marshal will be on you in no time," I said.

"What? No smoking in here either? This town is more backwards than I thought." He made no move to put out his cigarette. He tapped the ashes on his bread plate and placed the cigarette there momentarily. Mary reached over, took the cigarette and dropped it in her water glass. She looked at him with a challenging, devilish glint in her eye.

"You don't want to die young now, do you?" she cooed demurely.

"All my grandparents are in their nineties and still drive," he said obstinately. But he did not reach for another cigarette.

With dinner out of the way, the band struck up. Now it was truly impossible to have any meaningful discourse. People were eager to dance and the floor began to fill quickly. I looked around to check out the people I knew. Out of the corner of my eye I saw Dylan lean in and say something to Mary and a moment later they were walking together onto the dance floor. They began to dance on the edge of the crowd and then were swept up in the tsunami of dancers to the hidden core of the tumult.

I saw flashes of the two of them as the sea of dancers parted periodically and then closed again. Mary had a rhythm and confidence about her that was unconsciously sensual in its effortless grace. Dylan moved stiffly and usually a split second too late to the beat. The eye more than the ear caught the singularity. The band transitioned to a faster song. Dylan was red-faced, gazing downwards with intensity. His gyrations were erratic. His concentration was complete and insular. Once he looked up at Mary and she smiled. He flushed even more with sheepish embarrassment and even I felt his self-consciousness. Begrudgingly, I noted that with his enthusiasm he was managing to look endearing. Mary was totally without guile and when she laughed, the force of her attractiveness was like a tractor beam pulling me in from across the crowded room.

They were both a little breathless when they returned to the table. Dylan held Mary's chair for her and she was touched by the chivalry. The din made chatting useless. I caught Dylan's eye and for a moment I saw a spark of superiority in it. I was confused, but then I saw myself as Dylan saw me: a middle-aged man whose best days were behind him, cynical rather than idealistic, slowly losing muscle mass, eyesight acuity fading, an obvious inability to understand speech in a noisy environment.

"I hope you don't mind I stole your girl for a quick twirl around the dance floor?" Dylan shouted, pushing Mary and her chair back closer to the table.

I caught his eye as he took his hand off of Mary's chair. He looked a little smug for a guy who had just danced with a woman I cared for very much.

"Not at all," I replied with forced gallantry and a strained smile. I raised my hand to support the back of Mary's chair although I immediately felt my involuntary vulnerability and possessive gesture was too obvious. "The band is quite good," I offered. I tried to stifle the desperation suddenly creeping through me. Dylan turned his chair to face the dance floor. I could feel Mary's warmth in the seat next to me. Her heat radiated out in concentric circles with every deep breath. If I could feel her heat in my chair, I had no doubt Dylan could feel it in his.

Chapter 15

Mary and I started seeing each other more frequently. I realized it was so much easier to have a healthy, consistent relationship when responsibility for afterhours medical emergencies was taken out of the equation. The Indian Clinic was a volunteer public health effort. There was no on-call commitment. No late-night phone calls or emergency room consultations. The patients we voluntarily cared for during the day fell back into the health care safety net of private and public hospitals at night and on weekends. I believe Mary realized it as well and slowly her reluctance to get involved with a doctor seemed to fade. One day Mary came over after work and I grilled some salmon for dinner. She had unobtrusively brought along a gym bag. She stayed over at the cabin that night. It was all so natural and seamless. It became the highlight of my each and every day.

Soon thereafter came a gorgeous Sunday without a cloud in the sky. Mary said to me, "Let's have a picnic!"

"I'd like to get some exercise," I countered. "Let's go on a hike."

"Let's do both!" That sounded like an excellent solution.

She wanted to surprise me and would only tell me we were going on a short road trip to the "The Ngorogoro Crater of Tucson." Bewildered, I brought a book to read, thinking she might be trying to sneak in a museum visit. A little north of downtown Tucson we left the highway and drove east. After about 25 more minutes Mary had me turn north again and we passed a restored adobe outpost called "Fort Lowell."

"Pull into the parking lot for a minute," she requested. I stopped beside an artist's rendering of a time many years ago.

Mary pointed to the large painting and then with a sweeping hand gesture she took in the restoration project. "This was a U.S. Army post in the late 1800's. Multiple creeks flow off the Santa Catalina mountains," she smiled and pointed a couple of miles north from where we were. "We're in the foothills now. The Army placed the post here because it's where two creeks join to form the Rillito River. The Hohokam Indians had chosen the site centuries earlier for the same reason. This fort was very active during the Apache Wars. The cavalry protected the entire Tucson area."

There was a small building with the remnants of what looked to be an old cross on the top of the structure's A-frame adobe peak. A sign out front said: "For all thee that have abandoned hope."

"What is that structure," I asked.

Mary smiled. "A wedding chapel."

She pointed to a larger building. "The biggest building on post was the hospital. You might have heard of one young officer who served here: Dr. Walter Reed."

I was impressed. "He did the research on Yellow Fever."

"My grandfather was a patient at Walter Reed Army Medical Center in Washington, D.C.," Mary said. Her eyes darkened. "Unfortunately, he ultimately died there."

"I'm sorry."

"Couldn't be helped," she said looking away. "Too many cigarettes." Looking back to me, she said. "I'll tell you about it another time. This is our picnic day." She turned back to face the windshield. "Okay. Let's go." I squeezed her hand and pulled back onto the road. Mary did not let go of my hand.

Ten minutes later when I thought we were going to dead-end in the mountains themselves, Mary had me pull into a parking lot. I caught a glimpse of a small sign with the National Forest insignia as she directed me where to park. We picked up a map at the visitor's center and I read how the desert trails in the canyon led to waterfalls, swimming holes, deer, rattlesnakes and mountain lions. "Mountain lions?" I quoted out loud.

"Yes! Isn't that exciting," Mary said, eyes gleaming.

We hiked up the Sabino Canyon trail and were immediately surrounded by hundreds of saguaros. We veered off the trail, up a couple of switch-backs which brought us closer to a thunderous roar.

Turning out of a small ravine, we came down upon a dam waterfall spilling into a pool below.

"Sycamore Dam," Mary said. "Too early in the day and too little exercise under our belts to stop here for our picnic - especially for a big hiker like you," she said, with a wink. I could barely hear her over the sound of the water. "But I like this spot and I wanted to show it to you."

We rested on the rocks for a bit. My vanity didn't let me tell Mary the sun was getting high, the air hot and the backpack heavy. She stood up and I followed her as we continued to climb. Soon, the Tucson Valley was far below us.

"Where are the mountain lions?" I asked.

"A little further up," she smiled. "Let's go since we've already passed most of the rattlesnakes." I blanched and followed her meekly. We climbed higher as we followed the Sabino Creek. She said the winter snowfall fed the Creek from its origin at the summit of Mt. Lemmon.

We stopped at a deserted concrete picnic table overlooking thick bands of water dancing down shear rock to settle in a serene swimming hole. Fifty yards later the water exited the pool and began meandering over smooth rocks creating several stepped waterfalls. The rushing, falling water serenaded us as it continued its journey down the canyon. Laughing, we stripped down and skinny dipped in the bracingly cold, natural pool. Invigorated, we set out our picnic.

The food, wine and exercise fused to make us feel lazy and luxurious, so we took a siesta beside the swimming hole on the "lunch rocks", as Mary called them. I could feel the sun's heat burning through my swim cooled skin. Mary fell asleep for a short time with her head on my shoulder. Lying on her side against me, her profile was sharp against the clean, transparent mountain eddy. So was the curve of her torso that deepened and then lifted with each breath. I was stunned by the wonder of her. I had never felt happier. As the sun began to cast long shadows in the canyon, we leisurely made our way back down. Before we got to the car, we stopped at the Visitor's Center once again and I perused the book section. Mary pointed out a small, stuffed tiger.

"Isn't that precious?" she said. "See they're not all that scary."

"That's a tiger not a lion," I said, bemused.

"Same difference," she said, unfazed. She went to the restroom before we started the drive back to Patagonia. In the car, I handed her a bag.

"I bought you a souvenir of our picnic." She opened it. Her eyes lit up. "It's perfect!" she said, clutching the small tiger to her breast. "I'll put it on the couch in the cabin."

When we got back to Mary's apartment she wordlessly led me back to her bedroom. There she introduced me to her shy, calico cat, Embers. Looking straight into my eyes Mary unhurriedly took my clothes off. Then she slowly disrobed. We kissed. Very softly at first and then she leaned into me until we fell on the bed. As I explored and caressed her she moaned softly. Murmuring indistinct sounds. Her movements were graceful responses to my touch and my body responded to her fingers making soft, brushstrokes on my skin. Every motion of us together was an affirmation between us. Like the billions of lives before us who merged in this dance, our blood raced together, a rhythm was found, our breaths became sharper and more shallow, our embraces still tender, but stronger and more frantic as clocks slowed and outside world troubles diminished until we found that moment in each other where we tautened and building and building, exploded across the edge into that temporary blackness that transcends self and aloneness, while reaffirming our vital life force in an expression of beauty, need, purpose, dignity and love.

Afterwards Mary snuggled next to me and fell asleep in the crook of my arm. Her face was serene in repose against my chest. Both of her hands were clasped together as if in prayer with the fingertips grazing her chin. Her knees were bent and the left one hung lazily over my left hip. With my left hand, I stroked the line of her ribs as it plunged at her waist to abruptly rise to the round swell of hip. The dips and curves and turns of her flank rose and fell softly with her breathing. She was beautiful in the gathering darkness.

In the morning, I awoke and gazed for a few moments at Mary's tousled hair. She was languid in sleep. I slipped from her arms and crept out of the bedroom. After a quick reconnaissance of her kitchen, I made coffee and toast. I scrambled a couple of eggs, found a tray and padded back to the bedroom. Mary woke with a big stretch and propped herself up in bed against several pillows. She was warm and still sleepy. I set the tray on her lap, kissed her forehead and left for my cabin. I had to clean myself up before coming back into town as a respectable physician for the day's clinic.

Chapter 16

After Sabino Canyon, the next weekend we planned a movie night at the cabin for Saturday night. Mary arrived with a gym bag packed with some essentials and wordlessly left it at my cabin when we parted late Sunday morning. She had to keep Embers at her apartment because of my allergy to cats.

I spent the rest of Sunday doing all the things that need to be done on an off day to push life forward. Laundry, bills, cleaning, grocery shopping and exercise consumed the last day of the too-short weekend.

On Monday morning, we were half-way through our busy clinic schedule when I heard a commotion coming from the waiting room. I walked out of my examining room to see Mary carrying a young girl in her arms. Trailing behind Mary was a woman I assumed to be the child's mother. She was talking to Becky, the clinic's medical assistant.

"She's really sick, Doctor," Mary said with worry all over her face. She insisted on calling me 'doctor' when we were at work. We all moved into the second examining room. "Her name is Adele."

"Are you her mother?" I asked the woman who accompanied the child.

"I'm Adele's grandmother," the woman answered. "I watch her during the day while her parents are working."

"I'm Dr. Harper," I said extending my hand. "Can you tell me why you brought her in?"

"Last week she caught a cold and wasn't feeling very well. Wednesday night I was drying her off from her bath and I noticed some red marks on her stomach. I thought they were mosquito bites. She went to school Thursday but when she came home she was really tired and felt hot. I noticed the mosquito bites were all around her neck and some on her face. She had a headache and didn't feel well on Friday, so I let her stay home from school. All weekend long she wouldn't get out of bed. I brought her ginger ale and crackers, but she didn't want to eat anything. Last night in the middle of the night she vomited and this morning she was sleepy and talking gibberish." The grandmother started to cry. "I don't know where my ninita went!"

Mary placed Adele on the examining table and helped me take off her tee-shirt. She had a rose-red rash of elliptical, slightly raised lesions from two to three millimeters in size spread over her torso, face and head. I took out my penlight and looked in her throat. Small white spots were scattered through her mouth and the back of her throat. Adele was moaning words we couldn't understand. She was moving her right hand and leg, but not her left side. I grabbed the Thermascan ear thermometer and placed it in her ear canal. Her temperature was 102.5 degrees Fahrenheit. I stepped back.

"What's going on Doctor?" Adele's grandmother asked through her tears. Mary was taking the child's blood pressure and feeling for her pulse.

"She has the measles," I said. "Has she been vaccinated? I'm sorry I didn't catch your name, Ma'am."

"I'm Louise. Louise Waters." Ms. Waters looked down. "Adele's father doesn't believe in vaccinations. My daughter and he had a big argument about it. He said he wasn't going to let any doctor give his little girl autism."

I looked at Mary. She was distraught over the little girl's condition and was trying not to show her concern to Ms. Waters. "80 over 40 and 96," she said referencing the blood pressure and pulse.

"Get me an IV set-up, please. I'll need some decadron. Have Rachel call an ambulance and see if Becky can call University Hospital and get the pediatric doctor at the Children's ER on the phone." Mary hurried out and I turned back to Ms. Waters.

She spoke first, in disbelief. "But measles isn't so bad. Are you sure?"

"In some kids, the measles virus infects the brain and causes swelling. It's called Measles-Induced Encephalitis."

"Is it serious?"

"It can be serious, yes." Before I could say any more, Ms. Waters started wailing. She started to fall and I caught her. She latched on to me, sobbing uncontrollably as I gently helped her to a chair.

Mary came in with intravenous materials and the steroids. "I'm going to give your granddaughter some medicine that helps decrease the swelling in her brain," I explained to Ms. Waters. "Then we need to transfer her to the University Hospital in Tucson. They have an excellent children's hospital there and Adele will be in good hands. I think you should call her parents and have them meet you in Tucson." Ms. Waters steadied herself, as tears continued to stream down her cheeks. She nodded weakly. I put the IV in Adele's left arm and injected the decadron. Becky poked her head in to say the emergency room doctor from Children's Hospital was on the phone. "Can you stay with Adele for a moment?" I asked the MA. Mary and I walked out to the hallway.

Mary stopped me before I could get to the telephone "Don't you think you should tell her that there is a chance her granddaughter could have permanent brain damage or even die?"

"No. Not right now."

"I think you should," she said defiantly.

"You are right and I will. Just not this second. She's feeling awful right now. Somehow, she thinks this is her fault. Maybe she thinks she should have been Adele's advocate with her son-in-law and she's let her granddaughter down. Let me get this transfer arranged."

"She deserves to know," Mary insisted.

"I agree. The whole family needs to know. But I don't want to overwhelm Ms. Waters with the information at this exact moment. She feels horribly guilty as it is." I went to the phone. I could feel Mary fret behind me. She was right to be concerned and I knew she was worried for Adele. I just didn't know how much the grandmother could take all at once and the human being in me didn't want to mention this awful possibility while she was already wracked with guilt for not pushing her son-in-law harder for the vaccination. Encephalitis in a child was a difficult trauma for any family to endure.

*   *   *

Once Adele and her grandmother were safely on their way to Tucson, Mary called the Mountain Vista Elementary School. The principal said one of the teachers told him two students came to school that morning with a runny nose, cough, fever and a visible rash covering their bodies. They also had stomach pains. The children had been to classes and playing outside with the other children. The principal said his staff was quickly becoming frantic and didn't know what to do.

"Keep them apart from the other children and I'll be right over,' Mary said. "Have you been vaccinated for measles?" Mary asked the principal. He had. "Go ask your teachers that question and I'll be right over." Mary tried to sound reassuring. "Have all the students' health records available when I get there please."

Mary said she would call me from the school. Rachel was relieved Adele had come right through and not mingled in our waiting room. I nodded and asked her to bring in the next patient.

*   *   *

When Mary arrived at Mountain Vista the school was in chaos as small informed groups of students and teachers disclosed to others Adele's plight. The office had left a message for the parents of the two children with symptoms, but not heard back from them. Students with cell phones called home and parents began to arrive, demanding to take their children home. Other parents couldn't get out of work and were panic-stricken. Mary asked the principal to lock down the school until she could get more facts. She examined the boy and girl with the symptoms and made the diagnosis of measles. The children didn't know if they had ever been vaccinated but were sure they never had a rash like this before. They were starting to feel scared and wanted to go home.

"Is anyone pregnant at home?" Mary asked the students.

"My mom is," a young girl answered. Mary told the principal pregnant women and children under one year of age were at highest risk for severe measles complications and asked him to get word out.

Mary and the teachers quickly went through all the health records on file. Forty students had not received the Mumps, Measles and Rubella vaccine and were considered for the moment as non-immune.

Mary paused as the teachers murmured among themselves. She surveyed her audience. "I put a call into the Santa Cruz Health Department and we're waiting for instructions. Right now, you should tell the parents that if any of their family members demonstrate these symptoms," she began to hand out a paper with measles symptoms she had quickly penned and copied, "to call our clinic to see Dr. Harper. Don't just show up. We don't want to infect the whole waiting room. It is the pregnant, the immunosuppressed, the very old and the very young who are most at risk with this disease."

A teacher interrupted. "How long are the children infectious?"

"The time period between exposure and developing the rash is usually 14 days," Mary replied. "But the person is infectious from four days before the rash to four days after the rash appears."

"Oh my god!" someone whispered.

"Yes," Mary added. "This can be very serious. According to the World Health Organization, last year there were over 100,000 deaths from measles."

Chapter 17

After work, I needed to decompress. Mary was still wrapping things up at the elementary school. I walked down Naugle Ave. and turned left to head north on 4th Avenue. The Wagon Wheel Saloon was on the left and I went in. The large horseshoe bar was dark and quiet. I had a pint and reflected on the day. A different practice of medicine from the one I left in New England. Different people with their own dreams and expectations from life. I wasn't hungry and declined a second beer.

I left the Wagon Wheel Saloon and walked east. My jeep was parked a few blocks away. My path took me past the Benderly-Kendall Opera House on my left. The doors of the beautiful new venue for the performing arts were open to the street for ventilation and I could hear from the sidewalk a speaker pressing his message to the crowd inside. The poster advertised a meeting to discuss the Patagonia Town Council's official position on a possible extension of the border wall between the U.S. and Mexico. The mayor and the town council were preparing a resolution to capture the sentiment of Patagonia citizens. This resolution would then be published in the Patagonia Regional Times and become part of the town's public record on this issue. I took a couple of steps inside and ducked to my right, finding a spot to stand inconspicuously in the back-corner shadows under an arch. I could see a friend of Mary's, Bob Baxter, sitting in an aisle seat in the third row from the front. Baxter was the editor of the town paper. The head of a local chapter of a conservative political action group was debating the merits of a wall with a member of the Town Council. The conversation was spiraling into name calling.

"Your views don't represent this area."

"Because they aren't racist?"

The 'Fake News Media' was lambasted by the conservative and directed at the Town Councilman. 'Serial polluter' was lobbed back at the conservative by the representative. Violence was in the air and I wanted no part of it. I made my way to the exit along with many others dispirited by the enmity of the discussion and divisiveness of the issue.

I tried to reconcile this with the rest of the day's news around the country I had scanned on my computer before leaving the office. Dash cam footage of a black man being assaulted by white policemen; cell phone images of a gay teenager being dragged behind a pick-up truck along a dusty, backroad; a woman in a burka harassed on a big city subway.

People around me walked home and others started their cars. This meeting was over for tonight, but the issues were unresolved, left to be continued on another day. I wondered how the Town Council would vote. The traffic coalesced into a sea of red lights as the occupants retreated to the small corner of the world they called home. Houses here had been staked out with picket fences instead of a bollard wall. Cyclone for the moment, still only used to fence in the farm animals.

I saw Dylan as I was leaving. He was talking to a tall man I didn't recognize. They stood stiffly and the conversation appeared solemn until they laughed awkwardly over some exchange. I made a step to join them but the movement got Dylan's attention. He caught my eye and almost imperceptibly shook his head. I immediately understood he didn't want company at that moment. I kept walking. There was no personal threat as I crossed the Town Park and walked up the hill, but I could feel in the air the potential violent energy of this divided slice of humanity. The people I lived among appeared poised to defend, enforce and amplify their individual interpretations of the inalienable, God-given rights of all Americans. I walked up the deserted side street and longed for the perceived safety of my remote little cabin.

Chapter 18

The first thing I did at the office the next morning was to check on Adele's condition. She was still in University Hospital but her acute condition was improving. It was anticipated she soon would be transferred to a rehabilitation facility. The rehab doctors had consulted in the hospital and were cautiously optimistic she would walk again, but were concerned about potential permanent cognitive dysfunction.

Our Indian clinic was very busy all morning, but after seeing our second wave of afternoon patients, Mary and I took a coffee break together. Stepping out the back, the wind was picking up. The sun was bright and heating up the earth which would soon start its own little dance with the colder atmosphere. Spring was well on its way. We held our coffee with both hands as a chill lingered in the shade of the clinic's back porch. The trees were swaying and I listened to the wind tease the forest.

"How are you doing?" I asked. Mary had been very subdued all morning. I knew seeing Adele so sick had upset her.

She looked past me, copper hair flying in every direction. Her eyes were like heat seeking sapphires. It reminded me I should never even have had a chance with her. I had forgotten this during the euphoria of our courtship.

"I should be asking you that," Mary said turning to me with true concern. "How is your grandmother?" Earlier in the morning there had been a message for me from back East. My grandmother had been taken to a hospital. I had called the hospital and managed to talk to the doctor. They were treating her for congestive heart failure.

"I'm worried, of course. When I talked to the nurse this morning she said my grandmother was responding to the diuretic and they had increased her digitalis dosage. I'm actually glad to be at work and forced to think of something else for a short time." I risked putting my arm in the bend of her elbow. Public displays of affection in the clinic setting were not professional. Mary leaned into me. Then the back door opened and we were called back into the clinic. Mary flinched and quickly headed back in. I lingered on the porch gazing at the oscillating treetops. I was beginning to be able to focus on a vision of possibility; of the long run together I could picture of a life with Mary. I had felt the thrill of passion and in other moments, kindness. She had depth and substance. We laughed a lot. We were good together. Yet, I felt a nagging disquiet I attributed to the measles case the day before and the news of my grandmother. Contemplating the vagaries of fate, I turned and re-entered the clinic.

Mary had to leave work promptly after we saw our last patient. She had an appointment with her family doctor for her annual check-up. She still had close ties with the people she had worked with at the University Hospital and her physician was in Tucson.

I was in my tiny office mindlessly finishing my charting when Becky came in to say good night. She handed me a sealed note. I told her to have a good evening and opened the envelope. It was from Bob Deerdorff, the Vice Chairman of "Humane Borders, Incorporated." Humane Borders was a group of volunteers motivated by kindness to help save desperate migrants from the perilous journey on foot crossing the Sonoran Desert. The migrants rarely were prepared for the dehydration and exposure. Death ensued too often in the harsh desert environment. With permission from the landowners, they maintained a system of water stations along the Arizona-Mexico border south of Patagonia.

On a water run to replace one of the blue flagged barrels, he had heard about a sick child just across the Lochiel border, north of Santa Cruz, Sonora. His note asked me to go check on this child to see if I could help. Deerdorff said he'd have liked to go with me, but had to appear in Tucson Court. Volunteers from a sister humanitarian organization called "No More Deaths/No Mas Muertes" had been arrested for leaving food and water on federal land in the Cabeza Prieta National Wildlife Refuge. This despite the recent recovery of 105 human remains of border crossers who had died in Southern Arizona this year alone. Most of the deaths were exposure to the hot sun, cold nights or dehydration.

"I was subpoenaed as a defense witness and I'm to testify in the morning," Deerdorff wrote. He finished the note by saying the family of the sick child lived on the creek that flowed from the La Bola hills. In the envelope, he enclosed a hand drawn map to their home.

I loaded up a bag of medical supplies and threw them in my car. I needed to go home and get my hiking gear, but had to wait until dark before venturing across the border. I stopped at the Wild Horse to order some sandwiches for the trip.

I sat nursing a beer while the sandwiches were being made. I felt tired. Depleted. I wished I had not received the note about the sick child. It had been a long day and I didn't feel the energy necessary for the undertaking. I suddenly felt vulnerable going to help a patient on the other side of the border. There was too much going on. I did not want to get involved when I had Mary in my life. I felt a pang of selfishness, then anxiousness. All my life I wanted this peace. Now I had something to lose. It had occurred to me in New England it was foolish to think I could find happiness in a different place. Life was the same wherever you were. How could I expect to find love in a part-time volunteer position? Now I wondered, having found it, would I throw it away crossing the border at night to make a house-call? Death was the ultimate and absolute abandonment. My grandmother, a lifelong atheist, told me the last time I was with her that she hoped there was an afterlife so she could get together once again with my grandfather. My other relations all believed in God and trusted God. I could see the comfort there was in this. In that I envied them. I was much more afraid that Hawking was correct and the whole spiel was a fairy tale for people afraid of the dark. Now I was going out into the night to dodge soldiers, patrol agents and scared, blustering people on one side of the border, to hopefully aid a sick child on the other side. Death, of course, would take care of any of the pain and anxiousness I felt now. But I wanted my chance for peace and happiness. I also wanted that sick child to have a chance. Isn't that the reason I went into medicine I asked myself? Being alive is hope … and pain … loss . . . and hope again. Hope being the greatest courage.

"May I join you?" a voice from over my shoulder startled me out of my reverie. I turned. It was Kermer. I nodded yes. The barkeep came up with a large grocery bag.

"Here are your sandwiches," the bartender said, lifting the bag up on to the bar counter. I thanked him and paid.

"Going somewhere?" Dylan asked. He was totally ingenuous.

I thought before answering. Then I made my decision. "I've got a house call to make tonight," I said. There was a three-beat silence.

"Down south?" Dylan asked, his eyes widening. "Where?"

"Up south," I said. I couldn't help being a jerk. I guess I did resent his dancing with Mary. It was a

counterintuitive truth in Patagonia, but as one went
south to Mexico, the altitude increased.

Dylan looked perplexed, but he forged on. "Can
I come with you?" he suddenly asked.

"Do you have any gear?" I asked. "You do
realize there are venomous creatures out there?
Thorny vegetation lurks everywhere and is hard to
see in the dark. Not to mention the javelina, bear and
cougars in these mountains." All true, but perhaps I
was overstating the case to make me look more heroic
than I am and because I didn't want his company.

"Javelina never attack anyone," he said sullenly.

"Just get between a mama and her baby in the
dark and see how she likes it," I said.

"I've got stuff to wear," he said.

I sighed. I had given him informed consent. At
least he had been forewarned - I wouldn't be totally to
blame if something happened to him. I acquiesced.
I couldn't think of any good that could arise out
of Dylan coming with me, but I also didn't relish
the journey alone under the heightened tension of
recent events. It might be comforting to have some
company. I gave him a list of gear: sturdy hiking
boots with good ankle support, two pairs of wool/
cotton blend socks, long loose pants, fleece jacket,
rain jacket, canteen, insect repellent, etc. "I'll have
a map but you should bring a compass as well," I
added.

I checked my phone. Sunset would be at
6:53PM. I saw Dylan looking at my phone. "You
won't be able to count on cell service where we're
going," I said. We agreed to meet at the Fray Marcos

De Niza Historical Land marker off of Duquesne road at 7:00PM.

"Park in the monument lot," I said. "We'll go on foot from there." I picked up the grocery bag by its handles. "See you then," I said and headed out the door.

Chapter 19

I was the only one in the monument parking lot when I heard a car coming down the gravel road. Through the haze I could make out Dylan's Buick Skylark. He slid to a stop and parked. I walked over to the dust cloud he created when he slammed his brakes on the dirt and gravel.

He looked over at my car. "Where's your ladder?" he said in greeting. Then to me, "Thought you'd need a ladder to get over the wall."

"We won't need a ladder." Dylan looked dubious. I pointed to a spot a couple of 100 yards off the road. "We'll go in there and follow the stream." I started walking.

"How do you know where you're going? You haven't been in Patagonia that much longer than I have. You told me yourself."

"Dr. Weiskoff, my predecessor at the clinic, showed me this route. He overlapped with me a couple of days when I first started as an orientation. The house call responsibility is part of the medical legacy here. It's a rite of passage for any new doctor. A sort of handing off of the medical baton."

"How are we going to get over the wall without a ladder?"

"This is mountainous territory with many dips into ravines and several streams flowing off the mountains down the valley into Mexico. Then the higher mountains curve west to drain the streams into rivers which flow downhill back north to the United States." We both jumped over a small tributary. "The water doesn't know there is a border," I added. "The crossing we're going to use tonight is at one of the original wall sections built a few years ago. The stream has eroded the sand under the Wall, so we will end up walking under the wall and ducking our heads a little."

Dylan shook his head in disgust. "So that's where all the drug smugglers are bringing it in."

I kept hiking. One had to pay attention here. The massive oak trees with their rough patterned, coarse bark provided a shroud to our mission. In the dark - even with my flashlight and 500-lumen headlamp - it was difficult to gauge how slippery the rocks were as we made our way downstream. From a distance, this woodland scenery was a magnificent rolling green canopied vista with the stream hardly visible. Along the stream was a living, breathing habitat; full of nature and danger. Over my shoulder I said to Dylan, "Do you really think everyone who lives around here is part of one big smuggling operation?"

"I know they're getting into our country somehow."

"They are. But we talked about this. The vast majority of smuggled goods are coming through our ports of entry. The drugs are hidden in big tractor trailers and shipping cartons."

"Then this stream can be a highway for all the felons south of the border from Mexico to Central America."

"It's not exactly a highway," I said, as we struggled to keep our balance and not crack our heads open on one of the big boulders. I thought I saw deer off to our right in the woods, but when I looked again they must have scampered off. "You're talking about people who are usually being persecuted in their own country and trying to get to America to find a better life."

"They should apply for citizenship," Dylan said obstinately.

My roving flashlight highlighted wildflowers. I couldn't see the stars for the thick cover of the sycamore and walnut trees. There was a moon, however, poking out over the top of the left bank of the ravine.

Dylan broke the silence. "Where are we?"

"We're skirting Lochiel right now." I turned back to him and smiled. "You'd like the town. It used to be a port of entry with a U.S. Customs house and a real U.S. Border Agent."

"Here?"

"Yup. From the sixties to the eighties, our country's security was in the hands of one U.S. Border Agent who happened to be a young mother of two small children. Up to sixteen people would cross Lochiel in a single day. Now the chain link fence has some rusty, dull barbed-wire on top and the gate is held closed by an old bicycle lock. There's a short no-man's land before you get to the Mexican Customs house – now also abandoned. With a little imagination, the whole set-up looks as failed as Checkpoint Charlie and the Berlin Wall."

"What happened to the town?"

"It was an ideal little haven for a long time, serving the big ranches, the San Rafael Valley over there," I pointed east, "and the mining camps to the northwest. Pancho Villa used to rustle cattle and horses in this area."

"What happened to the mines?"

"That was big business down here. A smelting works was built to serve the mines. Lochiel had five stores, three saloons, a butcher, a bakery and a boarding house. If you want to step back in time you can still see the adobe one-room school house right next to the old adobe church, a bona fide ghost town." We passed a prickly pear cactus with oval pads freshly perforated where javelina had feasted. After biting off big chunks of the cactus they had kindly left some offerings at the cactus base which would make a good fort for packrat nests.

"But what about the mines?"

"Be careful you don't step into an abandoned shaft by the way."

Dylan stopped abruptly, his flashlight making a sweeping circle. Slowly, he began hiking again.

"Treasure Vault mine is around here somewhere," I went on. "Mining in these parts dates back to the

Jesuits in the 1680's. They used Indian labor to search for gold and silver. By 1853 and the Gadsden Purchase, the Apaches made mining too dangerous. After the Civil War, the miners came back." We were now climbing through manzanita and oak trees. The lush green ravine would soon turn to scrub oak.

"Everyone's gone from Lochiel then?"

"A lot of people here are concerned with what's happening in this area. When you put soldiers and other federal agents in uniforms with guns patrolling the area – essentially militarizing it – the entire habitat is altered. It feels different. People don't want to live in or visit a military state – it affects restaurants, small businesses, housing sales and of course tourism. The government has mischaracterized life on the border for political reasons and the citizens down here are having their lives permanently altered."

"It's only temporary for the security of our country. It's not permanent."

"Maybe, but actions have repercussions. Some irrevocable." I put my hand up. We stopped and listened.

"Can't the border patrol see our infrared signatures right now?" Dylan asked.

"Not yet. Not here. We're in between the technology at Lukeville to the west and Taco to the east. The mountains prevent a lot of visibility into the ravines." I looked at Dylan. "When you get your tower up around here though, we won't be making any more house calls."

He shrugged. "They'll just have to make a doctor's appointment like the rest of us."

I moved carefully down the hillside. Startled hummingbirds flew over my head. Their wings invisible in the dark, they were hardly bigger than moths. I wanted to shine my flashlight into the trees and spotlight a blue jay or a cardinal, but that would be careless.

"We're almost there," I said as we descended.

"Where is 'there'?"

"We're just west of the main stream of the San Rafael valley. These head waters form the Santa Cruz River which flows south into Sonora, Mexico. It then makes a U-turn and flows back north off the Mexican hills into the United States through Nogales, Tubac and Tucson. If the water is running, it continues to flow into the Gila River near Phoenix and west to the Colorado River. Those waters run south to the Sea of Cortez and into the Gulf of California." I looked down at the trickling water at my feet. "Quite a journey, don't you think?" Ahead of us we could see a large striated shadow. Dylan pulled up quickly.

"Is that ...?"

"Yes," I said. "Free enterprise in the shape of a wall."

Dylan was spooked. He heard vehicles. "Somethings coming towards us," he said, crouching. The night was so quiet it was easy to hear the sound of a motor trailing off north of us.

"That's Duquesne Road," I said, listening. "We're just south of the Lochiel Road and Duquesne Road intersection. It's just traffic. Lochiel Road ends at the old Customs site and we're clear of that. No worries." Dylan did not look mollified. We approached the wall. The egress point underneath was larger than my last visit with Dr. Weiskoff.

"This is like the Holland Tunnel!" Dylan exclaimed.

"Better. No tolls," I said, checking under the wall with my flashlight for any thorny brush that would obstruct our gateway. Dylan was mesmerized. "Let's go," I urged. I went under the wall first, bending a little so my pack didn't snare. Dylan followed me and when he reached the other side he stood up and looked around wondrously.

"Welcome to Mexico," I said.

"It looks the same," he finally said.

"As what?"

"The other side."

I touched his arm after consulting Dierdorff's map. "This way. We follow the stream for about 300 yards and then there is a fork. We take the stream on our left that's flowing west and there should be a small cluster of homes on the southern uphill side which would be on our right." The last bit of hiking was similar to our trek from the Monument. Dylan slipped on a moss-covered rock but I caught his arm and he righted himself. The night was cold now and the water looked dark and uninviting. We could see flickering lights up ahead.

A young boy was waiting for us. I guessed he was about twelve. He motioned for us to follow. We walked up the bank of the stream to a home that was more like a wilderness shelter. The shack was constructed of various woods flung together: plywood, old fences, branches. One part of a wall was an old school blackboard. The holes between this piecemeal arrangement were plugged with moldy carpets. The roof was several different sections of corrugated tin and aluminum. We stepped over a broken sled, a small pink bicycle and several old discarded appliances. We followed the boy along a clothes line with shirts and pants still hanging in the night air to a door which was yet another piece of carpet nailed to two-by-fours. It had a kite string handle. A trailing thread of string allowed the door to be latched to a rusty nail along the wooden frame of the home.

The boy spoke his first words. "In here," he said, holding the carpet door open for us. He probably learned his English from a school near Lochiel. Inside was an older woman sitting in a high-backed chair. On a makeshift bed, a young girl reclined, surrounded by pillows. The woman bowed her head to us.

"Buenos tardes," I said. I didn't speak Spanish, but I could try and be polite.

The boy sized up my language skills quickly. "My Abuela doesn't speak English, but she is thankful you are here."

I bowed to the woman. Then I turned back to the boy. "Is this your sister?" I asked. The boy nodded and I approached the young girl. I could hear her labored breathing from across the room. There was a whistling and then a squeaky sound with each breath. Dylan stayed in the doorway. The boy nodded 'yes' to his sister as if to say, "it's okay." I addressed the boy again. "My name is Harper. I'm the doctor," I said. I gestured to Dylan, "This is my assistant. What's your name?"

"Jesus," he answered, his eyes on his sister. There was a smell of cigarette smoke in the cabin.

"Is your father here, Jesus?"

"No."

He was around somewhere, I thought; smokers always think non-smokers can't smell their cigarette smoke. "How old is your sister?" I asked.

"She is six."

"What is your sister's name?" I asked, moving over to kneel by the side of her bed. The makeshift bed appeared to be a door set on some cinder blocks and covered with a threadbare blanket. I could see the hole on the side of the door where the knob used to be. I asked Dylan to move to his left as his head was blocking the light from an old Coleman lantern.

"She is Ariel," Jesus said.

"Does she speak English?" Jesus shook his head no. He said she could understand some English, but did not speak the language.

"Hello Ariel," I said. "I'm Doctor Harper. Can I listen to your lungs?" Ariel was tiny. She had dark lustrous hair, but her facial bones had a subtle curve to them and I suspected she had suffered from fetal alcohol syndrome when she was born. It looked like she was growing out of some of the earlier manifestations. I blew on the end of my stethoscope and rubbed it between my hands. "This might be a little cold, Ariel," I said and she smiled nervously. She might not have been able to speak English, but she did understand me. She had a beautiful smile. She

125

twitched abruptly as the cool diaphragm and metal of the stethoscope touched her skin. I could hear the bronchial spasm loudly with each quick breath. The wheezing was almost deafening as the air weaved its way through the spider web of mucous. "Can you cough for me?" Ariel just looked at me blankly. I looked at Jesus. He said something in Spanish and Ariel coughed, catching the goop in her left hand. I shined the flashlight on her palm. The phlegm was thick but clear. In the shadow of the flashlight beam I could see Ariel's face was sweaty and her lips looked bluish. She was also scared. "Has she had this before?" I asked.

Jesus nodded yes.

"Last year at this time?" I asked.

Jesus looked surprised. "Yes, I think so."

I stood up. I patted Ariel's shoulder in an attempt to comfort her. "Please tell your sister she is going to be okay." Jesus translated. She recognized the word "okay" and smiled shyly. She remained scared until after two inhaler efforts her sense of suffocating began to ease. I asked Jesus to translate to ensure his sister and grandmother understood what I was about to say. He nodded yes. "Ariel," I began. "You have a condition called asthma. What happens is the tubes in your lungs get red and swollen and it's tough to breathe. I suspect it's because of all the pollen in the air. It has been very windy lately and you might have some allergies." I looked around at the moldy carpets and imagined the mold spores floating in the air. A couple of dogs had found us and were barking outside the door. "Smoke is also a trigger, so whoever is smoking in here should do it outside."

I pulled two extra inhalers out of my bag to give to Ariel. One a bronchodilator. The second a steroid aerosol. I gave Ariel one more treatment with the bronchodilator and she improved immediately. I showed her and then Jesus how to use the two inhalers and wrote a schedule down for Jesus to follow.

"I don't think she has a bronchial infection yet," I told Jesus. "But she needs to go to the clinic in Santa Cruz, Sonora tomorrow." He nodded. Skeptically, I thought. The older woman had not spoken or moved throughout the visit. I moved to her chair and kneeled beside her. Gently I put my hand on a thin shawl covering her enjoined hands. I could feel a rosary bead chain protruding between the woman's fingers beneath the shawl. Looking at her I asked Jesus: "Does your grandmother have any questions?"

Jesus asked her. She said something softly looking only at Ariel. "My grandmother says thank you," Jesus said.

I stood and moved back to Ariel's side. I squeezed her shoulder for reassurance and shook Jesus' hand. Waving goodbye, Dylan and I left the shack. We were immediately accosted by the barking dogs and cacophony ensued. Jesus followed us out and said something sharply to the animals. They muffled their barks and circled each other, but did not follow us. We waved once more to Jesus and made our way back to the fork in the stream. "You were very quiet in there," I said to Dylan.

"Not my thing," Dylan said. We found the fork and turned north. "Couldn't she have just gone to this Mexican clinic in the morning?"

"Maybe. But asthma can advance quickly. You see how tiny she was? Not much room for error there. It's very scary too. For Ariel, it was like someone putting two pillows over her face and pressing down on them while she tried to breathe. Both Jesus and his grandmother looked frightened."

Dylan moved on. "Having kids can be scary, I guess."

"Yes, it can," I agreed.

"Mary wants to have children," Dylan said, but he really wasn't talking to me it was more a thought that he spoke out loud.

This jolted me. "When did you two talk about that?" Seeing our way back was even more difficult because the moon was now behind us and we were casting moving shadows with every step.

Dylan lurched back to the present, "A while back," he said vaguely. He was hiking very slowly. "Didn't you and Mary ever talk about it?"

"Not really." I started to feel an anxiousness that had nothing to do with the partially obscured, slippery trail. Mary and I had talked about children, but I wasn't about to share this information with Dylan.

"You didn't?" He seemed surprised. "You think you're too old to have children?" I looked at him. He really didn't seem to weigh his words before speaking.

I didn't answer his question. "Mary seemed preoccupied today," I said. "Any idea why?" We were almost to the wall.

Dylan hesitated. "I think that girl with the measles bothered her. She also said something about a run-in with the Sheriff."

"What kind of run-in?" I asked.

Dylan stopped hiking as we reached the wall. He turned to me. "I don't know. She wouldn't say." I started thinking about that, but Dylan nervously interjected. "You know, I like her a lot," he said and started to look for the cleared spot under the wall that we had used earlier. I moved along the wall as well.

"That's easy to do," I said.

"It's actually more than just fondness." This made me pull up and stop. At the silence, Dylan pulled up as well. He turned around. "I haven't done anything," he said. I was stunned by his almost boyish sense of decorum and privilege.

"What makes you think she'd let you?"

"What you did back there was fantastic," he went on. "But Mary's going to want children and you're a little long in the tooth for that, aren't you? No offense."

His innocent arrogance was annoying. "Mary has told me she doesn't want children," I said evenly.

"They all say that until their clock starts ticking. If you loved her you wouldn't put her in a "Sophie's Choice" situation between you and having a child."

He was right of course, but she had reassured me several times that the issue was not important to her. I suddenly felt the melancholy of impending loss. And I resented Dylan: his youth and his impudence.

"I think its Mary's decision, not yours," I said. Then it occurred to me. "You didn't come on this house call tonight to check border security, did you? You came to tell me this."

"I was interested in the illegal entry pathways as well," Dylan said.

"I'm not going to give her up, you know," I said.

Dylan dismissed this. "She looks up to you. That will pass when she does some critical thinking." I felt the necrotic breeze of being alone waft over me.

"You believe in a lot of nonsense," I said.

Dylan looked at me with genuine caring. "I hope we can remain friends." A palo verde tree swayed ominously in the reflection of my headlamp.

Dylan's puerile images of male bonding aside, I thought I understood Mary and she seemed to "get" me. Dylan believed everything he had said. Therein lay the trouble. Time enough to prove one's worth to a lover might even out the odds, but who waits for that? Why would Mary start anew when we seemed so happy together?

Dylan found our previous spot and ducked under the wall. I followed. We quickly found the trail and retraced our steps along the shifting sand of the creek side. We were soon back to our cars without incident. The moon was now very high in the sky. We said goodbye and drove our separate ways. Back at my cabin I was exhausted but couldn't sleep. Eventually as the sun began to light up the eastern sky, I got up and made some coffee.

Chapter 20

Mary didn't understand the feeling washing over her as she saw Dylan across the street coming out of Patagonia's only hardware store. It was a visceral, electrically charged blow – there was nothing cerebral about - it took her breath away and she felt vaguely faint.

The avalanche started with a snow ball - the chance dinner at the Wild Horse. Her interest had been piqued, her curiosity aroused. But when they had danced in the gymnasium she had felt deep stirrings. At the time, she had been able to tamp the strange longing down using her intellect. She saw it now like a bee sting. The first sting is a nuisance, but thereafter, behind the scenes your immune system is building an army for the next attack. She was infected at the benefit dance and now she was experiencing a sexual anaphylaxis. She had been trying to get him off of her mind since that Saturday night, but her mind had surrendered and was no longer involved. To see him loping across the street to his car aroused her beyond her experience. She wanted him. Nothing else mattered. She wrestled with the conflict out of habit, but it wasn't a fair fight. For someone who had always done the right thing all her life, she now realized she didn't care about anything else. Harper, her job, her friends, everything faded into a colorless background. She still loved all those people and the life she had built, but it all was secondary to this glory of desire.

Dylan didn't see her as he opened the door to his Buick and drove off. This was a good thing because Mary felt if she had caught his eye she would have thrown her life away at that very moment and taken him in the street. She felt feverish and didn't recognize herself. At the edge of this rapture was panic, because he knew she was off the rails. Out of control. She was being swept away by something she had never experienced and didn't understand. Even that was exciting.

Chapter 21

Soon after the school visit for the measles outbreak and our subsequent dealings with the State Health Department, Mary and I were invited to visit the Migrant Youth Shelter in Tucson. We were asked to staff a half-day medical clinic for the children sequestered there. It had not been publicized, but the State Health Department had received information that the migrant children were not receiving adequate health care at these private facilities and health officials were now attempting some stopgap efforts while the Department investigated. We were pleased to get out of town and curious to see the Tucson shelter. Just as we were preparing to leave town, the new Patagonia Regional Times issue hit the newsstands. The town was abuzz with the published resolution adopted by the Mayor and Town Council of Patagonia. I picked up a copy and Mary and I read it together before she started the car. The resolution was in its own section on page 5 next to the "Letters to the Editor" and "Council Notes." Under the byline of the Mayor and Town Council of Patagonia it read:

"*The Town of Patagonia hereby urges you to reject funding that would expand the border wall along the*

Southern border. Patagonia welcomes refugees and immigrants and we urge you to reflect these values.

The wall is contrary to what makes this country great and stymies efforts to protect our friends, our neighbors, our colleagues, ourselves and our vibrant border communities and borderlands.

Patagonia is concerned that important environmental laws that keep us safe, like the Clean Water Act and the Endangered Species Act, have been waived to build these walls. Please focus funding instead on protecting our land, environment and people.

We should be creating jobs and rebuilding our failing infrastructure. Congress should invest in our families, our children, our health, and our future."

We were leaving a region divided. Mary turned over the ignition and pointed her Prius towards Sonoita and Tucson.

Mary knew the way and had offered to drive. Mary was an excellent driver and had a true sense of where she was in space when she was behind the wheel. When she was sixteen her father had made her take the Bondurant defensive driving course in Phoenix before allowing her to obtain her license. Those good habits at an age of primacy had stayed with her. I was able to relax when she was behind the wheel, knowing I was in competent hands.

"What do you think of the resolution in the paper," I asked, as Mary maneuvered the car on the winding road.

"I hope your friend Bob Baxter doesn't get in trouble."

Mary glanced over at me dubiously, then turned back to the road. "Why would he get in trouble? He's just publishing the town council's decision on the issue."

"The mayor and town council are politicians and people expect platitudes from them," I said. "Regular folks know Baxter runs the paper and might blame him for publishing this. They will say it's liberal media bias or 'Fake News.'"

"He is originally from Philadelphia," she smiled, referring to our run in with Joe and Mike at dinner not too long ago. "He could be tarred with the East Coast brush they used on you."

"Do you think the mayor and the town council reflect the town's position on the issue?" I asked.

"Maybe a little more than half of Patagonia will side with this resolution. The other half will feel angry. They already feel they don't have a voice. Very few papers write what these people believe and only one television network airs what they feel is right. The internet and social media is their only chance to express what they think on the issues of the day."

"What about the rest of the Arizona?"

"Tucson has an eclectic population base, so maybe a majority of people there would agree with our town council, but Phoenix would hate it." She side-glanced me briefly again. "And Phoenix has three times the number of people when compared to Tucson."

The drive went by quickly and when we reached Tucson, Mary exited off Interstate 10 and turned north onto Oracle Road. We passed a local brewery on the left and a couple of small motels on the right.

"Is this the place the First Lady visited?" I asked Mary.

"No. She visited a Customs and Border processing center in Tucson but the detention facility she toured was the Southwest Key facility up in Phoenix."

"Is that where she wore that jacket "I REALLY DON'T CARE, DO U?"

"No. That was a week earlier when she went to see the McAllen, Texas facility."

"What do you think that jacket was all about?" I asked.

Mary looked at me. "I have no idea. Marriages - who knows what goes on?" she said, shaking her head. Mary moved into the turning lane and when traffic cleared, turned left into a nondescript parking area just off the main road. She parked on the outside of a fenced-in compound.

"This is right in the heart of the city," I said with surprise.

"Midtown Tucson isn't exactly midtown Manhattan," Mary said with a smile as she pointed to all the aged, one story commercial buildings surrounding us.

"True that. Looks like "Alice Doesn't Live Here Anymore," I said getting out of the car.

There were no road signs or marquees set outside this central Tucson converted apartment complex. It was eerily quiet - only the traffic on Oracle penetrated the silence. "It's hard to believe this is where they detain children. It's ominous," I said looking around. The place appeared shrouded in secrecy. It had taken the District's U.S. Congressman one month to get permission for an hour-long tour. The newspapers had pointed out how the delay allowed the facility a lot of time to prepare a good show for the representative.

"I have no doubt I saw this place at its best," the Congressman had said to waiting reporters outside the shelter upon completing his tour.

I grabbed my medical bag from the trunk of the car. Security was waiting for us at the front gate. The facility was encircled by copper colored metal, slatted fencing. We were led through a large twelve-foot-high gate of similar material. The gate was expansive enough to let a vehicle pass through if both doors were opened. The lower eight feet of the gate had metal mesh connecting the slats so nothing could pass through in or out. Four-foot metal saguaro silhouettes decorated the gate. We showed our ID's to the two security guards and a woman stepped forward holding two guest pass lanyards.

"Hi. I'm Sara James," the trim woman said. She had jet black shoulder length hair pulled back over her ears and appeared to be in her early thirties. "You must be Mary," James said, extending her hand. "I'm the one you talked to over the phone." Mary shook her hand and then introduced me. We draped the lanyards over our heads. "Thank you so much for coming," James continued. "Please follow me." We walked across the graveled driveway to a portico entrance. The architecture reminded me of numerous house calls I had made over the years to various nursing homes when a resident was too weak to travel to a doctor's office and yet not sick enough to merit an ambulance to the emergency department.

"I'm the Assistant Director of Services," James began. "So, medical care falls under my purview. We have contacts with some local practitioners but they insist the children come to their offices if they need care. I understand the doctors feeling they can deliver the best health care in that setting, but it is not practical for this situation. Plus," she added abashed, "we don't have a budget for those costs. We appreciate the two of you donating your time and services."

James gestured at the building with her hand, "Conditions were much better before the P 'zero tolerance' policy was enacted. The mission statement of the Shelter when I signed on, was to prepare the disenfranchised immigrant children for absorption into the unified public-school system. Now, however, the Administration's new policy has abruptly turned this shelter into a private prison." An expensive one at that, I learned.

I asked her why there was so little transparency in the work they were doing. "Few people know exactly what is going on inside these shelters," I pointed out. "News crews and cameramen have not been allowed inside. I've read reports the children were becoming less compliant and acting out more, requiring stricter discipline. The lack of disclosure implies you have something to hide."

James fidgeted and looked down. "These are private companies. They are not used to, nor do they like, public scrutiny. I'm doing the best I can for these children, but I don't make the rules. U.S. Health and Human Services has contracts with 100 similar detention facilities in 17 states. Even with the best of intentions, it's a big juggernaut with constantly changing rules. The children weren't supposed to be here very long in the first place. Now the longer they are here, the more they want to run away - even when they have no place to go. That's one reason why going to a doctor's office is so difficult for us. We don't have the staff to do that safely. But, we love our kids and try to do right by them."

We were closely accompanied by the two security guards as we walked with James. "I'm sorry, I couldn't get you cleared to actually tour our facility. But we have set up this meeting room for your visit." She ushered us into a small function room with a folding card table desk with two chairs. In the far corner of the room there was a gurney behind a three-part dressing partition. "We can start whenever you are ready," she said hopefully.

Mary and I looked at each other and she nodded yes and replied, "We're ready." A line of children soon snaked outside our door and down the corridor. They were accompanied by various staffers. The children were hauntingly quiet as Mary triaged them. She handled those cases she was comfortable treating and sent the others to me in the corner. Some of the staffers engaged us in conversation and tried to include the children, while others acted like zombies and were clearly just going through the motions. For the most part, the children were mute and would not make eye contact. The youngest was four and the oldest was fifteen years old.

One six-year-old girl named Isabella was so traumatized, she wouldn't talk, make eye contact or socialize with us. Isabella was curled up into a little ball on her side and wouldn't yield her fetal position. Mary was almost in tears by her inability to reach this young girl. The child had a swollen jaw I thought was a tooth abscess, but the parotid gland was right next to this tooth. A parotid gland tumor or infection was not something I wanted to casually dismiss. It was frustrating to be unable to make the definitive diagnosis in this primitive setting. Sara James was pessimistic about arranging a dental or ENT consult. "I'll see what we can do," was all she could promise. I prescribed a broad-spectrum antibiotic in the interim. Before a staffer took her away, Mary spontaneously hugged Isabella tightly. Mary was close to tears. The rest of us stood there until the staff person gently tapped Mary on the shoulder. Mary relinquished the girl and the staffer led her away. Mary turned her back to us, dabbed her eyes with a tissue, blew her nose, and took a slow, deep breath.

Another male employee, probably in his early twenties, explained to me: "In the past, these children would be placed with sponsors: usually relatives or family friends who would agree to house them while their immigration cases played out in the courts. Now the Government has announced all 'potential sponsors and other adult members of the household must be fingerprinted and the data shared with US immigration authorities.' ICE started arresting these people who applied to sponsor the children because a lot of the volunteer sponsors were in the country as undocumented aliens - even though the vast majority had no prior criminal record. People stopped applying to sponsor these children to avoid their own arrest and incarceration. Now the U.S. is creating a situation where thousands of orphan children will become part of the underfabric of our society. Even the adults who do come forward to help us are stuck with waiting times of up to three months to get through the fingerprint process."

An older social worker who said he'd been working in different settings for many years was escorting one little boy and stood next to me as I examined the child. The social worker introduced himself to me as "Ronald" and gave me some background on the current situation. "The longer these children remain in custody, the more they become anxious and depressed which leads to violent outbursts. We've had several children on suicide watches, but we don't have the staffing let alone the mental health training to do this right. We're having to put more and more of the children in discipline segregation which isolates the troublemakers but also sows seeds for gang development in our own facility. Some parents may never see their children again."

As we were leaving, an employee called out, "Ms. James." The two huddled for a moment as the person whispered something to her. "Oh no," James gasped. When she returned to lead us back to the front gate, there were tears in her eyes. Mary offered her a tissue and she gratefully accepted.

"I'm sorry," Ms. James said. "Two awful events were just reported. You'll hear about it on the news tonight so I might as well tell you." She wiped her cheek with the tissue one more time. "The first occurred north of us at our sister shelter in Phoenix. One of the care workers for the youths was arrested on charges of sexual abuse and child molestation. The second report is from a different facility, but also run by our parent company. A worker was arrested at this shelter after his supervisor find out he was sexually abusing the children . . . and he is HIV positive. We are working to have all the children he came into contact with tested. We don't know any more than that." Her face fell into her hands in despair.

The plight of the children had a profound effect on Mary. She was very quiet on the drive back to Patagonia.

"What do you think will happen to Isabella," she asked me at one point.

"I wish I knew," I said helplessly.

"I would have adopted her then and there if it were possible," she said, her eyes moist again. Lost in our thoughts, we were oblivious to the desert landscape passing by.

Chapter 22

Sunday, I received word my grandmother had died. She had been in decline, but this abrupt turn took me by surprise. The afternoon was a flurry of phone calls to arrange clinic coverage, obtain flights to the East Coast, commiserate with family and close friends, make funeral arrangements and begin to organize a memorial service - all under a blanket of deep sadness.

I flew out Monday and was gone ten days.

Chapter 23

I landed back in Tucson in the late morning thanks
to the time change. The flight was behind schedule
because of the strength of the prevailing westerly
winds aloft. I became edgy because now I would be
late to the afternoon clinic which I knew would be
overbooked on my first day back. As the plane made
its final approach, the engines abruptly changed to
full throttle and the nose pitched up acutely. The
pilot executed a go-around and once the plane had
leveled off he spoke over the intercom and apologized.
He explained that air traffic control called off our
landing because another plane had taxied onto the
runway in a miscommunication. Our plane now
had to overshoot Tucson to the west, bank around
'A' Mountain and reconfigure for landing once again.
This added another twenty minutes to the flight.
I squirmed in my seat. A powerless traveler in this
airborne, aluminum cylinder.

It would be a hectic work afternoon, but I was
anxious to see Mary as well. We had briefly FaceTimed
twice while I was back East, but the conversations
were only notable for their awkwardness. Trying
to comfort someone over the loss of a loved one is

difficult at best, but it seemed like we couldn't quite connect. Our conversations were halting. The pauses were pregnant, not poignant.

I had somehow hoped Mary would surprise me and be waiting at the bottom of the escalator to welcome me back. But, no one was there. It was probably an unreasonable expectation given the hour-long drive and the busy upcoming clinic. Still, I found myself downcast as the swirl of hugs and relatives bustled around me. I stood with my bag in the eye of this sweet storm of reunion of travelers and their loved ones until an opening allowed me to squeeze past and head to the parking garage.

I found my dusty car in the long-term parking lot and arrived back in Patagonia thirty minutes late for the start of office hours. There were some sympathy cards and a stilted hug from Rachel as she offered her sympathy. But there was also work to be done. Patients had been waiting and appointments were backing up. When Mary came out of an examining room to greet my arrival, I was overjoyed. She gave me a chaste embrace. We were at work, after all.

"How was your flight?" she asked, with tenderness, but her eyes weren't dancing to see me. They were polite, caring eyes. I sensed something amiss.

I told Mary about the headwinds and the landing go-around, but she was not concerned by the near runway incursion. "You're here now and that's what counts," she said. "Everyone is waiting to see you." She turned to lead me to the first examining room.

I felt the world had shifted a quarter turn and I couldn't put my finger on it. Something had happened. The fabric of my universe felt slack. Mary was warmhearted and familiar with me, yet I felt the breach. I sensed an ebbing of my good fortune. My intuition immediately suspected Dylan, but I didn't know what to do. I refocused on the work at hand and immersed myself in seeing patients.

Chapter 24

I felt awful talking to Harper while he was back east. He had sounded so sad and I felt such conflict: sad for him, joyous I could see Dylan.

I felt like such a traitor when I rang Dylan's room at the Stage Stop Inn from the lobby phone. It had only been a couple of hours since Harper's flight had left Tucson.

"Well, this is a surprise," Dylan said when he realized it was me calling.

"I'm in the lobby," I said. I could feel Sam Jacob, the owner of the Inn, behind the front desk, desperately trying to overhear my conversation.

Dylan was confused. "I heard about Harper's grandmother. Do you need me to help in some way?"

"No, it's not about that," I said. "Maybe it would be better if I came up."

"Sure, Mary," he said, after a moment's hesitation. "I'm in room . . ." I had already hung up the phone and was bounding up the stairs. When he opened the door to his second-floor suite I threw myself into his arms and wrapped my legs around his waist. Dylan stumbled back, but he didn't fall.

Now that Harper was back in town, I was confused again. It had been a wild ten days with Dylan, but my feelings for Harper flooded over me the minute I saw him in the clinic. I didn't know what to do. I felt my heart drawn to Harper. I felt everything else drawn to Dylan.

Chapter 25

There was no clinic the following day. Mary had mentioned she was going up to Tucson to meet some of her girlfriends from her college days at NAU. They had plans for shopping and lunch. I had received a call from Dave Nance upon my return from the east coast and there had been some "developments" since our last hike together. Nance wanted to have another excursion and we agreed to meet at the Feast around lunch time.

I used the free morning to make my own journey north and pay a visit to the Tucson Indian Health Care offices. Once I got through town and left Naugle Avenue behind me I had almost twelve miles to myself on the Sonoita highway. I turned left onto Highway 83 at Sonoita and was met by a mobile Border Patrol checkpoint. I counted twenty-four agents at the site and saw a lot of portable coffee urns. There was little traffic and I was quickly waved through. The next stretch was a quiet, winding drive with few cars and only small signs of civilization in the vast country. I was jolted out of my daydreaming as I came across Interstate 10 heading east and west. The sign said El Paso to the right and Tucson/ Phoenix to the left. My little vehicle tried valiantly to get up to speed as I entered the highway. A thundering twenty-two-wheel tractor trailer heading west at a great rate of speed was unrelenting as it prevented my smooth assimilation with traffic.

Despite considerable congestion on the highway, after twenty minutes I could see planes entering the landing pattern at Tucson International Airport. On this morning, they were landing into the prevalent easterly winds once again. For the benefit of the passengers on today's flights, I hoped the winds aloft hadn't slowed the plane's speed as they had on my last trip. In the afternoon, the wind direction would change and come out of the west. The pilots would then strain to see into the brilliant setting sun for the privilege and safety of landing against the wind. A mile further along I saw F-16 fighter jets circling the Tucson airport as they waited for an opening in the commercial aviation corridor to practice their own touch-and-go landings. A little further to the northeast, A-10 Thunderbolt Warthog jets were doing similar maneuvers at Davis Monthan Air Force Base.

I took Exit 258 to Congress Street and then made a quick right onto St. Mary's Road. The Santa Catalina mountains loomed out of the north with their high, intermittently jagged and then rolling peaks. At the top of one peak I could see red lights on top of communication towers and a spot of white which I knew to be the Mount Lemmon Observatory. I knew this because at Kitt Peak Mary had educated me.

"The Mt. Lemmon Observatory in Tucson also participates as an early warning station of ATLAS, the Asteroid Terrestrial-impact Last Alert System," she had said. Her eyes were sparkling as she shared the information. I could see her eyes and hear her voice in my mind as clearly as if she were now sitting in the passenger seat beside me.

I turned right on Stone Road. There, smack in the middle of the Old Pueblo, was the Indian Center. At the dead end of a hallway, I found the office for Health and Wellness Services. The placard on the door said "Dorothy Graham, MPH, Manager." Ms. Graham was pleasantly surprised to see me and then a look of worry came over her face.

"There's nothing wrong is there?" she asked.

"No, not at all," I said. "Just the opposite." Her faced relaxed and she half smiled.

"Is that why you drove up here? To say hello?" she teased. "I must say I have heard good things about your work." Then more darkly she added, "I also heard about that dust-up with I.C.E. Very unfortunate."

I nodded. "Actually, the reason I'm here is I would like to sign up for another six months. Extend my stay." Mrs. Graham paused, looking down at her desk and when she looked back up at me her face was pained.

"I'm sorry, but the next rotation is filled. One of our only semi-regulars is returning. She's been coming for six months every year and a half since we started the program. Without her commitment, we might never had gotten this clinic off the ground. I

can't turn her away." My disappointment must have
been obvious, because Graham took a deep breath.
"I'll tell you what I can do. I'll make a gentle inquiry
to see if she's at all flexible with her schedule and get
back to you. Is that acceptable?"

"I would really appreciate that consideration,"
I said. We made small talk for a bit and then I left
her office, feeling my life was on unsteady ground.
The sensation was uncomfortable and disconcerting.
Walking out of the Indian Center I was hit with a
blast of city heat. While living in the higher elevation
amidst the mountains of Patagonia, I had escaped
the oppressiveness of a Southwestern urban area
trapping the energy of the sun. The bright unsparing
light reflected off the building windows and cement
sidewalk like mirrors trapping me in a blinding Don
Quixote moment. The dark asphalt roads absorbed
the sunbeams and I saw a woman walking her dog
with booties on its paws to keep them from burning
on the hot surface. I could easily picture frying an
egg on such a veneer. It was only early spring but
the sun was relentless. Foolishly I had not erected
the windshield sunshade Mary had given me. I had
considered it frivolous. Now I couldn't touch the
steering wheel because it was so hot. I had heard of
Arizona residents keeping oven mitts in their cars
for this purpose, but had dismissed that as urban
legend. I opened all the vehicle's doors and windows,
then grabbed a towel from the trunk and put it on
the driver's seat so I could sit without burning my
back on the faux leather. My thin shirt wouldn't be
enough protection. I went to fasten my seat belt and

singed my fingers on the metal clasp. Pulling out my handkerchief, I used that to protect my skin and managed to connect the belt and harness construct. I felt lethargy seep through me as I used my hand as a shade to protect my eyes from the sun glinting off signposts and bumpers. I didn't see the speedbump and went over it too fast. My head hit the ceiling of the car and threw me off-kilter. There were too many speedbumps in my life all of a sudden. I was back on the highway before the air conditioner finally began to blast cool air out the vents.

In my first weeks in Arizona, Mary had laughed at my heat intolerance.

"I thought it was supposed to be cooler here because it was a dry heat," I'd said.

"So is an oven," Mary had replied, smiling.

Chapter 26

When I arrived at "The Writer's Feast," Dave was waiting for me inside the front entrance by the Zhivago poster. He was standing with a large coffee in one hand and his car keys in the other. He handed me the coffee.

"I made a couple of calls last night and there is someone we should talk to," he said and motioned to his white Dodge truck parked in front of the Feast.

"Where are we going this time?" I asked as we pulled out onto McKeown Ave.

"A ranch near the Valley. It's down Harshaw Creek Road. The MacKenzie Place," he glanced at me. "Did you know that Lochiel was named by a Scot?"

"The border town?" I asked.

"Yup. Named after his homeland back in Scotland about one-hundred and thirty years ago. His family has been working the ranch down here ever since. There used to be a lot of cattle in these parts. Most people mispronounce the town's name. It's 'Low-Keel' to the locals. The family pretty much keeps to themselves but they know what's happening along the Border. They can't help it. It's like knowing what's happening in your backyard."

"Who runs the ranch now?"

"The grandson. Colin. He wants to show us something." He looked over at me with a wry smile. "Who knew this was cattle country?"

"I wouldn't have guessed that myself. What does this MacKenzie want to show us?"

"He wouldn't say over the phone. But I know him. He's a serious man, circumspect. He wouldn't invite us down for some whimsical visit."

"Why is he even talking to us?"

"I called him while you were back East and told him about our little ride in the country," Nance said. "He was in the Feast a few days ago." Nance smiled. "He loves my overpriced coffee. He was pretty upset then about the Government's new priority of separating children from their parents in order to break the spirit of immigrant families." We passed a truck on the winding two lane mountain road that followed Harshaw Creek. "Colin has a passel of kids himself. He's a stoic person so I was surprised he was so vocal in my place. Made me think he had some skin in this game. Yesterday afternoon he called me and said to come down. He wouldn't say more over the phone." Nance looked sideways at me. "Mackenzie wasn't keen on you coming with me, but I vouched for you."

"Thanks . . . I think," I replied. We drove in silence for a spell. I was still thinking about Nance's revelations on our last outing.

"You said you could never go back to Russia," I began slowly. Nance turned his eyes from the road and glanced quickly at me. "Are you in hiding here?"

"Let's just say I like keeping a low profile in Patagonia. Putin believes all the "parasites of the West" – as he calls the outsiders who worked with Gorbachev – are traitors to Mother Russia and he has made catching them a personal vendetta. He's killed quite a few of my more careless co-workers from that assignment over the years. His signature death for them is a quick, but painful death by an illegal nerve toxin. It's his way of sending a message to his fellow Russians and the world: traitors will not be tolerated."

Nance turned down an unmarked dirt road. I noticed an inconspicuous wire fence on either side of the road almost hidden in the brush. After about a half mile we came out of the trees into a vast clearing. I could see several structures scattered over the gently rolling hills with the Patagonia mountains in relief behind the biggest building. On a small knoll, a two-story brick house sat in the shadow of three large deciduous trees in the midst of starting to grow their spring leaves. There was a large porch that wrapped around the house, making it look like a Mississippi River boat from a distance. Dormer rooms stuck out from the sharply slanted roof on all sides.

As we pulled closer I could see barns and various aluminum structures scattered over random distances. They were the growing pains of an old ranch with complexes built and dispersed as time and fortune dictated. We pulled up to a green gate with horizontal steel bars. The heavy steel gate rested on wide rolling casters and had been pulled open. On either side of the gate was a different fence that encircled all the buildings. It looked new, a labor intensive wooden structure made of fallen trees. On the right side, the wooden fence made a large circle on itself to create an expansive corral. To the left of the gate was an unpretentious weathered sign that said: "Mackenzie Ranch."

Flood lights were visible nestled in the low buffelgrass on either side of the entrance. We drove in past worn wheels of wood. The wheels had rusted metal sheets protecting the circular construct. Broken and intact wooden spokes irregularly fed into the axle. It had been many years since those wheels were married to wagons. Ranch equipment that had seen its day and been put out to pasture, littered the entryway. A small stone wall defined the grass lawn of the big house. The house sat on a high mound of earth overlooking the ranch. We turned in and parked on one side of the circular driveway.

Walking up to the house, we passed an old collapsed prairie wagon on the downhill side of the path. Its right front side had burrowed into the ground. Three rusted wheels were visible and one partially submerged spindle.

Colin MacKenzie was waiting for us in a rocking chair on the porch.

"I keep the wagon there to remind me of my roots," he said with an easy smile. The porch was littered with rocking chairs. He stood up as we approached.

"It looks like the tow truck never arrived," Nance said, shaking hands with the rancher.

"Aye. And I don't think it's coming," MacKenzie said. Nance introduced me. A rangy man, I placed MacKenzie at about six feet four inches tall. I put him in his late fifties. He had a deep tan, but his face, aside from some deep smile creases seemed almost wrinkle-free. His handshake was firm and he looked me straight in the eye.

"Would you like some coffee?" he asked, gesturing for us to have a seat in the chairs as he disappeared into the house. MacKenzie returned with coffee and a plate of warm biscuits. We sprawled in the rocking chairs and took in the sights. It was a fine day and a beautiful vista stretched out in every direction.

Dave went right to the point of our visit. "You said on the phone you knew Dylan Kermer?"

Colin leaned back in his chair. "Knowing a man is different than having a small business deal with him," Colin reflected. "He called me a while back and told me he was a consultant for the Government. Said he had a few shipments related to the new tower they're building and would like to store them in a safe place. We had just finished the loft on our new barn," MacKenzie gestured to a couple of men a few hundred yards away painting the trim on a new building. "We were using the old barn for storage to tidy up the appearance of the ranch a bit." He pointed to an old rectangular structure with a tall weathered A frame at one end. "We have lots of room now and a little Government money never hurts, so I said yes.

A couple of days later a step-van truck pulled up and unloaded some barrels and boxes taking up about twelve by eighteen feet in the corner of the barn. No problems. Cash right up front. They've been by two or three times to pick-up or drop-off some material. They always call first. I didn't pay them much mind."

"Then something happened?" Dave prompted. MacKenzie took a sip of his coffee and nodded.

"Two of my men were working at the far end of the shed," he pointed to the west end of the rectangular building with the flat roof. "Both of them started to feel sick. My foreman thought he smelled some fumes and called me. I took a stroll out to see what I could see." He took another sip of coffee. "I couldn't smell anything. I figured the boys had themselves some bad chorizo. But then I did stumble across something that took me back a ways. Would you like to stretch your legs?"

The coffee was strong and tasteful. I hated to put it down. MacKenzie led us on a crushed stone walkway to the shed. Behind the storage shed there was a path into a dense patch of trees. Through the opening I could make out a circular clearing beyond. It looked like a small amphitheater. "What's back there?" I asked and pointed to the path.

"An old offal," Mackenzie answered, after a pause. "There's also an ancient septic tank over there so don't go on a solitary nature walk. The ground is a little soft." He gestured to the shed entrance. "Watch yourself here," Colin added. "The first step is broken and it's hard to see when you first get in." We entered the shed. Mackenzie was right. I had to pause as the transition from brilliant sunshine to cloaked shadow was temporarily blinding. My eyes quickly adjusted, but not before I almost collided with a man in the shed apparently waiting for us.

"This is Duncan. He's my top hand. Been with me forever. He's one of those fellows I told you about that got sick out here," Mackenzie said by way of introduction

"It wasn't bad sausage," Duncan said irritably. He raised his arm a bit to acknowledge us, but didn't offer to shake hands. Duncan looked like a hard man. He was lean and chiseled from rugged labor. His features were dark from many years of working outdoors. He turned and led our party deeper into the building. Light leaped into the shed through various cracks in the casing and soon the visibility was no worse than the dimness of a movie theatre before the film started. As we walked down a make-shift aisle with storage supplies on either side, MacKenzie pulled out a flashlight. We stopped near the far end and the rancher shined the light on the wall. "There's a bay door here that opens up for easy access at this end. We keep it chained except for loading and unloading." Moving the light to one side he stopped to highlight a barrel. "Most of their supplies have been picked up. Just the odd few remain."

I leaned forward to read the label on the drum: "DIOCTYL SEBACATE." I pulled out my phone and turned on the 'flashlight'. There was a box next to the drum that said "low-viscosity motor oil." I turned back to MacKenzie. "I don't get it," I said. "Tractor oil? And what's this other thing?"

MacKenzie said ruefully, "You're too young." He looked at Nance. "You?"

"No clue," Dave said.

"They've already taken back the cyclonite and the polyisbutylene, so that's probably why you are puzzled." That wasn't why, but I didn't say anything.

Duncan shifted his weight. He had melted into the shadows like a phantom and I had forgotten he was there. Dave and I looked at each other and back at MacKenzie. We said nothing. As Lincoln would have advised: Better to be thought ignorant than to open our mouths and prove it.

MacKenzie sighed and leaned on a back hoe. "Neither of you were in Vietnam, I take it?" We both shook our heads no. "We used to play with this all the time in 'Nam. You felt childlike when molding the clay. The cyclonite is an explosive, the Dioctyl Sebacate – we called it DOS - is a plasticizer to make it moldable. The polyisobutylene - PIB - is a rubber binder you combine with the oil. That gives you a putty that's similar to modeling clay. The oil can get you high – or make you nauseous. Anyway, when you're done molding you have a small brick. That little brick is worth more than gold in the jungles of war."

"C-4," Nance said in a barely audible voice.

"Exactly," MacKenzie said. "A little gift from Alfred Nobel. I figured some of the other boxes had some blasting caps and detonating cords in them."

"I've never seen it, but I've heard of C-4," I said.

Nance turned to me. "That is the explosive which killed seventeen sailors of the USS Cole in

2000. It is now the device of choice for Al-Qaeda."
Turning to MacKenzie, "What is that stuff doing in
your barn?"

MacKenzie's face hardened. "That I don't know.
And since it's a Government deal, I don't want to
know. You said this would stay between us."

"And it will," Nance said quickly in a reassuring
voice. He looked at me. "If you don't need me
for anything, I've got work to do," Duncan said
impatiently. Mackenzie waved him off.

"Look, this is way out of my league," I said,
placatingly. "But why are you sharing this information
with us?" MacKenzie sighed and suddenly looked
much older. A slit of light from a seam in the wall
ran down the side of his face. His shoulders slumped
slightly. "I had a man - Carlos - who worked for me.
He spent years building these stone and wood fences
you see around the ranch. He would cross the Border
in the morning, work hard all day and cross back to
his family in Mexico in the evening. A couple of weeks
ago a gang member from Nogales, Sonora approached
him with a gun and handed him a cell phone to
deliver to a fellow in Sonoita the next day. The gang
member said if the Sonoita contact didn't call on the
following day to show he received the phone, Carlos
was a dead man. He told Carlos he knew where his
children went to school and he would kill them too.
Carlos knew the man, knew he was serious and so
were his threats. Carlos also knew this would be the
first of many such assignments and he wanted no part
of that dangerous, slippery slope. He talked it over
with his wife, Maria and they decided to quickly find

a Coyote to lead their family across the Border. After they had crossed, the family planned to go up and stay with Maria's sister in Phoenix. But Carlos made the mistake of paying the Coyote in advance. They were crossing the Border, when the Coyote ditched them and ran away. Border Patrol nabbed them and I.C.E. separated the family. They put Carlos and his wife in different holding facilities and the children in a detention center. No one would tell him where his children were. Carlo speaks English, but can't read it well. His wife, Maria, can't read or speak English. The Border Patrol pressured her to sign some papers she didn't understand. They said if she didn't sign the papers she would never see her children again. She signed them. We now hear the children are in Chicago somewhere.

The Border Patrol is charging Carlos and his wife with child smuggling and illegal entry. Instead of sending him back to Mexico, he's going to face a judge sometime in the next twelve months and then mandatory jail time in the United States. I've gone to the holding facility and tried to see him, but he has no rights. I've engaged an attorney from Tucson and we're trying to get a DNA test to prove the children are his, but the lawyer says there is no U.S. position on using DNA to prove paternity in immigration cases. The attorney also told me the papers the Border Patrol made Maria sign, waived her right to be with her children. The immigration attorney said the government has been doing this for months at different sites like El Paso. They are only now making the policy public. I remembered your call," he nodded to Dave. "I thought I'd bring you in on this. C-4 is rarely used with good intentions. If anything blows up around here, I don't want to be the only one with a bad conscience."

* * *

We were quiet on the ride back to Patagonia. I didn't have much to say. I was stunned by Nance's history. I couldn't make sense of Dylan and the C-4. What was he doing with explosives. Could it be possible he also was caching drugs in his Quonset Hut as Nance had suggested? Or was it possibly a meth lab he was operating in the canyon? Nance and I were lost in our thoughts when we pulled up to the Writer's Feast. We both had to snap back to our daily responsibilities. Those commitments needed our immediate attention. We parted with an agreement to keep in touch if either of us saw or heard anything that might make sense of today's discovery.

Chapter 27

The next evening, there was a gathering at the Patagonia town hall. While I was away at my grandmother's funeral, the U.S. Secretary of Homeland Security had made an appearance in Nogales, Arizona to tout the National Guard soldiers deployed to the area as support for the Border Patrol with "more boots on the ground." Dylan's prediction had come true. The Arizona Governor obediently trotted along as the Secretary toured the old Border Wall. The Homeland Secretary described a "crisis occurring on this border today with vast amounts of drugs and criminals, vast amounts of those who want to do our country harm, coming through areas we currently cannot properly defend." She also criticized the U.S. Supreme Court "as a further example of a system that undermines our efforts to keep our Country secure." Her visit had created unrest in the greater Patagonia/Sonoita area and a general discussion meeting had been called for by the Mayor with pressure from the Chamber of Commerce. U.S. Customs and Border Protection officials had been invited to attend. A captain in the National Guard had politely declined, saying he was too busy processing and assigning soldiers to their locations.

I entered the Town Hall and took a place leaning against the back wall. I scanned the crowd looking for Mary. I didn't see her but immediately noticed Dylan in the front row, standing and waving me up to an open chair. I shook my head no and motioned for him to go ahead and sit down.

The crowd noise began to quiet as Joe Theyman walked out on stage to the podium accompanied by a uniformed man the Mayor introduced as an assistant deputy director and a spokesman for U.S. Immigration and Customs Enforcement. The spokesman started speaking as to how the Homeland Secretary had personally asked him to attend tonight's meeting to answer any questions and allay any concerns regarding the department's actions to 'make America safe again.' I had a hard time concentrating as my mind kept wandering back to Mary - wondering where she was, how she was, and what she was thinking?

A question came from the audience: "I'm a teacher here in town and I want to know what we're supposed to do with the children left without their parents after that silly raid on our clinic? Those people were just trying to see the doctor." There was a supportive shout here and there and scattered applause and then silence.

The I.C.E. spokesman smiled obsequiously and started speaking in a folksy manner. "I'm sure you're aware that the people arrested during that mission were in this country illegally," he began.

The teacher interrupted, "And I'm sure that you are not aware that their children don't understand what happened. They're scared. They're afraid to go to school. They've been told you'll come snatch them up next. The ones who do show up to school are crying. We had our State-mandated standardized tests yesterday and one-quarter of the children were absent and the ones who did take the test couldn't concentrate. It's horrible what you're doing!"

"Where are these children staying now?" the director asked, deflecting attention and feigning compassion, but forgetting his audience.

"Well I'm certainly not going to tell you," the teacher said sitting down.

"It's about time we upheld the law around here," a man said.

Another different voice spoke up. "I hear you are especially looking for pregnant women so they can't have babies on American soil," he said. A wave of voices rumbled through the hall. The mayor stepped forward and put up a hand.

Theyman raised and lowered his hands. "Let's be civil here," the mayor said. "The man came to answer questions." He looked around the room. "Let's give him a chance!"

The spokesman nodded appreciatively to the Mayor. "You people don't realize there are bad people trying to get into our country: gang members, drug dealers and terrorists. We're trying to protect you," the Deputy Director said.

Theyman saw me in the back and decided to distract the crowd. He always thought he could turn on his charm like a light bulb. "Everyone, I'm not sure you've had a chance to meet the new doctor at our medical clinic." He gestured to me against the back wall. "Please give a warm welcome to Dr. Harper!" He started clapping. People turned around to look. There was polite applause. I waved awkwardly.

A man with a plaid work shirt and jeans stood up, took his hat off and said to Theyman: "Since you brought it up Mr. Mayor, I have a question for the Doc." He turned to me. Theyman started to protest, but the man talked right over him. "Doctor Harper, are there any health risks to these children being separated from their parents?"

"This is not the time or place …" Theyman began to interject, but the crowd shouted him down.

"Let him answer!"

"I want to hear this!"

People looked expectantly to me. "It's not good, "I said.

"Can't hear you!" "Speak up!"

"Children depend on their parents for safety and support. When that safety and support is shattered it leaves wounds that may never heal. A young child's brain is still developing," I said speaking louder and looking at some of the faces staring back at me. "Research shows that high stress hormones disrupt young brain development. Breaking up the family unit is associated with lifelong trauma such as depression, anxiety, suicide and post-traumatic stress disorders." The room was quiet.

"Thank you, Doc," the man who asked the question of me said in a soft voice and then sat down.

Another man raised his hand. I recognized him. He stood and calmly said his name was Phil Trevino from the Arizona Daily Star. "My question is for the Deputy Director." Theyman seemed to visibly relax. "I'd like to follow up on this gentlemen's question," Trevino said, gesturing to the man in the plaid shirt. "These parents are seeking asylum and then you separate them from their children. Most of these people are said to be fleeing persecution from their homeland. Do you feel that is the case?"

"We suspect many are posing as family members, but are really terrorists or drug smugglers. We at the agency, have a mandate we must enforce," the spokesman replied.

Trevino was looking for a newsworthy quote. "Let me re-phrase the question: aren't we subjecting these people to treatment that we as Americans have traditionally reviled and considered unjust? Aren't we becoming that which we despise in other countries?"

The town hall erupted as people argued among themselves. Many raised their hands frantically to be called upon. Friends and neighbors who supported the government's position wanted to be heard as well. The clamor grew. The I.C.E. spokesperson said over fifty percent of the Border Patrol are Latinos themselves. I could see Dylan arguing with a couple of men in the row behind him. Theyman recognized the raised hand of a young woman.

"I've heard these children being detained in facilities far away from their parents are being sexually abused by predators. Is that true?"

"We have heard rumors ourselves," the assistant Deputy Director answered. "As you know, the children are placed in facilities that the government has subcontracted to organizations expert in these matters to run in a safe and clean manner. We are sending investigators to explore these allegations as well as lawyers and psychologists to help the children."

"What's a five-year old child going to do with a lawyer?" another person shouted out.

"How do you think the parents in your jails feel?" someone else asked. "You've created a disaster!"

"They are the ones who decided to come here illegally," the frustrated spokesperson began, before people in the crowd started shouting at each other.

"He's got a point!"

"Boo!! Boo!!"

"You ought to be ashamed of yourself!"

The meeting began to break down. I slipped along the wall and went out into the night.

The street was empty. The high desert evening warmth was dissipating and the dry Arizona air made the night feel colder. The mild indoor sweat on my skin evaporated. I didn't feel like going back to my cabin. I knew it would be empty. I didn't want to engage with anyone at the Wild Horse. I walked up Naugle Avenue to the Wagon Wheel Saloon. I could still hear the distant arguing at the Town Hall, but when I entered the bar it disappeared and was blessedly replaced by a Lady Antebellum love song playing on the music loop. I sat down and ordered a draft. The bartender asked if I was expecting someone to join me. I said no and wondered if I should just go back to New England.

Chapter 28

I didn't see Dylan for several days after the night of the Town Hall. Our dead of night conversation as we hiked back from the Mexican house call had taken on a dream-like, ethereal quality. There was a buzz about town that Dylan was not a security consultant and his job description was a cover for some other secret enterprise he was engaged in. The talk bounced around that he was CIA or NSA and his mission had something to do with the Border, but of course no one knew anything.

Mary and I carried on at work and awkwardly tried to be friends but romance was wordlessly set aside. My fear of a romantic seismic shift occurring while I was at my grandmother's funeral appeared to be valid. I had not broached the Mexican house call dialogue with Mary and she had said nothing to me. I knew how important communication was in any relationship, but I felt our bond was so tenuous that to talk about it would destroy the fragile threads that remained. I couldn't do that in case I could find a way to rebuild our connection using those threads as a scaffold. At times, I thought I might be making too much of Dylan's bravado admission to me but then again, Mary had not been out to my cabin since I got back. I was surprised when I received a message at the clinic that Dylan wanted to meet for a drink around 6:00PM. The message asked if he could come to my place. I asked Mary if she wanted to join us.

"I think he wants to talk with you privately," she said.

"What about?" I asked, surprised that she was so well informed.

"Some project he's working on I believe," Mary replied. "I really don't know any details."

After work, I made sure to return to my cabin in a timely manner. As usual, Dylan was late. Eventually, I heard a vehicle drive up and there was a knock on my door. I opened it and greeted Dylan. He was backlit in the doorway, as behind him the daylight was giving way to evening. His eyes searched the interior of the cabin.

"She's not here," I said. "Meeting some friends, she said." He turned a little red.

"Would you like a drink?" I asked.

He surprised me. "A bourbon, please. Neat." I had pictured him as only a beer man. Conjuring up an image from his fraternity house days.

"You're in luck," I said. "I usually don't keep scotch or bourbon around, but I have some that a grateful patient gifted me." I opened the bottle from Kentucky and popped the cap off of a Blue Moon for myself. I handed him his drink and looked at him expectantly.

"I wanted to follow up on our talk the night we went to Mexico," he began. "Before . . . your loss. I'm sorry about your grandmother."

"Thank you," I said. There was a pause. We both took a sip of our drinks.

"We had talked about Mary," he offered.

"I remember."

"I wanted to discuss with you moving forward."

"I'm not sure what you mean by that."

"I want to act on my feelings."

"Like duel for her?" I knew it was snarky, but he caught me off balance. You bring this up in my own house, I thought? Really?

"You are so cynical, Harper."

"I'm not. I'm a realist. There's a difference."

He returned to my dueling remark. "I wouldn't recommend physical altercation by the way," he said with great seriousness. "I have youth on my side."

"Okay, the dueling is out, but I don't think Mary would like us talking about her as if she was a commodity." Just the mention of her name altered his countenance.

"You're right," Dylan added quickly. "We shouldn't talk about her like this. It's not honorable."

"Her honor or ours?" I asked. Dylan looked like he had swallowed something sour. "Shall we talk about your side project?" I asked.

His eyes widened. "What do you know about that?"

"Nothing. I heard you might be more industrious than I had thought." He looked at me trying to decide if I had insulted him. He appeared to decide I had not.

"I don't understand. How could you …"

"It's a small town," I interrupted. "No one really knows what they're talking about, but that doesn't stop them from talking. What is it you're working on?"

"I really can't say. U.S. Government contractors have to be vetted and sign non-disclosure agreements. The Government takes those agreements very seriously."

"I know your leader does."

"He's your President too." Dylan looked down into his drink and regrouped. This was not the discussion he had prepared so carefully for.

"So, it's not just the tower you are consulting on?" I asked.

"There's a little more to it than the tower," he conceded. "But it's all connected."

"Like the French Revolution was connected to the guillotine?" I re-filled his Bourbon without asking. He didn't acknowledge or resist the refill. He still looked uncomfortable.

"No, not like that. This is for the better good. We just have to be careful so people don't misunderstand."

"Yes, it's always very dangerous to let the people in on what's in their best interest," I said. Dylan looked wounded. "Are you going to tell Mary what would be for her better good?"

He said stubbornly, "I do know *who* is in her better interest." I took a long sip of beer and thought about countering that statement. As I did, I heard the sound of a vehicle coming down my dirt road. Dylan heard it too. He was up quickly and to the doorway before me. To give him credit, he was spry. He was right, I thought: a physical altercation with Dylan might not go well for me. He waited in the doorway as if it were his home. Mary pulled her car up to the front of the cabin. She turned the engine off and walked to the porch steps where she stopped at the sight of the two of us in the doorway.

"I decided to come over after all," she said.

Chapter 29

When I saw the two of them in the front room together, I immediately wanted to get back in my car and retreat. I didn't like Dylan's idea of meeting with Harper and telling him he was going to start dating me because it felt like the lie it was. Dylan thought it would be easier on Harper's feeling to offer up this white lie. I knew he really thought it would be easier on our feelings.

Pretending the clock of our relationship was just starting would spare me and Dylan the pain of feeling unscrupulous. It was impossible for me to believe the past two and half weeks didn't happen. I don't think Harper would have believed that either. So, I decided to show up myself. When I saw the surprise in their faces, my courage dissipated.

I didn't know how this play out. Once again, I had barged ahead without thinking things all the way through.

*   *   *

"Would you like something to drink?" I asked Mary.

"A chardonnay, please."

I opened a chilled bottle and filled the stemless glass she preferred. I brought it over to her and she accepted it, nodding slightly. She sipped her white wine elegantly while Dylan and I stood awkwardly. I broke the tension by sitting down in the easy chair kitty-corner to the couch. Mary and Dylan sat on the couch across from me. On opposite ends of the couch.

"This is sophisticated," I said.

"Don't be mean," Mary murmured.

Dylan cleared his throat nervously. He started a long soliloquy stating he was smitten by Mary from the very first time they met and although they had spent very little time in each other's company, he felt deep emotions for her and would like to court her openly. At this he sneaked a sidelong glance at Mary. She was staring into her wineglass. No one spoke.

"Well, Mary," I said. "You know how I feel about you. If you are not sure I'll tell you again here and now." She raised her eyes to mine with a barely perceptible pleading gaze not to do that. I wasn't sure whether she meant it wasn't pertinent anymore or whether she wanted to spare Dylan the discomfort of a scene. I feared it was the former. I wanted to make her happy more than anything. "It seems Dylan here feels he's the better man," I said, instead of professing my love for her.

She continued to look at me. "Are you going back to New England?"

I didn't want to tell her of my visit to Tucson. The uncertainty of extending my position at the clinic could be enough to derail my position. I could see

she was viewing me as a man of limited local options
- geographically undesirable now. I did not want
to confirm that supposition. But wherever I went,
couldn't she come with me? She must have thought
of that? Maybe she thought of it and discarded that
option. The possibility deflated me. Did she think
Dylan was going to settle down in Patagonia? Maybe
buy a little spread and begin ranching? I didn't want
to debate these thoughts with her. I wanted her to
read my mind and pick me on my merits. Clearly
and decisively. But, I wasn't too enamored by my
merits. I couldn't take that chance. "I asked for a six-
month extension," I blurted out.

"And?" Mary asked. Dylan's eyes were as wide as
a lottery contestant waiting to hear the last matched
number.

"They're checking into it." I heard Dylan exhale.

Emboldened by my uncertain prospects, he
couldn't contain himself. "I want to marry her!" he
almost shouted in his enthusiasm. Then he played his
wild card, albeit at a lower volume. "I want children
with her." She looked at him for the first time.

"Has he already asked you?" I tried to bring her
gaze back to me. She shook her head no. I couldn't
restrain myself. I wouldn't argue with Mary, but I
would with Dylan. To Dylan I said, "How do you
know you can even have children or how a marriage
would suit you?" I sounded weak, even to myself.

"I have family money," Dylan said. "I could buy
her a house."

This is ridiculous, I thought. "I have a house.
I'm sure Mary can find a man with a house."

"I happen to be right here, you know," Mary said to both of us.

"Have you had your sperm count checked?" I said before I could stop myself. "Proper courting etiquette, you know." It was lame. I didn't mean to go low. It just came out. Mary gave me a hard look. A while back, Mary and I had talked about the many children who needed adoption as well.

"I know this is unpleasant for you, Harper, but don't make fun of me," Dylan said. "I'm trying to be a straight shooter and above board here." I cringed at the "straight shooter" comment, but took the high road and let it go.

Mary spoke up. "I think you are both wonderful and this situation is . . . so unusual." Mary looked to both of us. I thought she might break into tears. But she didn't. "I am very confused," she said and put her head in her hands.

Dylan stood up. "I should leave. I've said my piece."

"Sit down," I said, but he was determined.

Dylan moved to the door, stopping in front of Mary. "May I call you?" he asked. Mary pulled her hands down from her face and looked up to meet Dylan's imploring gaze. I felt the forces of fear and love wrestling in my chest.

"Yes," she said, softly. Arizona didn't often get earthquakes, but I felt as if the ground beneath me had splintered and shifted.

"Thank you for the bourbon," Dylan said to me and he left.

I looked at Mary. I knew she believed, like the honest mass of humanity, that the path she walked in this world was a wide, safe place. Whereas in truth, it was a high, swinging, narrow, rickety bridge over a canyon of unfortunate events. Less the Brooklyn Bridge and more a wood and rope construct in the mountains of Nepal.

"When did you decide you wanted children?" I asked gently.

"I've been thinking about it a lot since Adele, and then when we visited the Detention Center . . ." her voice trailed off. She started to sob very quietly. "Those poor children . . ." I brought over some tissue and she pulled one from the box.

"Could I have a smoke?" she said.

"I know where you left some. I'll get it for you," I said, standing up to enter the other room where she had left a couple of joints hidden in a loose board. The Attorney General had made very clear to all federal prosecutors that possession of marijuana was still a federal crime. I was careful to keep Mary's stash hidden. I didn't want my DEA-prescribing license taken away. But that's not what I was thinking about as I went to pry open that board in my bedroom. I was wrestling with the triangle of fear, love and decay as I passed the full-length dressing mirror behind my open door. It was difficult to keep my anger at Dylan fueled. He was taking his shot at happiness in his own self-conscious way. If I really loved Mary I could see the advantages a life with Dylan could provide. But, self-preservation is a powerful drive in a person. I had a life to offer her as well. In my heart and in my mind the debate continued to rage. I stopped to see in the reflection of that long mirror a man with thinning hair and jowls beginning to droop. He stared back at me.

"How do we handle this and where do we go from here?" I asked Mary as I handed her the blunt.

"I don't know," she said, lighting the weed and inhaling deeply. The effort seemed to calm her even before the medicinal qualities kicked in. "I don't want to lose you."

I sighed. Could this be a passing squall I should ride out? I pushed down my feelings of rejection and unworthiness. The high road. Always take the high road. Then Mary clipped me at the knees.

"You're such an important friend to me. I want so much for that to continue."

I didn't have much of a rejoinder. "Our friendship is dear to me, too." The rest of our conversation was vague and laced with disappointment from my perspective. The smoke invigorated Mary and she appeared to become almost effusive, her thoughts emboldened with clarity. When she finished her joint, she gave me an affectionate hug before she departed. She did not seem to register my reserve.

Chapter 30

The next morning, fighting my emptiness, I took my coffee and walked down the path to the water. It had rained during the witching hour of the night and the cacti were responding to the moisture with their inner brilliance. The paddle shaped prickly pear cactus had sprouted a bright yellow flower that would fade to peach by tomorrow. The queenly saguaros in their stick-man brilliance had posted clinging blossoms and the cholla cacti were putting out a medley of red, orange and purple flowers. The cottonwood trees officially declared the advent of spring with their bursting buds. Soon, the willow trees and sturdy ash trees would follow suit. The path was still lush with the early spring grasses and wildflowers but when summer hit, the hot winds would wick them of their moisture and they would slowly wither until the monsoon, like the cavalry of old, swept in to revitalize them once again. Right now, many of these posies would only last a day and that brief sentiment mirrored my despondency. My memories and melancholy were always lurking in the shallows. The littlest thing could bubble them up out of the shoals of my mind until they erupted like a whale spout. If my sadness were a fish and you were sunbathing next to the cool, clean water of a Sabino Canyon pool you could see it swimming just below the water line. Ready to surface at any moment.

Chapter 31

To counter criticism of their no-show at the Town Meeting, the National Guard decided to hold an informational tour of the Border Wall a few days later. The flyer stated a Captain Leland Nielsen would lead the tour. Interested citizens could muster at Skye Master Memorial Park, a mile east of the Post office on E Hudgins St. The park was on the eastern edge of Nogales, Arizona. Only Santa Cruz County residents were welcome.

The press was specifically not invited. There had been a rash of bad publicity in the news lately. Many articles had documented the thousands of U.S. Citizens held in detention centers around the United States and targeted for deportation by mistake. One Associated Press wire story highlighted a man held in an immigration detention center for more than three years while he tried again and again to prove his citizenship. The articles concluded the wrongful arrests were because of outdated or incomplete government records and lackadaisical governmental investigation. It appeared children and citizens born outside the United States were unpublicized targets. Immigration Court, it was pointed out, does not have to adhere to the rights inherent in the U.S. Justice system. There's no guarantee to legal defense. You are guilty until you prove your innocence -the opposite of what Americans take for granted. One I.C.E. spokesperson incurred wrath for a statement which said: "If you and your children would carry birth certificates of your dead parents and work records showing you've been in the Country long enough to achieve citizenship, we wouldn't have this problem." The average person's feeling of powerlessness was washing over the historically disadvantaged southern border States.

The National Guard tour was on one of my off days, so I decided to attend. The drive from Patagonia only took me twenty minutes. Santa Cruz County Sheriff Frank Lorence was introduced, but did not speak. Since the event was scheduled to begin at 2:00 PM during the work week, the turnout was relatively sparse. Clever scheduling, I thought. Captain Nielsen introduced himself and then surprisingly, asked a Catholic priest from the area to start the government sponsored assembly with an invocation. The priest wore a long, black cassock and a tight white collar and I idly thought he must be hot in the sunlight. He talked about love and God and all his children. He ended with a well-known prayer and many joined in. A few so loudly it appeared they thought their volume could make it true. It was quiet when the priest finished and a smattering of applause was initiated by the captain. I heard someone clapping loudly and turned around to see Dylan on the fringe of the group. He stopped clapping to wave to me.

Nielsen intoned for all of us to follow him. We walked towards the wall. A group of six soldiers fanned out to the sides of the group to guide us along the path. With their uniforms and gear, I thought they must be as uncomfortably warm as the priest. They were all so young. I passed one soldier who had stationed himself on the left side of the trail. We did not make eye contact as he scanned left and right. His head was topped not by a helmet but rather a patrol cap, his closely cropped hair visible beneath the cap's sweatband. His face was impassive and he held himself with a ramrod straight posture. His pistol holster was on the side closest to me as I passed. I could see under his shirt was a protective vest of some kind. His belt held a combat knife and other small packs I couldn't decipher and his boots looked formidably sturdy. I recognized a canteen and gloves hanging from his belt. The most jarring item was the automatic rifle he held diagonally across his upper body. I had no idea what make, model or name was attached to the weapon, but a small wave of fear washed over me. This was lethal stuff. I felt someone come up on my side and I turned.

"Hello, Doc. I didn't expect to see you here," Dylan said jovially.

"I thought I'd come out and see what I could learn."

"That's the spirit!" He never realized when he sounded patronizing, but with his total absence of malice I couldn't work up any indignation. Dylan bulldozed on. "I'm awfully sorry about the other day.

186

I hope you're not sore." The group had stopped ahead of us. "We're still friends, right?"

"Sure," I said. "Of course." After all, he had repeatedly pointed out I was the much older party, so I should at least act with maturity.

I brought water in my fanny pack, but the hike to the wall was brief. We had reached the border wall in no time. Captain Nielsen began to speak and I drank my water. "As you all probably know," he began in a tone that implied he had given many previous briefings. He was accustomed to commanding and being listened to attentively. "Our first wall here was known as the "landing mat" wall. It was corrugated steel about eighteen feet high. The wall got its name because the fence panels of the wall had been used as portable touch down pads for helicopters in Vietnam. Sadly, it turned out they were easy to cut holes through since they were only made of aluminum. It was also easy to put ladders up and jump over. Border agents couldn't see through the walls so they didn't know what was happening on the other side."

The officer gestured with his hands to the wall behind him. It had a solid concrete base a few feet high that secured steel rods climbing well into the blue sky. "This is our new wall. It's called a Bollard Fence Construct and costs about twelve million dollars to replace the 2.8 mile stretch of landing mat fence between Nogales, Arizona and Nogales, Sonora. It's a lot higher – thirty feet – and agents can see through it to anticipate what is happening on the other side and respond to threats more quickly."

A man in our group spoke up. "Can't the visibility work both ways? If the illegals see no officers around, packages can be thrown over or passed through the openings?"

The captain hadn't asked for questions yet and I could see a flicker of irritation pass across his face but he reined it in quickly. "The steel rods are four inches apart," he answered. "They are very difficult to cut so it's harder for big loads to be transferred through the wall. Passing items across the Border is illegal activity you know."

"I wasn't asking for me," the man said dryly.

A woman raised her hand. Nielsen visibly resigned himself to civilian lack of discipline with an audible sigh and recognized her. She was undaunted by his presumed authority and didn't hesitate. "Don't people just go around this fence?" she said. "2.8 miles . . ." She shrugged dismissively. "That's not far. Wouldn't they just cross in more remote areas – you know, like the path of least resistance? Perhaps more dangerous for everybody?"

"We haven't completely stopped illegal activity," Captain Nielsen conceded. "But this slows it down. Desperate people will still find a way." He stopped, repeating his words in his head. Then he accepted them as answer enough.

"You got that part right," the woman said. A few more questions were lobbed at the officer. Finally, the inquiries from the small group were exhausted. We shook our heads no when he asked if there was anything else he could answer. The shadows were lengthening and Nielsen decided he had done all he could with this group and suggested we start back to our mustering spot. The small group retraced their steps under the watchful eyes of our armed escorts.

"You can see the problem here, can't you?" Dylan said to me in a low tone. "The people aren't in step with the government's vision."

I almost snorted, but I didn't want to get shot. "Yes, that's obvious to me, but I don't see it as a problem."

"Oh, it is. They need a wake up. Something to pique their senses. Something to make them really stop and think about these issues in depth."

"I'm not sure I understand."

"You remember how 9/11 united America to the threat of terror and educated the country to the dangers of letting those people weasel their way into our country?"

"What are you even talking about? Do you think separating parents and children of poor people is comparable to protecting our country from al-Qaeda?" My voice sounded sharper than I had intended.

"There you go muddying up the water again," he said. "Or you are making fun of me? I can't tell sometimes."

"I'm not making fun. I am all for keeping our country safe from people who want to do us harm. Our country spends hundreds of billions of dollars doing that. This is different. This is racist. Xenophobic. Cruel. Unjust. No wall would have prevented 9/11. This is just fear-mongering to keep politicians in office." We had reached the parking area. Good-bye and thanks were being exchanged.

Dylan was unmoved by my comments. I found talking to him about government policy enervated me for hours afterwards. "Follow me out of here," he said. "I want to show you something."

"Where are we going?"

"I heard it used to be a good picnic spot. Just follow me."

Like an idiot, I followed him.

Chapter 32

We were scrambling up a dirt trail through the thorny mesquite. I barely avoided catching my arm on a shoulder-high nopal cactus. Dylan moved quickly along the trail and I felt a pang of envy for his youth and enthusiasm. As the light began to fade, the streamside wildlife began to sing. The water would attract raccoons, squirrels, skunks, deer, javelina and a medley of birds. A great horned owl called in the near distance and echoed off the canyon wall. The trail left the stream and began to climb up the cliffside. As we hiked out of the flood plain, we detoured around a massive mesquite bosque on the edge of the stream terrace enabling us to ease between a century plant and a yucca agave at the entrance to the rocky cliff path. The route weaved around palo verdes threatening to bloom and of course, the stately saguaro. A prickly pear cactus caught Dylan's pant leg as he turned to speak. The spines easily passed through the fabric and Dylan howled. We stopped. I used a couple of credit cards and managed to pull the thick stems out of his lower leg.

"Are those poisonous?" Dylan asked anxiously.

"Naw. Just a nuisance." They came out easily because of their size. "I'd stay away from the 'Jumping Cholla' though."

"Jumping? What do you mean 'Jumping?'"

"See that cactus right there?" I pointed to a chain fruit cactus off the trail by only a couple of feet. "Those spine segments are numerous, small and very sharp. They are weakly attached to the mother ship. The slightest graze will detach them and the needles will find a way through your clothes, your shoes, socks and then your skin." I pointed to another cactus. "That's a teddy-bear cactus. Don't let the cute name fool you. Those spines will 'jump' too. The needles are clumped so densely, it's a real chore to extract them."

"Are the needles to defend the plant?" Dylan asked, rubbing his knee vigorously.

"Why? Do you want to build a wall around them?" I said. He didn't take the bait. He was fixated on his leg. With good reason, I admitted to myself. The cholla spines have backward pointing barbs which makes it easier to grab a ride on a human, but also more difficult to remove than the average splinter. Dylan was trying to rub the painful experience out of his thigh.

"To some degree," I finally answered his question. "They do defend the plant. These cacti make needles instead of leaves. The needles provide modest, but effective shade. The barbed spines also carry seed capsules. It's really a strategy of vegetative reproduction rather than trying to irritate your knee. When the spines are finally shed from a passing mammal they fall to the ground and growth of a new plant can begin."

Dylan was back on his feet, ready to go and began to hike again. This time when he spoke to me he kept his eyes on the trail and threw his words over his shoulder. "These people - the Mexicans, the Hispanics - you know why they are so dangerous? Why they just keep coming?" he asked. His pace had slowed as he carefully chose his steps and twisted his body defensively around the desert cacti.

"They want a better life?"

"No. It's because they have faith. They believe in God. It keeps them going. Against all these odds," he said as he threw his arm out expansively to embrace the high desert. Then he stopped and turned around. The sun was going down and he wanted me to see his face. To see his earnestness. He waited for me to say something but I remained silent. I knew there was more.

"And that's exactly what we Americans are lacking down here," he said. "There is a fading commitment to a Higher Being that is exposing our weakness."

"I'm still not sure I understand," I said.

"What we need is a little push. The people in the Southwest especially. A gentle shove to get us American citizens back to our center. Find our groove again. Realize what's at stake. Focus our attention on the threats to our country. A little wake-up call is all. To bring us together again. Look at what Pearl Harbor did for the U.S. It brought us together. America is unbeatable when we're united!"

"Is giving all of us a little push part of your consulting contract?"

He became coy. "Sort of. To analyze the problem. Recommend solutions. I think - that is, many people think - it's very important."

"How do you go about something like that? It sounds ambitiously ineffable," I said.

"We'll see," Dylan said. He extended his arm and pointed at some vegetation on a small mesa a couple of hundred yards away. Past the mesa was an expansive stretch of the high desert. "On the other side of that brush is Mexico. No Wall to protect us here. They'll be coming – the illegal immigrants. How they'll get through that thicket, I don't know," he said admiringly. "But you can bet they'll be coming and now you know why."

"We're not standing at the Alamo and those immigrants are not Santa Ana's army," I said.

"No difference," he said blithely.

Dylan's closing statement was disputable, but my fatigue prevailed over argumentativeness. Debating Dylan was always draining. The sun was about to fall behind the hills and we were poorly prepared for this little jaunt. "We better get back," I said. "If we can't see where we are going on that trail, we're going to look like we got in a fight with an army of cacti when we arrive back in town."

"Yeah, you're right," Dylan said summarily. "No need to go into Mexico tonight, even though it's so close. Let's go." He started past me, reversing our course on the path. "Do you believe in God, Harper?"

"Not since I was eighteen."

"You know you might be wrong. Billions of people believe in God."

"Many different gods. Sometimes that serves to divide them," I replied, trying to find a good hiking rhythm. We made our way around another small grove of mesquite trees. The path was parallel to the border before it turned north.

"Oh, it's still only one God, Harper. God looks different to different people."

"Like Mexicans or African-Americans do to us?"

"That's not the same thing and you know it." Dylan pushed a drooping palo verde branch out of his face. I had to duck when it swung back to the trail at me.

"I know nothing of the kind. I don't think you do either."

"You must believe in something, Harper."

"I believe in science. Gravity. The law of probability." I stopped in the shade of an Arizona walnut tree. We had reached the small stream. The tree was enjoying the moist environment from the stream as much as I was enjoying its broadleaf umbrella protecting me from the sun's last rays on the ridge. The light out of the west was almost horizontal and was piercing at eye level.

"Sounds lonely and depressing to me," Dylan said.

"The truth often is. That's why people choose not to believe in it."

"I don't envy you, Harper."

"On the contrary, there have been many times I've wanted to have faith. But sadly, that's not the same as believing. I do envy those who choose to believe. I see they get great comfort in their beliefs. I wish I could convince myself of such things, but I can't. I don't mind people with different beliefs except when they impose those beliefs on me or others. I find being an atheist or an agnostic is much more threatening to people who believe in god, than their believing in god is to me. I choose not to mention it unless it comes up, for that reason. It makes people very uncomfortable."

"If your life was in mortal danger right now, where would your thoughts go?" Dylan asked.

"To Mary."

"Me too."

I resented that. "Not to your god?"

"It would be a tie."

"One of those might be jealous of the other."

"It doesn't work like that Harper," he said curtly.

"Oh no? Check out those two snakes right there." He jumped as I pointed creekside. "See the one on the other side? That's a black-tailed rattlesnake. He's probably waiting for some rodent in the brush below that sycamore tree." Dylan visibly shuddered. "Whereas, here on our side we have a Sonoran whipsnake." I pointed to a long, slender snake nestled under a velvet mesquite. "He's probably waiting for us to get away from this lovely walnut tree so he can climb up and steal a young bird from its nest." Dylan moved away from under the walnut tree limbs and back onto the path, gazing up into the tree as he shuffled. "These two snakes won't bother each other much, but that doesn't mean they won't engage in combat. Usually it's not over territory so much as it is courtship. A gopher snake or a king snake will take on - and often prevail against - a rattlesnake if threatened."

"We were talking about Mary, not snakes," Dylan said. "Let's keep moving." He started on the path again, putting space between himself and the two snakes.

"Your tower seems like a snake to me," I said. "I know you feel strongly about it. Would you have last thoughts about your tower if you were in mortal peril?"

He tried to parry the question. "And you would have no last thoughts about any of your patients?"

"As a doctor, I have never felt irreplaceable. I always do the best I can, but know that if I'm not there, the world would go on just fine and that includes my patients finding another physician to take my place." We walked in silence a bit. I sensed Dylan was annoyed with the turn of the conversation.

So, I asked him another question. "Do you think your god worries about the plight of immigrants?"

"I believe God understands the Mexicans can't all come here or our country won't survive."

"Do you pray to him about the tower? And our country prospering?"

"Yes. You should try it."

"I might pray that our planet survives."

"A typical liberal prayer. I'm a Republican."

"Even conservatives will need a planet to live on. If we put our country before our planet, it might prove to be a hollow victory."

"For a man who doesn't believe in God, you sure like your idealism."

"Yes, but my idealism doesn't hurt other people."

"I suppose you think protecting the environment doesn't hurt people trying to get a job?"

"It might hurt the exploiters, but there are jobs in protecting the Earth as well."

"Tell that to the starving unemployed Americans whose jobs are being taken by foreigners."

"That is quite a segue: from climate control to unemployment. All solved by your tower."

"We have to protect and maintain our way of life. That's your own Darwinian natural selection." Dylan trudged ahead of me. He seemed pleased with his rejoinder.

"Natural selection doesn't believe in your god. You don't get to cherry-pick your beliefs like that." There was "thump" as something landed in the brush behind me and to the side. I turned towards the sound.

I never heard the shot. I was walking and then I was on the ground. I looked at my right leg and the outer part of my pant leg was gone. I felt no pain at first. Just wonderment.

There might have been more shots. I can't remember. Dylan had dove to the ground and now rolled over beside me. Somehow a gun had materialized in his hands. He fired a short burst behind me in the direction of the thicket. I heard voices and the noise of movement. Then it was very still and the pain started.

"You okay?" Dylan asked.

"No," I said. "I'm not okay. I've been shot." I pulled up the curtain of what remained of my trouser and saw my calf shredded in the upper, outer muscle. I felt my shin. My tibia was intact. I could see the upper part of my Achilles tendon and I reflexively tried to move my foot up and down. I could see the exposed meat of my gastrocnemius and soleus muscles. The tissue contracted and the foot moved. My outer calf muscles were oozing blood. The shock to the nerves was wearing off quickly and the numbness was turning to very sharp pain. I wanted to escape this pain. I looked down and didn't know how.

Dylan leaned in and looked at my leg. "You're lucky it wasn't a military weapon they used."

"I don't feel lucky," I said. But I knew what he meant. The mass shootings in Las Vegas and Florida had shown the public the destruction those bullets inflict on human tissue. "I don't think I'll ever dunk a basketball again."

Dylan, always so literal, was surprised. "You could dunk one before?" he asked. My look stayed the conversation and he glanced back at my leg. "We should get you out of here. Do you want me to tighten my belt around your thigh?"

"No, no," I said seeing in my mind the image of my leg rotting from his tourniquet. "Help me wrap my wind jacket around the wound. We'll make a compression bandage." We did. My face was grimacing now. The throbbing pain was beginning to overwhelm my thoughts.

"What just happened?" I asked Dylan.

"T-shirt cannon, I think."

"What?"

"Drug smugglers use a t-shirt cannon like you see in sporting events to throw a cache over the Wall to their accomplices on the other side. They mistook us for their friends and fired the load over the border. Then they quickly realized their mistake. They saw we weren't Border Patrol or military so they tried to warn us off. They probably didn't mean to hit you, just squirt up some dirt on the path, but . . ." Dylan shrugged his shoulders and looked around.

"You mean to tell me that some University of Arizona cheerleader is missing a t-shirt cannon and now my leg is shot?"

"Bad luck all around." It was very quiet.

"We should move," Dylan said. He was a different person under these circumstances. Competent and confident. He saw me staring at him with wonder. "Someone's going to be coming to get this cache," he said, raising himself on his hind legs. "And they might not be as nice to us."

"You call this considerate?" I said through the pain.

Nonplussed, he went on. "Plus, the yo-yo's that are supposed to be protecting the drop could come back. Can you walk?"

I tried to stand but my body was smarter than my mind and my knee buckled. Dylan caught me. Even though my leg, foot and ankle were intact I couldn't put weight on it. The muscles refused to contract and hold me erect. In a self-preservation act, they had shut down. Thinking a little more clearly, the concept of infection suddenly loomed in my head like an oncoming Death Star. "I've got to get this leg washed and debrided," I said aloud to myself.

"I know that," Dylan agreed. "Put your arm on my shoulder." I did. "How's that?" I could hobble on my left leg. My hamstrings could bend the knee of my right leg so the foot - weighed down by the bulky make-shift dressing – didn't drag in the dirt. My mind shifted back to the pain. I was now afraid of the pain; it hurt so much it took my breath away. I could feel every heartbeat as a pulsating, stabbing throb of pain through my leg. I closed my eyes as tight as I could but the pain found me and wouldn't go away. I became conscious of my breathing because every breath hurt. I tried holding my breath but that only made it worse. Any bearing down made it worse. Without crying, tears came to my eyes. I wasn't sad. It wasn't the dust. It was the pain.

I didn't want to move. It would aggravate that horrible demon inhabiting my leg. "Maybe you should go ahead and scout the path," I said. I wanted to stop moving. Maybe that would ease the pain.

"No, we're making a lot of noise. If someone's out there, they'll hear us and take cover," he said.

"I don't want to get shot again. I don't want you to get shot. That won't help anything," I protested. "Don't be a hero. Let me rest and you go ahead and check it out."

"We should be fine," he said in a voice not much above a whisper. "Any smuggler worth his weight in contraband will see we aren't sneaking out with his load. If they're out there they'll let us go by and quickly get their stuff."

I was starting to feel lightheaded. "How do you know so much about this stuff?" He didn't answer. "I can't believe I'm in the high desert and I drank my water," I said. It sounded whinier than I intended. I was starting to babble. "Stupid, bumbling, tourist doctor," I said to myself in a whisper. A downed tree was on the side of the trail and I abruptly sat on the trunk, almost tripping Dylan. "You go on. Get cell service and call me an ambulance. I'll rest here," I said.

"I'm not leaving you," Dylan said looking around. "Come on, it's not that much further." He hoisted me up amidst my protests. After an interminable trek, he stopped and looked around. "We're safe. They've passed us by." Easy for him to say. Sure, I'll be safe in a rocking chair with a leg rest. Should provide me with a comfortable view when I sit on my porch and wave to Dylan and Mary as they stroll by after church on Sunday mornings pushing a stroller with a yappy dog trailing behind. Dylan stepped on a rock and we both almost fell. That jerked me out of my trance.

"I don't want to be in your debt because you saved my life," I said.

"Don't talk so much. Save your strength."

We struggled along. Dylan, for all intents and purposes, carrying me. Is this the time that the faithful pray to a god? I don't want thoughts and prayers, I thought. I want morphine. "Was the car this far? I don't remember it being this far ..."

"Shhhh." He pushed me down on the ground. Something was moving in the brush. I saw the gun in Dylan's hand again.

"Where'd you get that gun?" I said too loudly.

"Quiet!" he whispered harshly, squeezing my shoulder hard with his left hand.

The pain in my leg began to crescendo with inactivity. Dylan's push to the dirt didn't help either. I heard some rustling but it was slightly behind us. A bear, I thought. I was about to tell Dylan there was a bear in the bushes when he abruptly pulled me upright with a sense of haste and said, "Let's go!"

I might have drifted off, since the next thing I remembered we were at his car. Then we were driving. "Aren't you going to call me an ambulance?" I asked dimly.

"No, I think I can get you to the University hospital faster if I just haul you there right now. Once we reach the highway and good cell reception, we'll call and tell them you're coming."

Belted in the passenger seat I looked out the window. The stars were coming out. Was that the Southern Cross? How could that be? I drifted off again and came out of it on the highway. I looked over at Dylan and he was staring out at the road. We were going very fast. "You should have left me back there. If I had died, you could have had Mary all to yourself."

"I couldn't let you die. She would have missed you too much if you were dead."

I wasn't so sure. Mary's memory of me probably would have faded like a bleached photograph left too long in the Arizona sun, but I appreciated his idealism this once. "Where are we?" I asked

"We just passed an exit to Vail. We're almost there."

"You seem quiet. What are you thinking about?"

He looked quickly at me and turned back to the road. A couple of seconds passed. "You just mentioned it." His eyes were on the highway. "Mary," he finally said. "I hope just because you got shot she doesn't get all carried away with you again." The road flew by and I thought about what he said for a second or two. But then, as was his habit, he distracted me with a different question. "Have you ever been in love before, Harper?" he asked.

"Yes."

"What happened?""

"I ended it."

"Why?"

"I thought she might be changing. I was afraid she might change enough to leave me. I didn't think I could survive that."

"So, you broke it off?"

"Yes.

"That's pretty dark. It's not like one of you cheated or anything?"

"No, this was more serious than simple philandering. The end of a love is a casualty of the heart one may or may not ever recover from."

"Did you recover?"

"The scar still aches at the odd moment."

"Why do you tell me these secrets?"

"Probably because my leg is killing me and I'm not thinking straight. But, mostly because telling stuff takes away the shame, Dylan. It takes away the shame. That helps close the psychic gate of pain. Gives a person a chance to heal."

"I'm not so sure, Harper. Everyone has secrets. Anyway, nothing like that is ever going to happen to me."

"I hope not. I really do."

"With Mary, I mean."

I'm too wiped out for this, I thought.

"Must be wonderful to know someone so well and they also happen to be your best friend," Dylan said wistfully.

"It is."

"I wish I had your experience, Harper."

"I wish I had your right leg." At the moment, it was not experience but the mileage in my body I felt. "Good judgement comes from experience. Experience comes from bad judgement," I said hazily.

Dylan glanced at me quickly and then back to the road. "I like that. See, I can learn from you. Who said that?"

"Either Socrates or some bartender in Maine. I'm not sure. Maybe when Socrates was a bartender he said it. Things are a little fuzzy right now. Don't let them sell me a boat or a timeshare at the emergency room."

"Always with a joke. I'm younger than you but I know what drives women crazy, Harper. Women *scream* after sex with me."

"That's probably because you wipe your hands on the drapes before leaving."

"You wisecrack, but young people can fall in love you know."

"Never said they couldn't," I said. "What's probably more a surprise to you is that old people fall in love too. We like to feel wanted just as much as your group. People seem to remain seventeen years old in their minds. We never quite stop fighting the battles of high school."

Dylan wasn't buying it. He shook his head in a 'doesn't compute' gesture and then added, "I thought you'd be tired of such things Harper."

"It's the stuff of life - being desired," I said as we pulled in under the Emergency Room portico.

Chapter 33

They took me right to the operating room after the X-rays showed no fracture. The anesthesiologist made me painfully roll over onto my stomach. She then found the pulse of the large popliteal artery which supplies blood to the lower leg and foot. With her finger protecting the artery she inserted a needle in the back of my knee adjacent to the popliteal artery in search of the nerve to my lower leg. As the sciatic nerve comes down the upper leg, it dives to safety behind the femur in the soft spot behind the knee. Then the popliteal nerve splits to make up the peroneal nerve and the tibial nerve. I knew that if she could numb that nerve before it splits she could anesthetize the lower leg, foot and ankle. It's a safe and powerful tool in the emergency setting. The anesthesiologist was talking to me as she worked, but with my face planted on my crossed forearms and unable to make eye contact with her, I was not much of a conversationalist. I felt a second needle prick and knew she was putting some of the medicine along the saphenous nerve as well.

Suddenly my pain was gone and I became almost chatty. She said the popliteal nerve block should hopefully last eight hours. She helped me roll back over and prepared to start a light general anesthesia for my comfort on the hard and cold operating room table. I gave over to her all control of my life. I would wake up or I would not. Up to her. I knew the odds were with me, but it was a helpless feeling nevertheless. It didn't hearten me to know from my physician experience how quickly life can change and how simply death came to many without forewarning. Death never cared. Quickly, stealthily and without prejudice it struck. I obediently started counting backwards, "ten … nine … eight …" and she put me to sleep.

I woke up in the recovery room and looked down at my leg. It was still there but covered in a mammoth compression dressing and a heavy posterior splint. It was all my quadriceps could do to lift the leg up off the bed a couple of inches. There was no pain.

I heard the voice of my surgeon ask someone at the nursing desk where they had placed me. "Bed four," they said. He found me and pulled the curtain back.

"I excised the devitalized tissue and washed out the wound with thousands of milliliters of saline to dilute and eliminate the contaminate," the doctor told me. "There was no vascular or nerve injury, but the nerves are stunned and probably won't conduct electricity for a couple of weeks until they get over their concussion." I think he knew I was a doctor, but he still habitually reverted to his lay speak analogies. I didn't mind.

Turning to the recovery room nurse, "Did he get his tetanus shot?" he asked.

"Yes," she nodded. "They gave it to him in the ER." She proceeded to use my IV to inject antibiotics as the surgeon continued.

"I loosely approximated the wound and we'll have you come back in seventy-two hours. At that time, we'll do a dressing change under anesthesia," he said. "If the wound is not infected, I will close the wound and put a fresh dressing on. If the wound looks questionable, I'll leave it open, clean it up and expect you to need a skin graft." He shook my hand and I thanked him. He left and I realized I had already forgotten his name.

The nurse fit me for crutches, put me in a wheel chair with my paper work on my lap and wheeled me out into the hallway where Dylan was waiting. It was 3:30 in the morning and he didn't even look tired. The car was at the curb and they both helped me get in.

"Keep that leg elevated," the nurse said. "Above your heart if you can. We don't want gravity to pull all the swelling into your ankle and foot. We want gravity working for us. If you don't keep that leg elevated it will take you weeks to get that water out. You will also increase your chances for infection and blood clots. But, if you do keep your foot up, all that fluid will drain back through your system. Your kidneys will go to work and you'll urinate all that excess water. So be diligent about for the next few days and you'll reap the rewards in a couple of weeks! It's going to start to throb when you get home. See you soon," she waved and headed back inside with the empty wheelchair.

"Thank you for staying," I said to Dylan.

"No worries, Mate," he said pulling away from the curb and into the quiet night. "I learned a lot at the coffee machine in the waiting room."

"What do you mean?" I asked.

"Well, you were lucky that was a low velocity handgun. Much less tissue damage than otherwise. A bullet from the high velocity guns like the AR-15 rifle causes a huge swath of tissue damage called cavitation."

I started to tell him I knew what cavitation was and how awful it is, but he was excited and I thought I'd let him vent his knowledge so I could rest. I wanted to drift with my thoughts during this window of comfort before the vise-like pain returned to my right leg when the nerve block wore off.

". . . as the high velocity bullet enters the body," Dylan went on. "It brings a large wave of kinetic energy that discharges into the tissue creating a huge wake of destruction. The bullet doesn't have to hit anything important, it only has to be in proximity to something to have a catastrophic effect." He looked at me for my reaction. I feigned interest. He continued. "For instance, if it's near a bone, it doesn't just fracture, the energy wave turns the bone into sawdust for a good six inches or so."

"How'd you learn this?" I mumbled.

"Like I said, at the coffee machine. A couple of trauma surgeons came out to talk to a Davis-Monthan airman. One of his buddies was involved in an accidental discharge earlier today during an exercise on the base. The docs were saying how discouraging it was for them to care for these high-velocity injuries. With handguns at least, they feel they can make a difference, but with assault weapons the wounds are so big, the organs are annihilated and the bleeding so comprehensive, they feel helpless. It was interesting."

My thoughts drifted. I had never counted on a long life, yet I had worried about it. Planned for it. Pined for it. I was more afraid of disability and loss of independence than I was of death. I didn't want to be a burden to anyone. Death would be hard on the people who cared about me, but the deceased never feel the pain of loss. I might have been more afraid of losing happiness - or never finding it - than I was of dying. Death would end that struggle. The fear of a future where one only looked back on the lost glory of youth would be snuffed out along with life. But also absent would be any opportunity for triumph in that lifelong tug of war between loss and joy.

I fell asleep and awoke to the sound of thin gravel crunching under tires. I opened my eyes and saw the driveway to my cabin.

Chapter 34

Dylan helped me to my bed and placed a blanket over me. He said he'd send someone from the Clinic over to check on me and would return after he attended to some pressing business.

I awoke a few hours later. My leg was throbbing and I was drenched in sweat. Mary had unbuttoned my shirt and was sponging my forehead, chest and abdomen. She was crying.

"Hi," I said. She flicked the sponge at the tip of my nose in a tender, familiar greeting.

"You're burning up," she said softly through her sniffles. She dabbed her eyes with a tissue and blew her nose. Then she continued to caress me with the wet sponge. She didn't meet my gaze. She worked, eyes on something above me, towards the headboard. After a while she stopped and dabbed my wetness with a small, dry towel. When she finished with the towel she reached into the drawer of the bedside table and extracted a pill from each of two prescription containers.

"Take these," she said and gave me a cup of water and a straw.

"What are they?" I said weakly as I took them.

It was difficult to swallow the big pills, but I managed to get them down. It was an exhausting effort to bend my neck to the straw and a relief to plop my head back on the pillow. I vaguely remembered I had wanted to organize the books in the front room that were accumulating and create for myself a small library. Did I pay the rent for this month yet? I couldn't recall. I didn't want to be late on that bill. And my shirts were still at the cleaners. Or had I picked them up?

"An antibiotic and a pain pill," Mary said softly. I noticed Mary's free left hand was holding my right hand. She squeezed my hand and I fell back asleep.

*   *   *

It was so hard to see Harper in such pain. I'd do anything to take the pain away. Sure. Big talk. I've probably caused him more suffering than that wayward bullet. What a hypocrite I am. His pride won't take this well. His temporary infirmity will make him feel less vibrant. If he only knew his vulnerability was far more attractive to me than how fast he could run the 100-yard dash.

*   *   *

I dreamed I was running in a track meet. My legs were like jelly and I couldn't get them to move faster. They were so heavy. It was a small high school track and the sparse stadium seats were adjacent to the infield. A woman in a smart red dress was standing up in an aluminum bleacher row as I ran by. She was wearing a big white flowing Kentucky Derby style hat and her hands were pushed together as if in prayer. I couldn't see her face but I knew in the dream it was Mary. Every step I took, it was as if my legs were thigh deep in sucking mud or quicksand. Then I was in bed with Mary. She was nestled under my arm. I peacefully stroked her flank. In the haze of afterglow, she played with my chest hair, drawing her fingertips back and forth from there to my abdomen.

*   *   *

When I awoke from my dream I looked around and didn't see Mary. I had a moment of terror, but then I heard her in the other room talking on the phone. My panic receded, replaced by a wave of security and I drifted into slumber once again.

*   *   *

I was playing left field in a Little League baseball game and the batter hit a high fly ball in my direction. I went back, back, back to the three-foot high fence. There was no warning track. The ball hung up in the blue sky between two large cumulus clouds. I felt the fence and jumped as high as I could, extending my gloved hand far over my head, my eyes on the ball. It would have been a home run. But I jumped an inch too high and the ball hit the heel of my glove, ricocheting down along my outstretched left arm to my face where it shattered my nose and rolled along

214

the ground. The center fielder picked up the trickling ball and held the batter to a triple.

*   *   *

It was the next day when the fever broke and my head cleared. There was a note from Mary that she'd gone into town for food and supplies and would return shortly. I saw my crutches propped against the easy chair. I wanted her to see I wasn't an invalid. I sat up and swung my legs over the side of the bed. Immediately, it felt like a dam had burst in my leg allowing gallons of fluid to escape down my knee into my foot and ankle. As the flooding seemed to fill my lower leg and stretch the skin to burst, a vise clamped down on my leg below the knee and began to tighten. The pain escalated to unbearable within two seconds, forcing me to reverse jackknife back into bed and thrust my leg back on top of the pillows. The floodwaters and the pain gradually subsided in this position and after several minutes I was able to catch my breath and my pulse returned to normal. Using the facecloth on the bedside I wiped the perspiration off my face. I was exhausted by the effort and gave up quickly any idea I had of hopping over to my crutches.

An hour later, I formulated a plan. I sat up, now forewarned and experienced, and draped my legs over the side of the bed. I forced myself to hold that position for a ten count. Then I backflipped into my supine state and stayed there until the throbbing in my leg stopped. Then I did it again. Slowly, I increased my tolerance. After a couple of hours, I was ready for my maiden voyage. I threw my legs over the bedside and hopped on my good left leg before my brain or my right leg realized what was happening. I reached the crutches and after a couple of teetering moments made it out to the porch, sunlight and redemption. I quickly sat down on the rocking chair and placed my leg up on the porch rail. The splint cushioned the hard wood edge. I noticed the lingering scent of smoked weed clinging to the porch facade. I smiled at the thought of my home nursing staff taking a blunt break. Somewhere in the back of my mind a flag of worry appeared and then dissipated as if an apparition.

Perhaps it's hard for us to believe we are lovable. Of course, a parent and one's own child have vested interests, but for a non-blood relation to truly love us for who we are is often difficult to fathom. I always wanted Mary to tell me more about our love. Platitudes would have been fine. But she never did. When she said things, she believed them. When she didn't offer soft, comforting words of endearment, it was because she didn't have that feeling at that time. So, I began to believe that with Mary there were no false moments.

When my strength returned after this vigorous first outing, I went back to the kitchen table and started a letter to Dylan. I thanked him for his assistance the other night, made light of my injury and mocked my skill on crutches. "I will soon switch to a cane as I will undoubtedly do much more injury to myself if I persist in employing these infernal

216

sticks." I concluded the missive by unfairly skewering him about Mary: ". . . she has been a doting, veritable Florence Nightingale and the occasion has brought out depths of our love we had not realized until this crisis. The silver lining of this injury is that it has brought Mary and I even closer together in a very special intimacy and for this I am eternally grateful." I finished with a little flourish of ". . . looking forward to sharing a drink with you at the Wild Horse soon." After I sealed the envelope, I leaned back into the chair and tried to think of how I could make the letter come true.

Chapter 36

The darkness crept in. I wondered if this was the time the blackness would never end. Just because it had passed in times gone by did not mean this wasn't the time the black dog would stay forever. I knew from my patients that any disease - pain especially - shares this phenomenon. When it comes on, how do you know this time it will ever go away? That the pain will stop? It takes tremendous courage to believe that this too will pass. But the condition doesn't always pass. Sometimes it kills you.

Through the kindness of Mary's friend, Bob Baxter, I was spared imposing on Mary or Dylan for my return visit to University Hospital. Bob came out to visit me at the cabin and immediately volunteered to chauffer me for my follow-up surgery. I jumped at the offer. Although I could drive with one leg, even my stubbornness recognized the danger of driving after anesthesia. I also remembered my surgeon had introduced himself as Tom Hanson.

It was déjà vu when Dr. Hanson swept aside the curtain in the recovery room for the second time.

"Fortunately, there was no evidence of infection," he said immediately. With the aid of another popliteal nerve block, I was feeling no pain, but relief still coursed through me. "I was able to do a primary closure of the leg wound. I put you in a removable, knee-high walking boot and I'd like you to return in ten days to have the sutures removed."

I thanked him profusely for his skill and care. "If the incision looks okay to me, would you mind if I took a photo of the wound with my phone and texted it to you? If you then agree the healing looked healthy, I would rather take the sutures out myself. It would save me the trip and save you the time."

Hanson looked doubtful. "I've never done this before," he said, mulling it over.

"If you have any doubts, believe me, I'll come right up to see you. I have no interest in anything but a great result," I implored. "But, as you can imagine, the logistics of getting back here are difficult and this seems like a good compromise."

Hanson reluctantly agreed and we shook hands on it. Baxter and I had a good ride back to my cabin as he regaled me with stories of life in his hometown of Philadelphia and was a trove of Arizona movie trivia.

Ironically, here in Patagonia it was work – that thing I left New England for – that helped to right my ship. The distraction, the concentration, the mind-numbing forms and documentation that left little time to stop at the dry-cleaners or squeeze in a haircut, all helped me heal, inside and out.

With no word from Mrs. Graham, I had to fleetingly think of the day I would leave Patagonia.

I had to push away the oppressive thought of a life without Mary. I didn't want to question Mary about Dylan. I knew that might force her to play loose with the truth and I didn't want to diminish my love for her. Questions and parried responses could fracture our friendship and impair our working relationship. So, I pretended everything was fine. But of course, it wasn't.

I couldn't help but hear the whispered talk about Dylan. Stories of little incidents and activity just south of us near the Border. Meanwhile, the rhetoric continued. The debates strained civility at the Wild Horse. On one side was the fear in some local people of change they didn't quite understand. Many had known little else than what they'd grown up with in this area and were scared of being left behind in the confusion of economic uncertainty and strange faces. Others thought their neighbors were jousting with windmills. They argued that more Mexicans and their families – including children born in the United States – were leaving the United States and going back to their home country than there were actual Mexicans migrating to America. No matter what the second group said, the first group wanted a wall. That seemed a solid, tangible answer to all problems. Something they could see and feel. Something they could understand. Every debate ended in the same stand-off. Berlin be damned. Give us a wall. Look how well it worked for China.

Chapter 37

Work exhausted me more than I let on to anyone. My calf was like a tapped keg – the standing depleted me as the energy poured out. Back in town I dreaded crossing paths with Dylan. He had saved my life, stolen my girl and now was perhaps involved in something nefarious that I didn't understand. Walking down the streets in Patagonia, I felt the other metaphorical shoe was going to drop every time I turned a corner. I had eschewed my cane in favor of pride and walked with a limp. My world seemed unsteady. My own vulnerability as a hobbling, cuckolded, old man shamed me.

Habit helped me cope. Going to the office. Seeing patients. Attending to all the paperwork. It helped stave off the two-headed demon of worry and anxiety. Otherwise I would have been sitting in bed at home watching British mystery dramas all day long.

Walking through town I had stopped by the newspaper offices to give Bob Baxter a book and thank him for his favor to me. One thing led to another and I asked him what he was working on.

"There is a lot of back and forth between journalists about the Army erecting huge detention areas for immigrant children separated from their parents when caught crossing the border. Right now, we don't have any leads or hard evidence. Just rumors. I'd love to break the story though. It'd be a coup for our little paper."

Two days after talking to Baxter, an afternoon consultation from the army base east of Patagonia helped me forget myself for a few hours and proved an unusual source to confirm Baxter's suspicions.

Captain Neal Mitchell had been sent over from Fort Huachuca in Sierra Vista for a second opinion. Mitchell had demanded the civilian consultation because he felt he was getting the run-around at the base. The referral request said he had a "fever of unknown origin."

"Good afternoon," I said, introducing myself to the captain and his female companion. Mitchell had changed into an examination gown and did not look well.

"This is my girlfriend, Carla," Mitchell said. I shook hands with Carla and then looked at the flow sheet Mary had left for me after she did her patient intake. Mitchell's fever was 102.5 degrees Fahrenheit. His blood pressure was 148/90 and his pulse 96. He shivered in his gown and cross-wrapped his arms tightly around his torso.

"His pee turned black this morning," Carla blurted out. Neither Mitchell or Carla looked as if they had slept in quite a while, despite both appearing to have fading suntans.

"Have you had a bowel movement lately?" I asked.

Mitchell nodded his head yes. His expression was one of distress. "Diarrhea actually. My stomach hurts bad. One of my buddies said it was a ruptured appendix." I asked him to lie down on his back. His abdomen was soft to my probing and there were no specific pressure points. He had no pain when I let the pressure off abruptly.

"It doesn't look like appendicitis. How long has this been going on?" I asked.

"It started the day we came back to Huachuca to get our stuff," Carla said.

"We've been at Fort Bliss in El Paso for the last three months," Mitchell added.

"He's been working so hard . . ." Carla said with exasperation.

"I'm an Army liaison with Homeland Security and Health and Human Services. We're erecting a family detention area at Fort Bliss."

"It's a big job," Carla interjected.

"It's going to have 20,000 beds there for youngsters who arrive in this country and are separated from their parents," he said. "And the brass wants it done yesterday."

"He's been under so much pressure," Carla added. "No one planned for this."

I tried not to show any surprise they were sharing this information with me. Patients tell their doctor many things that have nothing to do with their medical care. "You both look pretty tanned," I said. During the abdominal exam, I noticed Mitchell had no tan lines.

"We did manage to get away three weeks ago for a vacation."

"Long overdue!" Carla added.

"We went to the Hotel Las Hades," Mitchell said. "That's where Bo Derek was honeymooning in the movie "10". We've always wanted go there."

"It's beautiful," Carla said blissfully.

"Is that in Mexico?" I asked.

"Manzanilla. Just south of Puerto Vallarta. Right on the ocean. Gorgeous area," Mitchell said and then groaned painfully, holding his stomach. He shivered and hugged himself again. "Can I use your bathroom?"

"Of course," I said. I reached into the cabinet and pulled out a specimen cup. "Can you put some urine in this? It might sound gross, but if you have some stool please don't flush the toilet. We'll want to test that as well. Do you need some help?"

"No. I can manage," Mitchell said gamely, rising to his feet.

"I'll come with you Honey and be right outside the door if you need me," Carla said taking his elbow.

I waited for them in the examining room and took out my phone to do some research while they were gone. When they returned, Carla handed me what was indeed, a black urine sample.

"What is this?" Carla asked, pointing to the dark liquid in the cup.

"I need to get a blood sample and check your blood count," I answered. "I'm worried you might have malaria. While you were gone I checked the Center for Disease Control website and they have cases of malaria in Jalisco, Mexico - the region that Manzanilla is in. It's more common north of Jalisco, in Sinaloa, but there are cases where you were."

"Malaria?" Carla said with surprise. "But the hotel told us to take Quinine while we were there."

"And we did. Conscientiously," Mitchell added.

"That doesn't work as well as people think," I replied. "What happens is the mosquito parasite destroys your red blood cells and the debris in your bloodstream – especially the hemoglobin - makes your urine dark. That's why a lot of people refer to it as Blackwater Fever."

"I always thought Blackwater fever was from drinking bad water," Mitchell said with astonishment.

"No, it's actually from malaria," I said.

"What can we do now, Doctor?" Carla asked, her concern obvious.

"Let's check your red blood cell count now. I'm going to call an ambulance to take you up to Tucson. You'll be admitted to the hospital and they will give you antimalarial medicine. You might need some dialysis to help your kidneys filter out the destroyed red blood cells, but fortunately it looks like we caught this early and otherwise you look in great shape." I turned to Carla. "This far out your own chances of being perfectly fine are excellent, but it would be prudent if you were checked out too." She nodded.

By the time the ambulance arrived Mitchell's hematocrit had registered as twenty-two against a normal of forty-five. An IV was started in the back of the ambulance and I ordered fluids to restore Mitchell's vascular volume and help dilute what the kidneys had to clear. Carla gave me a spontaneous hug and promised to call me later with a report. She kissed Mitchell and hopped in her car to follow the ambulance to University Hospital. I had called ahead and hospital personnel would be awaiting Mitchell's arrival. I shook hands with Captain Mitchell and the attendant closed the bay doors of the vehicle. Carla gave one final wave as the convoy of two vehicles left the parking lot. I turned to Mary, who was standing beside me waving at the departing car.

"Malaria . . ." she said to me as she dropped her hand. "You don't see that every day."

I agreed with her. Not too long ago I would have shared with her my quandary as to whether it was ethical to tell her friend, Bob Baxter, what I learned from Captain Mitchell about the Fort Bliss construction. I missed the comfort of a companion I could trust and counsel I could respect. I was pretty sure telling Baxter would be a HIPAA violation.

Chapter 38

I decided I couldn't tell Baxter. As much as I wanted to help him and his small paper, it didn't feel right. From past experience, I knew if it didn't feel right, it probably wasn't right.

My own meager attempts at avoiding confrontation with Mary and Dylan did me in. Instead of going to the Wild Horse for a pint after an exhausting day of clinic, I went to the Wagon Wheel Saloon off of McKeown Avenue. I saw Mary and Dylan at a table off to the right the moment I crossed the front door threshold. Simultaneously, they looked up and saw me. The light was murky inside the bar but I thought Dylan's hand was on Mary's as I walked in. However, by the time my eyes adjusted to the dimness, the hand was gone.

"Hello Harper," Dylan said, half standing. "Please join us." He was so energized I thought he was going to ask me to be his Best Man then and there. I hesitated, but Mary smiled warmly and turned an adjacent chair sideways. I acquiesced and sat down. A waitress came by and I ordered a beer.

Dylan pulled a letter from his pocket. "Mary and I were discussing this," he said.

I recognized the handwriting. I wanted to reach across the table and grab the letter but I squelched the impulse. Dylan continued. "There might be a couple of inconsistencies," he said in a scolding, disappointed tone.

"Not to me," I said with forced bravado. Dylan turned to Mary who was looking at her clasped hands on the table. "That was the truth as I knew it at the time," I said, wincing inside and feeling like a witness changing his testimony on the stand. Mary looked up and our eyes locked. The stale Wagon Wheel air between us was charged with words unspoken. Behind us, a loud, competitive game of darts was taking place between two regulars.

Dylan was still mulling over my 'truth.' He decided to accept it as a confession. "Well that clears it up. Things change and life moves on," he said with what I'm sure he saw as magnanimity.

"Does it?" I asked, directing my query to Mary. With her head down, she reached into her purse, pulled out her own letter and handed it to me. I saw my name on the envelope and stuffed it in my pocket.

"Excuse me," Mary said as she left the table and crossed the barroom in the direction of the lavatory, totally halting the dart game.

"I love her," Dylan said leaning over the table as if that settled the issue.

"You confuse romantic notions of love with true love," I said evenly. "I don't know what exactly Mary feels for you. You've confused her. But when the dust settles, there will probably be just three broken hearts because of this emotional recklessness."

"I saved your life!" Dylan said self-righteously. "You're just embarrassed."

"You are also the one who put me in jeopardy of losing my life. You probably thought that was a good idea too. Just like you think toying around with plastic explosives is good for Patagonia and our country."

Dylan looked as if I'd slapped him. "Plastic explosives?" He was a poor liar.

"Probably another idiotic scheme born of hubris, innocence and ignorance," I said standing up to leave. "I wish you weren't basically a decent person, Dylan. Then maybe you wouldn't so quickly assume the people you work for are decent people. You might be able to open your eyes a little more and see through their agenda - all the way to the top."

"I'm going to give her children - and security!" Dylan blustered.

I looked over in the direction of the restrooms. There was no sign of Mary returning. "She's scared, Kermer. I'm scared. And you should be scared too." I walked out of the Wagon Wheel. I didn't look back. I wanted to take one last look to see if Mary was returning to the table, but instead I shut the door. I was proud of my idiotic discipline. I wondered again what Dylan was up to and did my jealousy color my reasoning? Or was it because, as with Mary, he felt love excused all his actions?

Back at the cabin, I sat in the armchair and looked at Mary's familiar scrawl on the envelope. I noticed my hand was shaking as I pulled out the stationery.

Dear Robert -

I know your leg is healing well. After all, I do see you at work. I wonder how everything else is healing? I'm sorry to have been so distant and I should have talked to you before this but when I meet your eyes I become a coward and I don't recognize or like myself at those moments. So, I'm writing this because I don't trust myself talking to you. I know there are other parts of you that need healing besides your leg and I feel absolutely miserable that I may have caused you the pain I sense. I'm so sorry.

I guess I do want children. I didn't really know this until recently. Although you would be a wonderful father, even if you changed your mind our children would go through school with talk behind their backs about their father's age. I fear you would not be able to be as active with them as you would like. The big point, however, is you might not be around to share their milestone moments: graduation, marriage, children of their own, and so on.

Dylan says he loves me. I know you do too, but Dylan is so unabashed by it all. I feel his "all in" commitment that is sometimes elusive with you. I'm going to have to stop loving you but I will always love our days together. Please don't be angry with me. I hope we can be good friends. I'd like that so very much. You are a prince of a fellow, just not my Prince anymore. I firmly believe you'll be okay. (I have to!) You'll find a person who loves you. I know by my doing this now with Dylan I have given you enough time to meet another person. Have one last great love. I know you won't be alone as you grow older.

I find such comfort in that we were always so kind to each other.

Sweet love to you now and forever,

Mary

I put the letter down. I tried to remember what I had said to Dylan at the Wagon Wheel, but now it seemed blurred, fuzzy and tinged with regret. Mary was so enthusiastically optimistic about her new life with someone else. It left no room for argument. I felt so helpless. I knew I couldn't convince her to try harder with me. If someone loses that will to try … that belief in the couple. . . the belief that should be stronger than any religion . . . well, there is no place for the other party to go, but away; the unloved left flailing silently in a vacuum like an astronaut with a broken tether. Love is not a college debate. You can't win the counterargument if the other person has given up on you. Morphine couldn't help this pain. I would merely wake up again to realize that no new scaffold had been created, no sinew healed, no collagen synthesized, no mineralization had occurred. Honesty and fidelity don't keep a relationship from ending. They are guidelines for the possibility of success but come with no warranty. Memories of Sabino Canyon kept washing over me. I kept going back to the way we fit together perfectly, the warmth of her next to me, her tender touch, the odd love note left in the unusual place. I would prefer Mary had shot me in the leg and stayed with me. That I could recover from.

Chapter 39

Writing that letter to Harper was one of the most
difficult things I've ever done. I had to get off the
fence. I was being cleaved in two and felt my health
slipping. I didn't think I could say the words out
loud to him, so I wrote them down on paper. When
I handed Harper the letter and saw the crestfallen
disappointment in his face, I had to leave. I couldn't
bear watching him read it at the table.

*　　*　　*

Those days after seeing Mary and Dylan at the Wagon
Wheel Saloon were desperate for me. The intense
Arizona sun did not seem to shine as bright. The stars
in the nighttime sky had lost their clarity. That awful
dream kept recurring - where I was running but my
legs were leaden and mired in deep mud. Mary was
kind to me in the Clinic. Almost too solicitous and
gentle for my paranoid state. We met for various
meals but conversations that had been effortless and
intimate before were now forced and stilted. I avoided
asking too many questions under the premise of not
forcing any indiscretions: a communication disaster

for any relationship - friendly or intimate. Physical contact, by unspoken agreement, was limited and proper. I ate, worked and was lonely. It was all I could do to not lash out and become someone I despised.

Sleep was hard to come by. Even after a late-night totty, the induction of sleep was elusive. My body felt exhausted but my mind was too active. Many times, I threw a blanket around my shoulders and walked out on the porch to gaze at the night sky. I enjoyed looking into the past. Knowing I was viewing light shed millions of years ago from stars that might not even be there anymore. Starlight was only just now making it across the universe to my cabin. If the sun exploded we'd have eight minutes of normal sunshine until our world ended. About the same amount of time I had when I realized Mary had moved on, I thought dolefully. If I could see the past in the sky, why couldn't I go there and change a few minor details? But we can't go back in time. We can only go forward. After a while, the musings would fatigue my mind, I would retreat to bed and try again to sleep.

One night was more eventful. In moving from New England to Arizona, I had unwittingly traded a geographic prevalence of ticks for scorpions. Lyme disease for a neurotoxin. I was warned that scorpions were everywhere in my cabin but you would rarely ever see them. If you wanted to give yourself a fright you could shine a black light around at night, but my friends didn't recommend it. "Ignorance is best. Just keep your bedcovers off the floor," they said. In retrospect, this night the scorpion must have climbed up the logs on my side wall and then on to the ceiling over my bed. Most likely in search of water evaporation in one of the ceiling vents. The worn log afforded poor traction and the scorpion fell onto my soft bed. I was sleeping on my right side. I wore a t-shirt to keep the night chill off of my shoulders. My right wrist was propped on a side pillow, creating a yawning tent between the upper sleeve of my shirt and my triceps. Using 400 million years of stimulus/reaction experience, this nocturnal invertebrate decided to crawl up the cotton in search of my warm axilla. Asleep, I stirred at the tickle. I reflexively adjusted with my left hand what I thought was a bunched-up crease in the bedsheet. I woke with a start at the painful sting on my upper arm. Bolting upright and now very awake, I stared at the bed. I only saw pillows and the bedsheet. Then I felt the tickle again under my t-shirt. I whipped my shirt off to see the scorpion tumble onto my pillow. I snapped at the scorpion with my t-shirt and flung it off my pillow to the floor. I turned on a light, but it was gone. I turned on all the lights of the cabin and warily searched everywhere, but never did find the desperado. The sting only hurt for about an hour, but there was no going back to sleep that night. I knew it was still in the cabin, waiting for me to let my guard down. I thought for sure the little scorpion was going to come back and finish me off.

Most times I would eventually drift off to a half-awake/half-asleep state for two hours until I was wide-eyed again. From there to dawn it would be a blur of zombie trips to the bathroom and the refrigerator to break up the mental spinning of my wheels on the ice of my thoughts. Sometimes a wisp of REM sleep would occur. I could always tell because I would start awake, vaguely feeling melancholy from some dream unrecalled. Or then some person or setting I hadn't thought about for thirty years would appear in my sleep. Where did that come from, I'd ask myself? What was the significance of the rain in that dream? What was the deer doing there? What was *that* all about? Finally, a gaze at the clock told me there was no use trying for more sleep. Might as well get up. I would drag my feet to the shower, knowing I was going to feel drained and depleted all day. The hot shower water would cascade over me while I dully wondered why on Earth did I have that dream and what could it mean? In an attempt to feel more human, I'd make a double expresso before leaving for work. Instead of feeling more alert by the caffeine, my energy was supplanted by a jumpy nervousness and a touch of impatient irritability. I could feel that surfacing as I started the car and headed out the driveway.

It was right about this point in my desperation that I got a call from Dave Nance. Colin MacKenzie wanted to see us again and there was a tinge of urgency to the request. We made the trek back down Harshaw Creek once again.

MacKenzie was waiting for us. He was all business and he asked us to pile into his Range Rover. He made no reply when I commented I was surprised he drove the same vehicle as the Queen. Dave looked at me sideways and I went silent.

We bounced around a poorly maintained ranch road through a saddle of the Patagonia Mountains. From the crest of the road there were arroyos visible cutting back and forth below us as we weaved through their maze. Oaks and cottonwoods blocked the view as the road dipped lower. Coming around a hairpin curve to a relative straightaway I could see wisps of smoke lay ahead. We pushed through some sagebrush until MacKenzie pulled up and stopped at a charred, still smoking piece of the mountainside that looked like a small, well contained forest fire.

"What happened here?" Nance asked.

"My men heard a thunderclap in the bunkhouse last night. Not uncommon this time of year, but when morning broke, the sky was clear and it hadn't rained. They drove out to clear some land east of here," the rancher said as we piled out of the Rover. "That's when they saw smoke entrails over this way. They radioed the foreman and discovered this. Duncan called me."

"What would cause this?" I asked.

"I wondered that myself," Mackenzie replied. "I had a suspicion, so I went into town and picked up some odds and ends to satisfy my curiosity. Come with me."

We walked around slowly, taking in the charred hole in the forest and the flickering red embers still smoldering in afterglow. Lost in our thoughts, MacKenzie motioned again for us to follow him. He led us up to a sizable tree trunk. On the jagged top of the trunk were small particles of gray residue. He slid a fanny pack around to his hip, unzipped it and pulled out a Swiss army knife. Fishing around in the pack, he found some oval shaped white paper that looked like a coffee filter and two small bottles that resembled travel shampoo containers. With the knife, he scraped the residue off the tree trunk and onto the white paper.

"What are you doing?" Nance asked.

"Another little trick I learned in 'Nam," MacKenzie answered. He opened one of the small bottles and gently shook some of the contents onto the white paper. "These are thymol crystals," he said while working. "Can be picked up at any chemical supply store." He opened up the second bottle and found an eye-dropper in his pack. "This is sulfuric acid. A few drops of this . . ." We watched as the residue became more distinct. ". . . and then the grand finale." He reached into his bag and pulled out a smaller bottle with a dropper built into the stopper. "A little ethyl alcohol," he said looking up at us before applying it to the residue. We watched as the residue turned rose colored.

"There you have forensic proof that someone has been testing C-4," MacKenzie said.

"Wow!" Nance exclaimed. Our eyes met.

"Exactly," Mackenzie said. "We're going to have to find a time to get together and talk this over. I've got work to do right now I can't put off. Let me drive you back to your car and we can touch base tomorrow. I can come into town if that would be easier for you both." We agreed and headed back to MacKenzie's Range Rover.

Not much was said as MacKenzie drove us back to his ranch. "Did your men see any strangers lurking around the forest here last night or this morning?" I asked.

"I questioned them myself. They didn't see or hear anything. We figured it was done late at night, towards early morning. Frankly, my crew is a little spooked that this could go on while they were sleeping only a couple of miles away."

Everyone was lost in their own thoughts. As we parted, we exchanged promises to be in touch tomorrow. On the way back to town I said to Nance, "We have to get a closer look at that Quonset hut." He was thinking the same thing.

"You should stay out of this," Nance said, maneuvering the truck around a slow-moving tractor and then crossing back into our lane before the road turned sharply around a curve. "Whatever is going on is serious business and a doctor nosing around is only going to lead to collateral damage."

"Shall we mention this to the Sheriff?" I asked.

"Now I know you've lost your senses," he said disdainfully. A few seconds ticked by. "You do realize who we're dealing with here, don't you?"

"Not exactly," I said.

"I spent a little time in D.C.," Nance said. I looked at him with surprise. "Remember I told you I looked up that guy meeting with Kermer at Writer's Feast?

"Yes."

"I didn't stop there. I called a couple of people I know at Langley and found out a little more." He glanced over to me.

"I'm listening."

"You have to understand Washington. The CIA isn't supposed to operate domestically - that's the FBI's job. The National Security Act of 1947 makes that clear. But the National Security Council - part of the Executive Branch - has the power to perform functions in the interest of national security. The head of the National Security Council is the President. Do you see where I'm going with this?"

"I think so," I said slowly, mulling over the implications of what Nance was getting at.

"None of this came to light until Nixon's Dirty Tricks people were exposed in the early 70's. Even then, the special group of intelligence operatives part of the National Security Council never got exposed. Overseeing this group is virtually impossible because their funding is swallowed up by the NSC's budget and everything is protected by executive privilege. The President just has to cry out "National Security" and his powers become unchecked and any inquiry is immediately halted."

"So," I summarized. "Under the best of circumstances a President can use this small intelligence group that reports only to him, for sensitive missions to further our national interests without the exposure and rule of law that our recognized intelligence community operates under. Is that about right?"

"Correct - under the best of circumstances. However, as Nixon showed, this power can also be abused."

"Abused by directing this NSC outfit to perform functions that are not necessarily in the country's national interest, but rather in the President's political interest?"

"Exactly. Many a President gets infused with power and starts to believe the country's best interests are whatever he or she thinks them to be. The corollary to that is when the President thinks: I am so important that whatever keeps me as President is in the best interests of the country and therefore a matter of national security."

"A slippery slope from there to dictatorship."

"Yes. Especially when you attack the American restraints on such power."

"Like a free press."

"Yes. When the political party of the President is also the party that controls the House and Senate those skids get dangerously greased. It totally eviscerates the checks and balances our Founding Fathers intended to have in place when they formed our government."

"But what of the other members of the National Security Council? Surely there must be some good people to stand up to what amounts to blatant wrongdoing?"

"These are busy people - the Secretary of Defense and the Vice President for example. The Defense Secretary manages almost 3 million employees and a budget of over 700 billion dollars. There is a crisis in our military every single day. Events and meetings demand attendance. International travel. The Secretary has a lot on that plate. The Vice President travels a lot and is kept in the loop purely at the whim of the President. Many Vice Presidents chafe at this limbo situation, but end up accepting with resignation the prestigious job that has little formal responsibility, excellent perks and an unspoken possibility for advancement."

"You're telling me this because …"

"Something subversive is happening here in an attempt to promote some political agenda. Seeing that fellow from the Photographic Society - essentially the operational section of the National Security Council special intelligence group - in Patagonia is too much of a coincidence. Plus, I don't want you to get hurt."

Chapter 40

I couldn't let it go. I had to go back to Dylan's staging area and see what I could make of things on my own. Nance knew things I was not privy to. He had his own agenda. I just wanted to be able to make some sense of what was going on around me.

I had some trouble finding the correct dirt road in the hills above Patagonia Lake, but I finally stumbled upon it. The wind was picking up as the sun heated the morning's cool air. The hotter air was rising to stir the atmosphere. It made for mesmerizingly sensual soft rolls and swells on the lake behind me as I climbed up the mountain. When I found the last turnoff, I had crested the mountain and could no longer see the familiar water behind and below me. I was more cautious this time around, so unlike Dave, I didn't drive to the crest of the hill that led to the ridge above the ravine. I parked and walked up the slabs of stratified, sedimentary rock. The spiky, desert scrub was harder to ascend than I anticipated because my right calf still couldn't push off with much power and the mudstone kept fragmenting. Plus, my leg hurt. I tried to think of it as therapy, but that didn't help. It still hurt.

I dropped to my stomach to get a good look at the small canyon. I was screened by the growth around me. This early in the day the sun was at my back, so I wasn't as worried about the glint from my binoculars giving me away. But I was still worried. I was not nearly as brave without Nance by my side and I felt like the lonely, foolish physician that I was.

Even in the morning I could feel the dry heat of summer coming. The effort of my climb produced sweat that evaporated like last night's dream. I could hear a faint rumble in the ravine. At first, I thought it might be the echo of a distant helicopter but then I focused the field glasses on the back of the Quonset hut and saw a portable generator parked there. It was covered by netted camouflage. Part of a green tarp had fallen off from constant vibration revealing the bright orange casing. Two black rear wheels were also visible. A long thick power cord snaked into the Quonset hut. After first scan, I thought the security guards were not on duty. On my second scan I saw a glint of light reflecting from under the tree canopy near the access road. Security was definitely on the case. They were wisely on duty in the shade.

Nothing was going on that I could see and the banality of evil enterprise was boring me. I was beginning to think my physical therapy excursion was a waste of time when I heard an engine just before I saw Dylan's Hummer come around the corner of the opposite canyon wall to the flat. This brought two security guards out of the trees and three people came out of the hut. Everyone was casually dressed and that surprised me. I had subconsciously expected

243

people in uniforms. There were no I.C.E. jackets. No Border Patrol shirts. No military uniforms. I guess I expected a garrison. The security guards kept their distance from the Hummer. Dylan conferred with the others. Through the glasses I could see they were all male. Then the four of them went into the hut. I waited.

Time slowed down, like watching the clock and waiting for the bell to ring at the end of a school day. After ten minutes, there was finally movement. All four men came out of the hut carrying different-sized boxes. They loaded the boxes into Dylan's H2. I turned my binoculars on the open door of the hut and could barely discern what looked like a tool and die machine inside. I couldn't make out any other details. The four men talked briefly and then Dylan got into the Hummer and drove off. I couldn't think of anything more productive to do so I shimmied away from the rim's edge and scrambled back down to my car. I didn't want to run into Dylan on the road so I took what I thought to be a circuitous route back home. It wasn't until I was on the Pena Blanca Lake access road that I noticed my heart was still racing and I was lost.

I reversed my course and eventually saw a sign for Rio Rico. I-19 south led me to Route 82 and I was back on track. When I finally got back to my cabin I turned on the coffee machine. As I looked at the pod selection and made my executive decision of a Lungo and Espresso combination, a wave of uneasiness passed over me. Something did not feel right. Others might call this intuition, but I knew it was a combination of unconscious clues not quite coalesced. I put the Fortissimo pod down and looked around the cabin. In the bathroom, Mary's hairbrush was missing. I pulled back the shower curtain. Her shampoo and conditioner were not there. I went to the bedroom. A lingering familiar scent was barely perceptible. I opened the master closet. Mary's spare clothes were missing. I went back to the bathroom and looked behind the door. Her floor length fleece bathrobe was not hanging on the hook. Finally, I returned to the front room. I examined the couch. The small stuffed tiger from Sabino Canyon was gone. I had to get some air. I couldn't stay in the cabin. The walls felt like they were closing in on me.

I remember the numbness. The agonal pain that led to dry heaves, tears and hopelessness would come later. I remember my mind shutting out the terrible overriding thought that my best days of happiness were behind me. Somewhere I hoped I would survive and pull myself back up. After all, I had left lovers too, but that gave me no solace for I didn't believe in true justice in matters of the heart. And I was not young anymore.

*   *   *

I hadn't heard from Nance or Mackenzie so I decided to go to Dylan's office. I remembered him telling me he was working out of a red adobe two-story building close to the Patagonia Market on Third Avenue. I didn't have any trouble finding it. There aren't too many two-story buildings in Patagonia. By big city standards, this was more of a converted large family house than an office building. There was a small directory at the entrance and "Security Consultants of America" on the second floor stood out next to "The Hummingbird Preservation Society" and the "Patagonia Arbor Day Council." I went up the stairs and down the second-floor corridor, found the office and opened the frosted door. An efficient-looking woman was working on a computer screen in the small anteroom and looked up as I approached.

"Can I help you?" she said.

"I'm looking for Mr. Kermer."

"He's not in the office right now."

"Do you know when he'll be back?"

"Let me see." She turned back to the screen and made a few entries on the keypad. "He's out all day surveying. Can I leave a message?"

"No, thank you," I said, realizing the futility of this fool's errand. I turned and left. Back in the stairwell, I caught my breath and leaned against the cool wall. I felt hollowed out. I realized I hadn't had anything to eat. But that wasn't it.

Chapter 41

When I went to the clinic the next day, I didn't see Mary as I walked in. Becky, our medical assistant, was at the front window checking in patients. Becky was also our de facto office manager and today Rachel was taking a vacation day for some event with her boyfriend so Becky was serving as our receptionist. She already looked frazzled. I said good morning to her as I headed to my tiny office.

"Morning Doc," Becky called to me over her shoulder. "Mary called in to say she forgot she had a doctor's appointment in Tucson this morning and won't be coming in." The patient back up began almost immediately, but then tipped over the edge of reasonableness when I went in to see Mr. Rodriguez.

Mr. Rodriguez' blood pressure was through the roof. When I asked him why, he covered his eyes with his hands and began to moan softly without any loss of dignity. He said yesterday he had been in Federal Court. His niece Mariela had left Guadalajara the week before with her two young boys and managed to get the three of them to Nogales, Sonora. Mariela had been beaten several times by her husband over the last six months and his alcohol abuse was

247

making the domestic violence worse. At first, Mariela had told her uncle her husband was just depressed because there had been no rain and the crops were dying. Her husband ranted and raved about climate change destroying his livelihood. Mariela knew he felt powerless and was lashing out at life. But when he started beating her little boys, she knew she had to escape. Her uncle was her only family. Mariela was caught crossing the border into the United States at El Sasabe and arrested with her children. Tears were quietly streaming down my patient's face. I excused myself to get Mr. Rodriquez some tissues. I didn't know where El Sasabe was and asked Becky. She told me it was west of Nogales and east of Lukeville.

"I was the one who told her to cross there," Rodriguez keened, when I returned. "The Altar Valley is supposed to be safer than Lukeville or Nogales. I was going to meet her at Sasabe on this side but there was a new sky tower on the outskirts of Sasabe that I'd never seen before." I cringed at Mr. Rodriguez' confession of meeting his niece, thinking of the I.C.E. raid not too long ago and that they might have put listening devices in my office. I didn't know anything about the area around Sasabe. Becky had heard the sobbing from outside the examining room. She knocked on the door and entered, asking if I needed anything. I motioned for her to stay. After several deep breathes, he continued emotionally in Spanish.

"Bajo la operación fue arestada rapidamente para enjuiciamiento," he said. I looked blankly at Becky and she translated.

"He says because of Operation Streamline his niece was fast tracked for prosecution," she related. Rodriguez went on to say that yesterday he had been at the courthouse and had heard his niece ask the Judge when she could see her children again and the Judge could not answer. Rodriguez had asked a public defender in the hallway where his nephews might be. The lawyer had said once the children are separated from the parent the United States deems them unaccompanied minors.

"Unfortunately, the government doesn't yet have a tracking system in place for the children, so they could be anywhere," the attorney said. "You might try the Office of Refugee Resettlement. They might be able to help you."

"What am I to do?" Mr. Rodriguez wailed to me in English. "My niece thought they might all die if she stayed in Guadalajara, but she didn't know she would be separated from her baby boys. What choice did she have?" I put my arm around him. I felt powerless too. All I could do for him was listen, give him a hug and increase his blood pressure medication.

Chapter 42

I went home straight from work that evening in the gloaming hour. I was exhausted. Stressful days often left me feeling depleted. At work, I felt a transference of my energy to my patients as I absorbed their challenges. The electronic medical records at the end of the day sapped whatever vitality remained. I would often sit in my desk chair and stare out my small office window at the people walking up and down McKeown and Naugle Avenue. Sometimes a couple would stop and share a bench in the town park between the two main streets. Relaxing from their day, the couple would appear to share the small events that occurred earlier to each other and when totaled, make up a life. To a couple in love, those events never seem real until shared with their partner. On the drive home, I felt acutely the absence of such intimacy. I pulled up to the cabin and saw someone sitting on my porch. It was Dylan and he stood at my approach.

"Dylan," I acknowledged. "What are you doing here?"

"Hi Harper. I heard you were at the office yesterday looking for me," he said. "I thought I'd check and see what you needed."

I passed him on the porch as I unlocked and opened the front door. "I don't need anything," I said entering. I half-turned back to him. "I suppose you might as well come in." I threw my backpack on one end of the couch and motioned for Dylan to sit on the other end. I slumped into the easy chair across from him.

"Why did you come by the office?" Dylan asked. As with many of our conversations, he looked uncomfortable and very dutiful. Which made me uncomfortable and irritable.

"I was out and about in the general area and saw you playing with fire," I said. "How's that going?" Dylan didn't answer. At first, he tried to look confused. Then pained. Finally, it was as if I had caught him with his hand in the cookie jar. He started scrutinizing the stonework on the fireplace. "And speaking of playing with fire, how's Mary?" This perked him right up.

"She's great," he said with some enthusiasm. "Really great."

"I hope you're not dragging her into whatever lame-brained scheme you have up your sleeve."

"I think you should mind your own business about my 'schemes.' Better for you to stick to medicine."

"Why should I do that?" I asked with a little frustration and some sharpness. "It's my country too."

"Because you don't have the grit for it," he said evenly. This was as honest as he had ever been.

"So, it takes grit to support these callous policies of our Government? I think not.

"Taking a firm stance on an issue is not callous or cowardly. It's called leadership."

"It comes off as meanness."

"You touchy-feely types always think hard policy decisions are mean."

"Maybe someday your car will be stopped by a cop because you're white, Dylan. That scares the daylights out of you. This country is going to be a majority of minorities and you can't stop it. You should embrace it. That's the future. Make it the best it can be."

"You don't understand. I told you before: this is a war," Dylan retorted. "Congress may not have declared it, but their financial and military support is consent enough. They have given us free reign. The people want this. I have all the information, Harper."

"Yes, but you misinterpret your information. If you saw two dogs doing it you'd suggest they switch to the missionary position and make a baby instead of a puppy."

"The wall will make this country safe again, Harper. You should be able to see that."

"You can't wall off America and expect it to grow and prosper. America is not China, trying to keep out the barbarians in 220 BC. The world has evolved."

Dylan stood up. "You mean well, Harper. Please stay out of this. For your own sake. You're out of your league. Turn on your cassette tape player, put on some folk songs and chill. This is the future where I'm going. Your dreamy days have passed you by. With your lectures, you're starting to sound like my father."

"Your father?"

"Yeah. With him it was always one way: his way or the highway."

"That must have been difficult."

"It was. Because, unlike you, he was right all the time.

"No one is right all the time. Even fathers." I stood up as well. "Don't do this Dylan. For Mary's sake. You can't trust the people you're aligned with. They aren't going to make the world a better place. Just better for them and only for a very short time. Feeling something strongly doesn't make it right. You are on the wrong side of history here."

Dylan walked to the door. "I really do like you Harper. You're a good friend," he said looking back as he opened the screen. "But this is my path."

"Then change your path!" I said, as he walked away, "there's still time." I shouted after him, "Hitch your wagon to a brighter star!" But he was gone. I heard the jeep start up. He must have hidden it in the bushes.

Chapter 43

A couple of days went by. I still had not heard back from Tucson regarding my extension request. I was being ghosted by Nance and Mackenzie. The tower was being built. Fractious elements were still in debate. Congress was balking over payment for a wall. Families were still being separated. The Courts were overextended. Ranchers continued to ranch. I was in conflict regarding whether or not to extend the lease on my cabin. Life went on, such as it was. I was about to start my afternoon clinic when two Border Patrol agents burst into my office. This time they were looking for me.

"One of the tower construction workers fell off the upper scaffolding. He can't feel his legs and no one knows whether to move him or whether they'll make him worse by helping. His moaning is awful. The helicopter from University Hospital is not available. It's transferring a sick baby to Phoenix and a haboob on I-10 has everyone else grounded. We called for an ambulance but there's an accident on Route 82 and the road is closed. Their ETA is about two to three hours out. Can you come with us and check him out?" the agent in charged asked.

"How far did he fall?" I asked, grabbing my medical bag. Becky nodded. She knew what to do and would tell the patients. Mary was still at lunch with Rachel.

"About 25 feet," the agent said.

I hopped in their souped-up white SUV with the yellow and black insignia of the map of the contiguous United States on the side. With sirens blaring we sped to the construction site. The agent who was driving told me there was a unit of the National Guard at the site. They were placing concertina wire on top of the perimeter fence surrounding the tower as a training exercise for when Congress allocated funding of an enhanced border wall. We pulled up to a large gate that had been rolled open on its casters. We were emphatically waved through by a National Guardsman.

I found the injured worker at the foot of the tower scaffolding. He was surrounded by a circle of National Guard soldiers in full gear. The soldiers parted as we approached. The worker was in agony. His eyes were squeezed shut but he was breathing and conscious.

I kneeled down and gently touched his shoulder. "I'm Dr. Harper. What's your name?"

He opened his eyes. "Joe," he grunted.

"We're going to get you better, Joe. Where does it hurt?"

"My back and my legs."

"Does your neck hurt?"

"Yeah." He started to move it and show me.

"Don't move it yet, Joe! Wait until I examine you. Stay still unless I ask you to do something."

The pain appeared to be localized to his lower back and ankles. He was conscious and said his name was Joe. He knew where he was and what had happened. His neck was sore, but he had no bone tenderness which usually rules out a fractured neck. He probably stretched some cervical muscle and ligaments muscles when his head whiplashed in the fall. He could move his arms freely. His right wrist was swollen tender when I pressed on it.

"Ow!" he said.

"Your wrist looks broken, Joe." The wrist looked like a dinner fork from the side.

He still had his heavy boots on which cast doubt on the briefing I had received in the car on the way over. They said he couldn't move his toes. Through his boots, the foot and ankles on both sides were very painful when I felt them. I suspected that the landing from the fall fractured both of his heel bones and compressed one of his lumbar vertebra until it resembled more an accordion than a building block.

"I'm going to try and release some of the pressure down here, Joe. Bear with me." I used the big bandage scissors from my bag to cut his boot laces and the top leather down the middle.

"Oh Doc, that feels so much better!" Joe said, the relief evident in his voice. He went to move his feet and yelped with pain as his hand grabbed his lower back.

"Hold still, Joe. We need to get you on a stretcher."

I left the boots on as a splint for his feet and ankles and then filleted his white socks so I could feel the pulse over the top of his feet. The pulse was strong on both sides and all his toes were pink. When I asked him to move them, they wiggled. He was reluctant, but he moved his legs for me until his back pain stopped him. He hadn't soiled himself, but lying in the dirt was obviously not comfortable.

The construction crew had an excellent medical aid pack. I held Joe's head and neck in a secure neutral position. "Okay, Joe. We're going to slip the back of a neck brace under you." I nodded at one of the soldiers and he placed half of the cervical collar under Joe's neck.

"I'm going to keep holding your neck, Joe and now we're going to put the top half on." The soldier connected the two pieces and we velcroed the two halves together.

"Your cervical spine is now secure, Joe. Now we're going to get you out of the dirt and on to a stretcher. You ready?"

"Yeah."

With three soldiers on one side charged with lifting the chest, pelvis and legs, and a fourth soldier at the feet, I controlled the head and neck as we log rolled Joe onto his left side. We then slipped the spinal board under him and gently moved him back. We made lateral supports for his head and neck with rolled blankets and I taped them in place, first with a wash cloth over his forehead and then along the sides of his torso to keep him from being jostled.

"Doc, can I have something for the pain?" Joe pleaded.

"You sure can," I said. "I just need to put an IV in and I'll get you some pain medicine. Please tell me if you get nauseated." I still kept a vial of morphine in my bag. I had been tempted to take it out as the opioid epidemic grew into a frenzy, but now I was happy I had procrastinated.

"The ambulance will be here soon, Joe. Right now, we're going to put some ice packs around those ankles. That will help." I nodded to one of the soldiers and he started placing the ice packs on the side of the boots. Then with six soldiers to help, we lifted Joe and the spinal board out of the dirt and carried him to the shade of a large cottonwood tree at the edge of the clearing. The first aid kit contained a liter bag of Ringer's Lactate and IV tubing. I put the IV in the arm without the wrist fracture and hung the bag on a low hanging branch. I grabbed a syringe and needle, drew morphine sulfate from the vial and gave Joe one cc to see how he'd handle the medicine. After a minute with no discernible reaction, I gave him two more. Ten seconds the strain in his face visibly eased.

"Thanks, Doc," Joe said, the relief evident. His eyes darted right and left. "Thanks guys," he said to the soldiers. The men gently patted Joe's right arm and murmured good wishes.

"Hang in there, man," one said with a thumbs up. Slowly they drifted back to their comrades. Their commander had assembled the unit at the one side of the tower and they gathered next to the large coils of razor barbed wire. Some of the guardsman walked around looking for their heavy gloves and wire cutters to resume their task.

I sat down next to Joe on the grass to wait for the ambulance. He was much more comfortable out of the sun, splinted and with some pain medicine on board. Some of his fear and anxiety drained away as we talked about some of the possible treatments for his injuries and the rehabilitation required.

Joe closed his eyes and tried to rest. I gazed out at the expanse. The sky was turning to a dark purple over the mountains. Up high, it looked like more rain or perhaps some late season snow was on the way. The majority of the soldiers had finished gathering their gear to resume maneuvers, while a handful were relaxed on the ground throwing dice from a paper cup. The men were laughing quietly and one gave a playful, frustrated shove to the last man to throw down who apparently had eked out a victory.

I smiled at the luck of the throw and then the diorama disappeared as the clearing exploded. Dirt showered over me and I reflexively covered Joe's face. I felt the concussive shock wave and a split second later, a wall of heat sluiced through and past us. Abruptly the blast wind reversed course and swooshed back over us, seeking the vacuum of air at the tower vacated by the detonation. Then all was silent. I could see leaves, twigs and dirt settling to the ground but I couldn't hear them. From a far distance, I could hear wails and screams. Then those screams became louder and closer as my hearing returned. Everyone had been hit by dirt and debris. In the clearing by the tower the air had been shredded by metal fragments traveling faster than the eye could register. I stood up and looked at Joe. He was unscathed but his eyes were wide with fear.

"I'll be right back," I said. Joe looked beseechingly at me. "I'll be right back," I repeated and turned to the tower.

The structure was still there but one side was kinked, blackened and melted in an unnatural posture. The scaffolding had collapsed and the National Guard soldiers were scattered. I made staggered steps towards the center of the clearing and slowly my muscles started following commands. One soldier was motionless on his back. Almost peaceful in repose, blood and clear liquid was leaking from his nose and ears, his neck pierced multiple times. Another Guardsman was thrown hard on his face and lay with his arms and legs at grotesque angles. A reservist was walking in circles, his hands clasped over his ears. A servicewoman was on her side, all her clothes torn from one side of her body exposing her burnt skin melded with uniform fragments. Another soldier was holding his stomach and moaning loudly as he tried to push his intestines back into his abdomen. One uniformed man was on the ground vainly attempting to pull a tree limb out of his thigh. I counted five dead. Some of the injured must have sheltered their comrades. Their uninjured mates were now swarming around the fallen colleagues. My hearing was coming back for I could hear a siren in the distance. Joe's ambulance, I thought. Then Joe's voice came through to me.

"Doc! Don't leave me! What's going on?" I realized his head and neck were taped. He was forced to stare up at the Cottonwood tree and didn't know what had happened. All he could see was the tree. All he could hear were the shrieks and shouts. Joe's ambulance pulled up to the gate. I vaguely noted the windshield glass of the Border Patrol SUV we arrived in was shattered. I didn't know where to turn. I thought to quickly comfort Joe who was still only a few feet away and go tend to the wounded. I started back to Joe and then somehow Dylan was at my side.

"Harper! What are you doing here?"

I looked at Dylan, confused. "Kermer? . . . What? . . . How? . . ."

"Harper, you aren't supposed to be here!" Dylan said. He looked at the soldiers. "They weren't supposed to be here!"

I was still confused. "What are you talking about."

Dylan was muttering to himself as he looked at the carnage. Then he turned to me. Desperately he mumbled, "I sent their captain an order to cancel today's maneuver." His eyes looked into mine beseechingly. "I sent him a message!" he said, pleading with me.

Pieces started to click in place together in my mildly concussed brain. "Dylan, what have you done?" I asked.

"No one was supposed to get hurt," he said, not to me, but to the clearing. The paramedics were coming for Joe. I left Dylan there talking to the

261

carnage and rushed to the soldiers to see what I could do to help them.

The next day, press coverage was led by the President's sensational tweet: "Terrorists attack our soldiers at the Arizona Border. We need a Wall now!!!"

Chapter 44

The Clinic was closed when I got back from the tower explosion. Mary was not there. I went looking for Nance and found him at a back table in the Writer's Feast. He had company. Even from behind I could tell it was MacKenzie. Nance caught my eye when I walked in and tilted his head to the empty chair beside him.

I realized what a sight I must have presented by the way they looked at me when I sat down. "We heard about the soldiers," Nance said.

"It was awful," I said. "They were just kids."

There was a long silence. I asked Mackenzie why we hadn't heard from him after our last visit in the mountains. He looked at Nance and then answered me by saying he got tied up with other business. Then he embarked on an angry, menacing ramble about finding answers to the tower "fiasco" and serving up justice. Nance looked at me wordlessly. He knew it was Dylan.

After hurling a few more curses and invective at the bloodbath, MacKenzie excused himself to get back home. "I'll be in touch," he said in parting, more to Nance than to me. "I've got to make some calls."

"Does he know?" I asked.

"Not yet. But it won't take him long to find out. He is well-connected and I was his first stop." Nance looked at me with a hardness I had not seen in him before. "Kermer needs to be stopped."

"He says it was an accident. He meant no harm." I felt the lameness of my words as they came out.

"Tell that to the families of the dead and maimed," Nance said harshly. "The press will be all over this town. Our quiet life here will be extinguished." It dawned on me international press coverage would not be in Nance's best interest. I was silent.

After a long pause, he asked, "What do you think he'll do next?"

"Blunder some more, I suppose," I said wearily. I knew it to be true. Dylan had a knack for destruction. My relationship with Mary had only been a warm-up. He stood ready to lash out at people he didn't know and those he would never want to know. Casualties of his ignorant war. After this last campaign, who and what would he devastate next? Until he finally looked around and there was only one person left.

Nance came to a decision. "Ask him to dinner with us at the Wild Horse for tomorrow night. I think we can probably talk some sense into him."

"What will we say that's any different?" I asked. "I've been talking to him for weeks and it's been water off a duck's back." Where was Nance going with this? Were we any better than Dylan or was it only that we thought we were? Dylan had his beliefs. Who was

PAWNS OF THE WALL

to say what was true. Who was to say what methods were fair?

"We'll think of something," Nance said with finality, pushing his chair back. "Someone has to take a stand. I have to run up to Phoenix in the morning on some business, but I'll be back in the afternoon." Nance stood. "Let me know tonight if he can make it. You look awful, by the way. Go home, take a long, hot shower and make yourself a drink. Get some rest," he said in parting. "And call me later."

I left wondering why Nance suggested the Wild Horse. Such a public forum for what might be a heated discussion. It seemed odd. Nance had many connections in the area and surely, we could meet Dylan in any number of more private places. A more intimate setting seemed appropriate for such a delicate discussion. I wondered whether he assumed that MacKenzie would be at the dinner too. That wasn't clear to me. Dylan knew Mackenzie from his barn storage deal. How would Dylan feel if MacKenzie showed up? There was so much about this town I still didn't understand.

Chapter 45

I couldn't reach Dylan that night. He called back the next morning and agreed to meet for dinner. We settled on 6:30 PM at the Wild Horse. I called and left a message for Nance telling him the dinner was on. I told him when and where we were to meet. Mary was not at work again. Becky said she had a doctor's appointment.

"Another one?" I asked. Becky shrugged. "Female problems," she said.

* * *

I did have a doctor's appointment in Tucson. But before I left for the appointment, I met Dylan for breakfast. I asked him about the Tower explosion.

"Horrible," he kept repeating. "Horrible. I got there as soon as I could."

I had never seen him look shaken or uncertain before. Then he made some comment about my shoes.

* * *

At 4:00 PM, my clinic cleared out fast. At 4:30 PM, there was a knock on my back door. Another patient forgot their phone, I thought as I walked to the door. I opened the door, but it wasn't a forgetful patient. It was Dylan. He had a bottle of single malt scotch in his hand and two plastic cups. We went back to my office.

"Something came up and I can't make dinner," Dylan said. "But I was happy to receive your invite, so I thought I'd come by. I was thinking you were upset with me."

"I am."

"But the soldiers were an accident," he said off-handedly. He had already forgiven himself. "Besides, the President was pleased. It looks like it won't be a problem."

"The President has probably forgotten all about it by now," I said.

The words wounded Dylan. For a killer, he wounded so easily. "Don't be like that, Harper," he scolded me. I felt anger building up within me and tried to suppress it.

"Don't you see I'm doing this for you?" he added.

"For me?" I said incredulously. "I don't want any part of your glory or your guilt. You can't refashion this using me as a pawn in your chess game. I don't want any part of it."

"I don't mean just you. But rather you and all the citizens in this country. Not everyone is privileged enough to be in a position to act. Yesterday was terrible, Harper," he went on. "But already a lot of good for our goal has been realized." He spoke as if at a pep rally. Then his mind when on to the next event. "Since I can't make it to dinner, I wonder if I could stop by your place later tonight? Mary is going to join us." There was a disconnect here that I didn't comprehend. But he often jumped around in conversations. I wondered if it was something I'd ever be able to bridge. "Oh, and my bosses are setting up a fund to take care of the soldiers' families. It's all coming together." He was ignorantly blithe to the pain he was causing others. He was almost giddy as he spoke and it made me forget to ask why were we meeting with Mary later. I thought of Nance and how I'd have to tell him Dylan was cancelling. The thought made me uneasy. Nance would be annoyed. Then Dylan added, "Besides the cause is greater than any one life."

"Not if it's my life. Or Mary's. Or I dare say, even yours."

Dylan actually chuckled. "Sometimes even more so, if it is your own life." He was high on his success. Getting in the last word came effortlessly for him.

His conceit worried me. "What are you doing that you can't make our dinner tonight?" I asked.

Dylan shrugged. "Work. Some meeting was called. I told you: we're in a war and these things come up," he said breezily. "Although, I must say, I'm getting to hate meetings. Nothing gets accomplished and it's usually a great waste of time." He was almost garrulous. As he rambled on I tried to identify the anxiousness that had come over me.

"What if Mary had been hit by that blast?" I asked suddenly.

"Please, Harper," he said disapprovingly. "Those were soldiers. Not civilians." My alarm and my disquiet vanished as my anger flashed. Before I could respond Dylan stood up looking at his watch. "I've got to be running. Can't be late. Good to have this drink with you, Harper. Hold on to the scotch for me, will you? I'll get it from you this evening. About 10 o'clock?"

I was worn out. I remained in my chair. The effort to stand would be exhausting and I did not want to afford Dylan that decency. "10 o'clock then," I replied, not looking up.

*   *   *

While Harper was seeing patients, Mary was visiting her doctor in Tucson and Dylan was putting out political fires, Dave Nance made the drive to north to Phoenix. As he passed the airport he turned east and pulled into a strip mall. In his rear-view mirror, he saw the deputy sheriff's SUV pull into the parking area and stop. The car was following so close behind him Nance could make out Sturgill's features. Nance parked about 100 yards down from a donut shop and stuffed a baseball cap and a thin windbreaker into the front of his shirt. Then he walked over to the donut shop. In the window of the donut shop he could see Sturgill get out of his vehicle and saunter in Nance's general direction.

"Two glazed in a small bag," Nance said, when it was his turn at the counter. He paid and backing up, bumped into the man behind him roughly.

"Watch where you're going," Nance said heatedly.

The man pushed Nance hard. He went with the push and it took him to the wall, out of sight from the plaza. "What do you think you're doing?" the stranger said.

"Sorry," Nance muttered. "My fault. I need to use the bathroom." The man stranger seething and rubbing his foot, but Nance quickly retreated to the back of the store. He went right past the restroom and out the back door where he threw on his hat and windbreaker. Circling back to his truck, he backed out and drove east. When he was sure Sturgill was still checking out the donut shop, he headed north on the 101.

Just south of Scottsdale he pulled into the parking lot of Viscorelli's, a small family-owned Italian restaurant popular in the neighborhood. It was lunchtime, but there were spots open at the bar and Nance took a seat and ordered iced tea. He didn't want to be disappointed by another establishment's coffee. Soon, the stool next to Nance was taken by a thick man with a Slavic appearance. He wore an expensive suit, but no tie. His white shirt was open at the neck to the third button. He set his folded copy of the morning edition of The Arizona Republic on the bar counter between himself and Nance. He made eye contact with Nance through the mirror behind the bar.

"Are you prepared?" he muttered quietly.

"Yes," Nance replied. He figured the man was from the Ukraine.

"What you need is right there." He almost imperceptibly tilted his head to the Phoenix paper. "It *must* be done this way or our pardon is rescinded," he added intensely.

"I understand," Nance said. "How will I know the pardon has been granted?"

"You will be alive." The stranger stood up and threw down a ten-dollar bill. "For your drink and your troubles." Then he left. The bartender hurried over.

"I was just going to ask him what he wanted to drink," the barkeep said, somewhat agitated. "I got tied up with that couple down there," he pointed to the other end of the bar.

Nance shrugged his shoulders, grabbed the newspaper and stood up as well. "I think he just received a call." Nodding to the ten-dollar bill, "Keep the change." Nance walked briskly to his truck, careful to not let the contents in the fold of the newspaper slip out. Safely in the cab of the Ram, he opened the paper. He involuntarily blanched at the syringe in his hands. Ten milligrams of this colorless, odorless liquid would kill a human being in minutes. So quickly there was no viable antidote. This was a twenty-milligram syringe, and it was full. The syringe was for his protection, he knew, because VX nerve toxin was quickly absorbed by contact with the skin or lungs. 100 times more powerful than Sarin, this chemical weapon was classified by the rest of the world as a weapon of mass destruction. Nance shuddered. He couldn't take his eyes off the syringe and knew this act would haunt him for the rest of his life. For years he'd had contingency plans to disappear from Patagonia at a moment's notice. Was it really worth it to be alive with memories that ate at your soul? He put the syringe back in the fold of the newspaper and then put the folded paper in the glove compartment. He pushed the keyless go of his ignition and the automobile roared to life. He now had to find MacKenzie.

Chapter 46

I couldn't concentrate on the work piled on my desk. I called Nance to tell him Kermer had cancelled dinner, but only got his voice mail. I left a message that I was still going to go to the Wild Horse for something to eat and hoped he would join me. Listlessly I walked down McKeown but didn't feel like the bustle of the Wild Horse. I turned north on Fourth Avenue and crossed Naugle to land in the Wagon Wheel again. It was dark inside and mercifully quiet as I took a seat at the window. The waitress brought me a beer and then left me alone. From my perch, I could gaze out at the fading daylight, wondering what Nance would have to say at the Wild Horse. If Nance was late to dinner, should I stay and wait awhile? I didn't feel like eating by myself. Why wouldn't Nance come? Just because Dylan couldn't make it? How come I couldn't reach Nance? Was he stuck in Phoenix? Was he with Mackenzie? What was Dylan really doing? I vaguely wondered if the god that Dylan believed in was looking out for him. A physician mentor had long ago told me: "Once a surgeon makes a mistake, you can attempt to minimize the damage done, but there is often no way to alter the avalanche of events that flow from that act." I took a long draught from my beer. All actions have consequences.

It was twilight as I walked down Naugle. My feet carried me to the Wild Horse. I went into the saloon. The place spelled of onions, French fries and grilled meat. The bartender looked blankly at me when I asked if he had seen Nance. Then he shook his head from side to side and went back to buffing the counter. I went into the restaurant and asked the young hostess for a table as far away from the bar as possible. The waitress approached me. It was Trish. Thank goodness for a friendly face.

"Will anyone be joining you, Doctor?", she said pleasantly, handing me a menu. She was teasing me with her formality.

"One person for sure," I said. Trish raised her eyebrows and canted her head. "No, it's not Mary." Trish did not hide her chagrin. "But could you leave the one extra setting please?" I thought perhaps Mackenzie might come too. I ordered another beer.

"Would you like some water?" she asked. I elected for tap water. "No ice, please."

"I knew that" Trish said, smiling and replaced the dinner setting she had reflexively removed. "Coming right up."

Where was everyone, I asked myself? To buy time, I ordered a salad as an appetizer - almost unheard of at the Wild Horse. I decided to give Nance a chance to join me if he had received my message late. I picked at the salad and sipped at the lager. The feeling of unease crept back. I thought of going by Dylan's office again. Did I really want to? I convinced myself it would be locked up for the night and if he really was in a meeting he wouldn't appreciate the interruption. I ordered some food and looked at my watch. It was half past seven.

"Can I join you?"

I looked up to see Phil Trevino of the Arizona Daily Star. He registered my hesitation, then I nodded at the empty place setting. "Sure. Have a seat."

"Thanks. It looks like you're expecting company, so I'll just have a quick beer." He motioned to Trish.

"Did the paper send you down from Tucson because of the tower accident?"

"Not exactly. I was in Puerto Rico doing a follow-up piece on the aftermath of Hurricane Maria. It's hard to believe it's been a year already. A lot of people in Tucson and Phoenix have relatives in Puerto Rico," Trevino said, accepting the beer from a different waitress. "I finished that story and was told to come straight here. I arrived about an hour ago."

He looked at me with questioning eyes, but I didn't bite. He could find out all the recent details from his sources, not the local doctor. "How is Puerto Rico faring?" I asked as he took a gulp of his beer. Trevino made a face as if the beer was spoiled.

"It's a mess down there. 3,000 people dead. Many still without power or clean water. No roofs on homes. It's horrible."

"What are they telling you about the incident yesterday?" I asked casually.

"Everyone is still trying to rule out an act of terrorism, but that is beginning to look less and less likely now. They're saying it could have been

an accident. So far, we know a worker fell off
scaffolding at the new tower just before the explosion.
Speculation is the tower construction struck a subsoil
pocket of methane gas. There's a press conference
tomorrow. Word is there will be an investigation into
why a ground gas pre-construction assessment wasn't
performed." Trevino fished for his something in his
shoulder bag and pulled out a notepad. I tried to hide
my astonishment over his account of the detonation.
Trevino stuffed the papers he had disrupted back in
the satchel.

Organization completed, Trevino continued
and I had composed myself. "Personally, I think
they rushed that tower through without doing all
the construction due diligence," he said, closing the
pouch. Trevino looked up after getting his notebook
poised and ready. "This wouldn't be the first time the
government has cut corners," he added. "I've seen
it before. I understand you were on site when the
methane pocket blew?"

I raised my hands, palms up to him. "I was only
the doctor called to care for the worker who fell. I
don't know anything more than that." My face was
flushed, but I couldn't help it.

"You hadn't heard about the methane?"
Trevino asked with surprise, noting my expression of
bewilderment.

"Or the press conference," I said. "I worked in
the Indian Clinic all day. It was very busy. No chance
to check on the news."

"What did you see when you were at the site?"

"An injured worker and then a big explosion."

"Like a methane gas explosion? Did you smell gas?"

"It was a large trauma scene. I was with Joe - the construction worker - under a tree waiting for his ambulance when the explosion occurred. Then I pitched in to help the injured until the first responders arrived," I replied, evading the methane gas question.

Trevino's phone rang. He excused himself and took the call a few yards away. I used the distraction to try and think. He returned, but thankfully didn't sit down.

"That was my editor. I'm sorry but I have to go. There's a teleconference call I have to be on." He started to fish in his pocket for some money, but I waved him off.

"I've got your beer."

"Thanks. Can we finish this later? I'll get the next round."

"Sure," I said. Like hell, I thought. He shook my hand and left.

When Trish set my food down in front of me, I knew no one else was coming. I called Nance but his phone went right to voicemail. I didn't leave a message. I suddenly felt the potential menace of Nance and Mackenzie. I became aware of music playing in the restaurant. It seemed unusually loud. Then I thought of Mary for the first time in hours. Where was she? What did she know of her new beau? Could she sense the danger? Was that what attracted her to him? The questions were confusing me.

My muddled brain now wanted to talk to Dylan again; to warn him. I called his cellphone. Right to voice mail. I left a terse message. I wanted to give him the chance the soldiers did not have. He didn't deserve it, but no one in this world deserves anything that happens to them, good or bad. I pushed away the untouched food and left enough cash to cover the meal and a generous tip. Trish would be sore, but I didn't feel like waiting to pay or small talk. Everything I knew and loved seem so tenuous, life felt like one big ambush about to happen. I walked outside and looked at the mountains looming over the little town. It all looked so peaceful and pastoral. So idyllic that nothing could ever go wrong here. I remember thinking how tranquil it looked when I arrived that first day. But New England looks tranquil. Some Revolutionary War soldier probably thought it looked beautiful and peaceful the night before a battle where men were slaughtered.

I realized I really didn't know Dylan. I could judge him, but I knew nothing of what formed him as a child; what lurked below the surface perhaps even he didn't recognize or understand. Heck, I didn't even know myself and I had been privy to the party from the beginning.

I turned and started walking back to my car. I decided I would drive around town for a while and look for Dylan. I wouldn't spend all night searching though. I didn't want Mary to arrive at an empty cabin.

Chapter 47

When I reached my parked Wrangler, a stranger came out from under the shadow of a tree. He headed me off as I approached the driver's door.

"Excuse me," I said. "Do I know you?"

"My name is Becker. I know Kermer's father. Could we talk a minute?"

I wanted to look for Dylan and knew I had to get back to the cabin. "He never talked about his father," I said, stalling the decision.

"He wouldn't talk about his father," Becker said, looking around the lighted area. "I'd rather not talk here in the street by your car," he said, his attention now back on me.

"I don't have much time. I have to be …"

"How about by the church up there?" Becker pointed. I followed his finger to the Seventh Day Adventist Church a half a block up 3rd. It was much less conspicuous up the hill a hundred feet. "I'll only take a minute of your time. I promise."

"Okay," I said reluctantly. He might be able to help me find Dylan. I was going to drive around aimlessly anyway. The information might be useful.

I kept my car key in my palm. We began the short walk.

"General Weathers. Ever hear of him?"

"No."

"He's Dylan's father. He was Central Command of Army Intelligence in Asia. A real hard liner. He's in the Pentagon now. He has a low profile, but he's pulling strings all over the world. You may have seen him last week on C-Span. He was testifying before the Senate Appropriations Committee."

"I missed it," I said.

"He and Dylan had a 'Great Santini' type of relationship. Dylan hated him – even changed his surname to his mother's maiden name to spite the old man. But every day he still seeks his father's approval." I didn't say anything, but I remembered what Dylan said about me and his father. "He may not have talked about his father," Becker said. "But Dylan and I used to be close. He was like a younger brother to me. Not so much now," Becker admitted.

"Do you and Dylan work together?" I asked.

"Not exactly. I know he is . . . on a project. He said to me once he was the "keystone of the arch" but I don't know if he was kidding, boasting or serious. Does he talk to you about his work?"

"He is very vague about his actual responsibilities."

"I see. Very good of him."

"Is that why you're really here? To see if Dylan told me about his clandestine life? To see if I'm a threat to the security of this country or to you and whatever farce you're all involved in?" My frustration washed over me. What were these people doing down here? Meddling in the lives of others over some ancient tribalism. "I don't know anything about what Dylan really does."

Becker was unmoved. "I was hoping you could tell me where to find Kermer. I've looked around town, but without any luck so far," he said casually.

"I have no idea where Dylan is. In fact, I'm looking for him myself."

"I thought you two were buddies?" Becker said.

"We have some history together. He has a girlfriend who might know where he is, but she's probably on her way back from Tucson right now. She has a lot of friends up there."

"Oh yes, the girl. No answer when I called her. Now I see where you're coming from. I heard about that nasty business. I can see why you're sore," Becker said.

"No, you can't. You don't have a clue. Go back and tell your people that I'm no threat. You all are safe from me. All I want is for everyone to have a chance in this world."

"We make that possible, you know," Becker said.

"Make what possible?

"Americans having a chance. We keep you safe so you can enjoy those soccer and tennis games you people from the East seem to care about so much."

"Some of you do, but I'm not sure you're one of them. Sounds like something you tell yourself to help you sleep. Please leave me alone. Drink some of your own Kool-Aid on your walk back to wherever you came from," I said, turning downhill towards my car.

Becker's hand pressed on my shoulder. He had made a decision. "There's something else I'm going to tell you. Which may help you concentrate on the search to find Dylan." His firm grasp held me in place. I hesitated. Becker forged on. "In the late 80's there were some Americans and Brits in the Ukraine working with Gorbachev on legitimate economic stimulus packages to help the Soviet Union adjust to his policies of glasnost and perestroika. However, those reforms were sabotaged and exploited by opportunists which ultimately led to Gorbachev's resignation and the fall of the Soviet Union in 1991. These same opportunists, many of them KGB, used the ensuing chaos to steal the nation's riches with new corporations and become oligarchs. They also went after the westerners who had helped Gorbachev to exact revenge. Some were caught and terminated. A few lucky ones fooled the Soviet agents by heading East instead of West and home. The U.S.S.R. was splintered and confusion reigned everywhere. The few outside advisors that escaped capture hid out in the Caucasus mountains between the Black Sea and the Caspian Sea at the base of Mt Elbrus. Eventually these Americans were able to sneak out through Turkey to Greece and make their way back to the States."

"Why are telling me all this?" I asked impatiently, looking at my watch.

"Because I want you to understand what I'm about to say. President Putin was a young KGB agent in 1991 and he personally has taken on the mission to exterminate these traitors to Mother Russia. We recently spotted one of the Americans who had escaped to Elbrus, in Phoenix. Unfortunately, we lost track him. We suspect that Russia made an overture to this man, an offer, if you will: work with us on a delicate matter as a favor to the American President and we will give you a stay of execution. We'll call off the Soviet hit on you."

"A pardon of sorts?"

"Exactly. This Russian favor is to prevent embarrassment to the U.S. President. Politicians hate embarrassment more than traitors, so Putin understood and agreed to help. Of course, Putin may also need a service from us some day."

"I still don't see where all this fits in."

"Dylan's father is worried for Dylan and his involvement in this tower fiasco. He's seen as the only link to the real backstory to Washington's involvement and therefore he's in grave danger. His father wants to save him and he asked me to help. We're following all avenues. It's a rather tricky situation. I went to tell Kermer about this today, but I couldn't find him. I'm sorry you don't know where he is. I fear he is in some trouble."

"Kermer was a baby when the Soviet Union fell why would he be in danger? Who is 'we'?"

"I can't go into that. But Dylan may be in danger from Russians asked to help cover up a recent operational failure here locally. There are favors in this business between the most unlikely of allies, enemies and countries," he said slowly, cautiously and ominously. "Not at my level, but much higher up. Money and power drive decisions for all politicians. The fear of failure, embarrassment and exposure make strange allies of desperate leaders. Favors are exchanged between leaders to protect each other from decisions or behavior gone wrong." Becker looked at me closely. He was trying to discern if I understood his meaning. Then he seemed to decide he had said enough. "I know you are in a hurry. Thank you for listening. As I mentioned: Dylan and I were close at one time. His father is constrained by his prominent profile and asked me to look into this on my personal time. I'm not here in any official capacity."

"Listen. I really don't know where Kermer is. He said he had to work. I don't know what I can do with the information you gave me," I said. "But I'll keep it in mind - and keep my mouth shut."

"I appreciate that," Becker acknowledged. I still didn't favor him, but my opinion had shifted slightly. He reached in his coat and I stiffened. He pulled out a card and gave it to me. It only had a phone number on it. "If you find Dylan, call me. You'll be able to reach me through this exchange. Give them your number and I'll call you back." I agreed and we parted. Back in my jeep I checked my watch. I still had some time. I could drive around a bit to see if I could find Dylan. It would be just like him to have no clue powers were in play to cover up the tower explosion and he was the wild card that needed to be dealt with. I started the car and looked at Becker's phone number. Sometimes the most ominous presents come in small, simple packages.

Chapter 48

I stopped at McKeown Ave. and tried to make a plan. Looking up at the mountains, I could see the foothills had received a dusting of snow that resembled a confectioner's sugar. Where could Dylan be? I tried his cell phone but it just rang and rang. It didn't even go to voicemail. Maybe he didn't want a cell tower to ping his location. I turned right and parked in front of the Stage Stop Inn entrance. Looking up from the street I could see Dylan's corner suite was dark, but it was so close I thought I should check the room in case he had fallen asleep. I rushed in the front door of the Inn and took the immediate right that led to the stairs to get to the second-floor rooms. I flung my arm up at the proprietor behind the desk in greeting, but did not even make eye-contact in my hurry. Reaching Dylan's door, I pounded on it forcefully but received no response. I ran back downstairs to face the curious owner, huffing and puffing from my exertion.

"You're out of shape, Doc," he said with a twinkle in his eyes. "You should take some of your own advice and work out more."

"Sam," I said, catching my breath. "I think Kermer might be asleep up there. He missed a dinner appointment with me. Could I have the key to 221?"

"I can't give you the key, but I can go up there with you," Sam said, nonchalantly coming around the alcove. He lumbered up the stairs at a leisurely pace and I followed, suppressing my urge to tell him to hurry. Sam knocked on Dylan's door and when there was no answer he fumbled with his key ring, found the master and opened the door. The suite was dark and we walked in. Sam called out, "Mr. Kermer?" Nothing. Sam flicked the light switch. We looked around but Dylan was not there. I thanked Sam and left him. "Always in a hurry," I heard him mutter.

Back in the car I decided to drive to Dylan's office. In two minutes, I was outside his building. All was dark in the old renovated Victorian. The front door was locked. I called Mary's phone, but there was no answer. I drove to Mary's apartment building. She had not changed the access code to the common door and I bolted up to the door of her unit. There was no answer to my knock. I put my ear to the door but could hear no sound from within. I still had a key to Mary's apartment, but she evidently had changed the lock because it didn't work. No one was home. I was convinced of that. I heard an apartment door opening down the hall and I turned my back as if I were leaving Mary's place after locking the door. Then I hurried down the stairs.

Back in my car, I called Mary's cellphone but it went to voicemail. She was probably with Dylan, saw it was me calling and didn't want to answer. I wondered if I had time to check Dylan's staging area? Maybe he was at the Quonset Hut. But could I even find it in the dark? I decided to try but first to check the Writer's Feast before I left town. I circled back to McKeown Ave. and pulled in front of the coffee shop. It was closed and that was unusual. It never closed before 11:00PM. My watch said it was 8:30PM. I turned the car around and headed west on Naugle.

I got out on the Patagonia Highway and reached the point where the Sonoita Creek crosses under the road. Suddenly three vehicles appeared out of the darkness speeding down Salero Road on my right where it comes down the mountain to end at Route 82. They fishtailed their turns in front of me as I slammed on my brakes. I recognized the first car right away. It was Dylan's Hummer. He regained control of the H2, pulling himself out of my lane and back into the eastbound lane. His cabin was highlighted by the headlights of the vehicle chasing him and I could see Becker in the passenger seat. Dylan zoomed past me, immediately followed by Nance's 2500 Dodge Ram truck and Mackenzie's Range Rover. I made a hard U-turn and followed their dust. No sooner did I have them in my sights when Dylan made an abrupt right turn. This one onto Flux Canyon Road which headed straight up Patagonia mountain. Nance and Mackenzie were fast on his tail. I guessed Dylan planned to ditch them at the dirt logging road that would soon come up on the right. That would require a roostertail, teardrop turn. By the time Nance and Mackenzie circled back,

Dylan could disappear on the back roads and hike into his staging area. No one could track him in the dark, among the many unsurveyed back access roads and hiking paths. It was a good plan, but what Dylan didn't know is that Nance knew of his hideout and would not miss the hidden service road. We were going straight up the mountain and my headlights outlined patches of snow below the trees.

My headlight beams were bouncing up and down from the rutted road, but I could see Dylan make his acute turn without slowing down. Nance couldn't adjust in time and plowed into the Hummer's right rear panel just behind the back wheel. The Hummer spun hard to the top of a berm along the dirt access road and Dylan overcorrected as he hit the power. He kept himself from going down the side of the hill, but shot out of control up the other side of the road. He would have been fine on a highway but these backroads were serpentine and tree-lined. The Hummer lurched up the road, which made a sharp turn north to stay above the water-carved gully of the arroyo below. Dylan couldn't make the turn. His wheels were up in the air from hitting the second raised bank. Steering and braking no longer existed for him. He went straight into a ledge-side tree and the Hummer's forward progress was stopped instantaneously.

Nance's Ram pick-up and Mackenzie's Range Rover slowly pulled up to the rear of the Hummer, blocking any possibility of the vehicle backing off the tree. I stopped about fifty yards shy of the other three cars. No one paid any attention to me. If they noticed me, they thought me inconsequential. The Hummer's doors opened. Dylan and Becker cautiously exited. Nance got out of his driver's seat and moved to the front of his truck. His right hand held something but his arm was down at his side. His eyes were fixed on Dylan. Mackenzie moved around behind his Range Rover coming up on the passenger side. Across his chest he held a shotgun. Everything became very still. The still spinning front wheels of the Hummer were the only sound. Even the forest seemed on edge, watching.

"Run Dylan!! Run!!" I yelled. It just came out. Some primitive survival reflex.

Becker's arm came up quickly as he pointed a gun at Nance but Mackenzie was quicker and his shotgun blast hit Becker as he fired. Becker's bullet went harmlessly up into the canopy of trees. Dylan turned to run through the forest and Nance went after him. Without realizing it and despite my aching leg, I had caught up with Mackenzie. He turned to me and pushed me hard as he said, "Get out of here Doc or you're going to get killed!!"

My heels caught on the berm with the force of Mackenzie's shove and I tumbled backwards down the gully, making one full, graceless somersault. Sliding down the steep bank, I was pushed sideways as a fallen tree branch jammed into my right side, knocking the wind out of me. I came to rest at the verdant streamside of the arroyo. I was upside down, sideways, dazed and disoriented in the dark. I couldn't catch my breath and time stood still.

Chapter 49

Nance was running as fast as he could, chasing Dylan up the hill. He shouted as he ran.

"Dylan! Stop! I only want to help you!" Dylan kept running. He was fast, Nance thought as he began to feel the blood throbbing in his temples with every heartbeat.

"Dylan this is ridiculous. Talk to me!" Nance shouted again. Dylan looked back briefly, but this was enough for him to not see the large, exposed tree root in his path. He caught his forefoot on the root and went sprawling face first. Nance caught up with easily. Dylan rolled to his side and leaned on his elbow. He noted Nance's gun. It was not pointed at him, but hung like an afterthought at Nance's side.

"What just happened back there," Dylan said, panting softly.

"It looked like your friend was trying to kill me," Nance said, still breathing hard. "I'm lucky Mackenzie was quick."

"He said you were going to kill me."

"Who said that?"

"My friend."

"He sure acted impulsively. I've never seen that man before. Come on," Nance motioned with his free hand. "Let's go back and see if we can get your car back on the road. You're in danger and I'm here to help you."

Dylan got up slowly. Still wary, he saw the sense of getting out of the dark forest and knew Nance's truck could pull his Hummer off the berm. He passed Nance, who took a step back as Dylan drew close.

"You're the one with the gun drawn," Dylan said, as he went by. Nance made an elaborate motion to put the gun away under his belt in the small of his back. He followed Dylan back to the cars. Nance immediately noted the absence of MacKenzie's Range Rover.

As they reached Nance's Ram 2500, Dylan started to turn back to Nance as he asked, "Do you have a rope strong enough to hook onto this hitch and . . ."

Nance had the syringe out with his right thumb on the plunger. As Dylan's neck reached a 45-degree turn, Nance thrust the 14-gauge needle deep into the side of Dylan's neck. In the dark, Dylan never saw the syringe coming. Nance pushed with all his might down on the plunger and was surprised at the resistance. The VX fluid was more viscous that it appeared. Dylan managed to get his right arm out and grab Nance's jacket, but the effect of the nerve toxin was almost instantaneous. Dylan had a violent seizure and Nance felt the 'thud' of Dylan's shoulder dislocate from the violent muscle contraction. Then he heard a loud "crack" as one of Dylan's long bones snapped. Nance felt unnerved as Dylan stared at him incomprehensively and his eyes begin to bulge out of their sockets as foamy saliva poured out of Dylan's mouth and nose. The grip on Nance's coat went slack and Dylan fell to his knees, coughing and gasping agonal breaths. Nance knew Dylan's lungs were filling up with water and he was drowning in his own secretions as his diaphragm became paralyzed. Rivers of sweat suddenly poured out of Dylan as all communication with his nerves ceased. Dylan shook with one long reflex episode of projectile vomiting and then fell forward, lifeless. Only a minute had passed.

Nance looked away for a moment, took a deep breath and opened the back hatch to his truck. He spread out a thick blanket in the bed of the truck and then laboriously lifted Dylan up into the truck bed where he wrapped the body with the blanket. He closed the back hatch, shaking it vigorously to make sure it was secure. He knew right where he'd dump the body on his way out of town. He thought to himself as he walked around the truck to the driver's door: I'll shoot him when I dump the body and if they're careless, maybe they'll think it's gang-related. No use getting blood all over the truckbed.

Chapter 50

My head cleared as if a veil had slowly been lifted. I crawled sideways until I was facing uphill and the blood stopped pounding in my ears. My breathing slowly returned to normal. I felt my ribs on the right side. They were sore, but I couldn't feel any disruption in the bony contour. I managed to sit up. I had no idea how much time had elapsed. I heard the sound of an engine's ignition, but then all became ghostly still.

I made a wide half-circle as I scrambled up the hill, making as little noise as possible. I picked up a rock with my right hand. I had no idea what to expect as I poked my head up over the top of the berm.

I didn't expect to find everyone gone. The Hummer was still there, but the Ram 2500 and the Range Rover were gone. There was blood on the snow where Becker had fallen. From there I could see the path where his body had been dragged through the sparse snow and buffelgrass to where the Rover had been parked. There were deep wheel gauges and ruts where Mackenzie had peeled out of the damp dirt. I had a pretty good idea where the rancher would dispose of the body. Becker would spend eternity in an offal pit with dead farm animals.

I called out Dylan's name several times and explored the direction up the hill he had taken attempting to escape Nance. The brush was thick and my phone flashlight was of little help. I could see broken branches, but I found no blood and no body. I could feel the hopelessness of the task as it counterpointed with my own helplessness. Finally, I gave up, hoping Dylan had somehow escaped Nance and was hiding out at my cabin. I went back to my car, turned it around and drove recklessly to the cabin. It seemed so eerie this all took place six minutes from my home. When I arrived at the cabin I searched desperately, but there was no sign of Dylan. I was in the shower when I heard Mary come in. When I came out, we began our vigil in the hope that Dylan would show up. Eventually, we heard the deputy sheriff's truck coming up the gravel road.

Chapter 51

Several weeks later

I hadn't seen Sheriff Lorence since our dust-up in Dylan's apartment when Mary was picking up her clothes. After the initial flurry of investigative activity regarding Dylan's death, it had all stopped abruptly. I kept expecting the sheriff to jump out from behind a bush, but for some reason he must have been avoiding me. There was still a whisper in town of some run-in with Mary, but I didn't know more than that. I was surprised to see Lorence sitting at a table at the Mercedes Mexican bistro on Naugle Avenue, where I often stopped to get a breakfast burrito. My habit was to order takeout and then eat it at my office desk while I tried to make a dent in the messages from the day before. The Sheriff was half-way through his chili rellenos when he saw me and waved me over. They had placed two sunny-side up eggs on the rellenos which I surmised were at his personal request. I sat down and gave my order to the solitary waitress, emphasizing the "to go" part.

"I like that burrito myself," Lorence said with a mouthful of food as a way of greeting. "Especially the hash browns they throw in there. Adds a nice crunchy touch." The waitress quickly brought me my coffee. She was overstretched with the morning workload, but very efficient. I poured a dash of cream and opened a packet of Splenda into the plastic cup, stirred the brew with a spoon from the table placemat and replaced the top.

"Hear anything more about your friend?" Lorence asked as he slurped his own personal mug. I idly wondered if he travelled with that mug wherever he went or just kept it here.

"Are you still working the case?" I asked.

He frowned. Then he shrugged. "Some people want us to. Other people don't."

"Let me guess. The people who don't are more powerful than the people who do."

"The people that don't want me to look into this case crap out little sheriffs like me with their morning constitutional." He stopped chewing to look straight at me. "They want me to close the case as a drug deal gone bad. The pressure to put a lid on this comes from the highest level." Lorence shook his head in disbelief. "I'm not used to dealing with the upper echelon." He went back to his food. "Doesn't mean I'm not still curious, Harper."

"You're too savvy a cat to be killed by curiosity," I said.

"Yet," he said, taking a big bite of his food and again talking with his mouth full. It wasn't pretty to watch. "Satisfaction brought that cat back. I think you know more than you've told me, Doc."

I looked up at the television over the bar. The Kilauea Volcano had erupted. A woman from Hawaii was thanking the volcano god Pele for destroying her home. "It was an honor to be chosen by the volcano god," she said to the reporter.

"Do you really think I'd kill Dylan out of revenge for his taking Mary away from me?"

"Naw," the sheriff said, chewing unselfconsciously. "You're much more of the suffer-in-silence type."

"Yet, you still think I'm involved?" I said to the sheriff. "Wouldn't that get you in trouble with your higher ups? Stirring the pot like that?" The waitress dropped off my breakfast. I gave her a twenty and told her to keep the change. I wanted to get out of there quickly. I stood.

Lorence let the thinly veiled sarcasm go. He was not one to let a foolish doctor ruin a perfectly good chile relleno. "I like to know what's going on in my county. I don't like to be blindsided. Especially by government employees who make more money than I do. I want to talk to you again, Harper," Lorence said. His voice was flinty. This wasn't a request. He could make my life miserable in many different ways. "How about after your clinic this evening?" Taking my silence as assent, he added, "I'll leave a message at your office this afternoon once I see how my day is shaking out." He went back to his breakfast. I was dismissed.

I picked up my burrito. Lorence was intently working on the second chile relleno when I walked out. The runny egg yolk was dripping down his chin.

*   *   *

It was late in the afternoon when the Sheriff called my office and left word that he would stop by my cabin after dinner. He had requested I be alone. I knew Mary had a night with the girls planned. I heard his car come up the gravel driveway at eight. I waited for him at the door and after he had stomped his boots free of dirt I asked him if he wanted a drink.

"Do you have whiskey?" he asked. I said, in fact, I did have some Scotch.

"I'll have a Scotch then. Neat."

When I returned with his drink – a good three finger pour - he took a deep swallow. "I heard you have decided to stay on in Patagonia."

"Yes, I have." I was surprised he knew of such things and said so. "You have a better information system than Google," I added. Lorence preened with self-satisfaction.

"Part of my job," he said with false modesty. "Any particular reason you are continuing to bless us with your company?" he asked.

"I like it here. I like the people and I love the country." He looked around the cabin and I suspected he was looking for traces of Mary. I was right.

"Miss Durant around?"

"She's gone out for the evening."

"How is it for you the second time around?"

I felt annoyance creep in to my heightened awareness. Probably just what Lorence wanted. I feigned boredom to keep me from rising to the level of Lorence's rudeness.

"Excellent, thank you. I recommend it." I knew he had been married three times.

The sheriff scowled. He abruptly decided to get down to business. "Tell me again what you were doing that night Kermer was killed?" he asked.

"As I told you before, I was waiting here with Ms. Durant. Kermer was supposed to swing by for a visit. He never showed."

"What was the visit about?"

"I don't know. Kermer was the one who suggested we get together."

"And he wanted Miss Durant there for the meeting?"

"Yes. You still think I killed him because of Ms. Durant?" I thought I'd juke him with that line again, but he didn't take the bait.

"No, I told you that already. But, I wonder what you were doing before she came over."

"Speaking of Ms. Durant," I said. "What ever happened between you two?" Lorence looked as if I had struck him. His face paled and he reflexively took a long swig of his scotch. After a couple of long seconds, he gathered himself.

"I acted a little foolish," the Sheriff said with a school yard smirk.

"Why wouldn't Mary tell me about it?"

"I took it that she wanted to protect you."

"Why would she think she had to do that?"

"You tell me," Lorence said. He took a long draw from his glass, almost emptying it in one big swallow. He leaned forward. "I believe you didn't kill Kermer, but you're not telling me the whole truth. In my book, that's the same as lying. You didn't come down to this part of the country to get mixed up in this whole thing. I know that. But somehow you did. There are two things we found with Dylan that were never released to the public."

"I have no idea what you're talking about."

"I know you don't." He played with a silver and turquoise ring on his left small finger. "One of them was a dead cat. There is also this item we found in Kermer's windbreaker." He reached into the inside pocket of his leather jacket and brought out a plastic evidence bag. I couldn't see what was in the bag.

"What is it?"

"A stuffed animal. A small tiger."

I was stunned. Lorence enjoyed my startled expression. The cat I knew about. Embers' demise was meant to be a harsh warning to me. If I kept my mouth shut, nothing would happen to Mary. I had no idea the sheriff knew about it. I was beginning to see whose side he was on. Why was Dylan carrying the tiger in his pocket? "What does a stuffed animal have to do with me?" I said lamely. Lorence held up his glass and I refilled it. He knew I was hedging.

"Miss Durant says there's a history behind this little dust ball." He held up the stuffed tiger so I could see it clearly through the plastic.

"It was hers to do with as she pleased," I said. Lorence drained his glass again. I looked at the empty crystal.

"Don't worry. I'm good to drive," the Sheriff said, reading my mind. "But I'm thinking you saw Kermer earlier that evening."

"I've already been through all this with you. What about that pressure on you from way up the food chain that you told me about?"

Lorence looked at his glass and twirled it in his gnarled hand. The light refracted off the cut edges of the crystal and made little rainbows that came and went as he rotated his hand. He looked mesmerized. The prism light bounced off of the plastic encircling the small, stuffed tiger in his other hand. "They want to make sure all the loose ends are tied up," he said absently.

"Am I a loose end?"

"As loose as they come. Those higher ups are saying Kermer was a loner with a mistaken zeal to help advance the administration's policies and he fell in with the wrong crowd. They think that drug smuggling is involved in some way and they want to make sure you agree that's all there is to this."

"I've told you everything I know time and again, Sheriff. I'm happy here in Patagonia."

Abruptly, he stood. He might have swayed a little. Or it could have been me.

"Yes, you have," he said as if the rainbows in the glass had provided the answer to him. "Thanks for the drink." He put the glass on the coffee table, stuffed the evidence bag back in his jacket and gathered up his notebook before starting for the front door. As he reached the door, he turned back to face me. "That night when you had dinner at the Wild Horse alone …"

"When Kermer didn't show," I interrupted.

"Yes. What time did you finish eating again?" Lorence asked.

"About ten."

"It couldn't have been closer to nine, could it?"

"No. 10 PM."

"No one could blame you if you got the times a little wrong. An hour here, an hour there." He looked at some notes. "You called Dylan," he flipped through the notes again. "At 8:30PM."

"Yes. I told you that."

"Your voice seemed strained in the message you left."

"I was peeved. He's so careless with other people's time."

"Some might say you sounded worried. Were you worried about him?"

"I was irritated that he had blown off our dinner."

"You made one other call right after that one. To Dave Nance. No answer and you didn't leave a message. Why call Nance?"

"I thought he might know where Kermer was. I think that call was before the one to Dylan."

"Oh yes, I got the times wrong," Lorence looked at his book again with greater focus. But I could immediately tell he knew the timeline and was trying to trip me up. The ploy rankled me, but I fought the provocation down. The sheriff looked up at me again. "Why would Nance know where Kermer was?"

"Kermer hung out at Nance's coffee shop a lot." Lorence wrote something in his book.

"Word has it you talked to a reporter at the Wild Horse before you left."

"You've certainly checked up on me." I knew he would like the homage to his competence.

"Part of the job," he said reflexively. "I don't remember you mentioning that item."

"So unimportant it slipped my mind."

"Have you seen Trevino since then?"

"He's called, but I never got back to him."

"Why not?"

"Not interested in talking to him."

"You never mentioned you stopped at the Stage Stop Inn and checked for Dylan in his room."

I sighed with exasperation. "Wouldn't you do the same if your friend lived a hundred yards away and didn't show up for dinner. I'm bad with people's names at parties too. I suppose you could even make that sound suspicious."

"Old Sam says you looked worried and were in a hurry. He couldn't remember the time though. Dinnertime, he said," Lorence said, shaking his head in mild disgust.

"Sam told me I was out of shape going up the stairs. That's probably what he meant."

Lorence was like a dog with a bone. "I still don't feel like I'm getting the whole story. Some pieces don't fit and some are missing."

"Sheriff, you know as well as I do that life seldom works out like that puzzle you do with friends on a Saturday night."

"You're satisfied with how things are then?"

"I'm sad for the soldiers and I'm very sorry Dylan is dead, but there's nothing I can change now."

Lorence stood to leave. "We haven't seen Dave Nance since Sturgill lost the tail at that donut shop in Phoenix." He looked at me expectantly.

"You told me about that tail during our first interview. I remember how annoyed you were at your deputy."

"I suppose you have no idea why Dave Nance left town so abruptly?"

"No, I don't, Sheriff. I really didn't know him that well."

"The only thing he took with him was that ugly movie poster," Lorence mused more to himself than to me. "Just doesn't make any sense."

"You're right on that account, Sheriff. It was an ugly poster."

Lorence looked at me hard. Then he seemed to make a decision. "Okay. That's all we have to know. Sorry to trouble you. Good night then."

After he left, I sat alone in the dark. I went over the nuances of our conversation once again. Embers and Tiger. I felt stained in some way. It was how I always felt when I told a half truth.

*   *   *

"Did the Sheriff come to see you?" Mary asked when she got home. I poured two glasses of water and we sat down on the couch.

"Yes. He didn't stay very long."

"Did you tell him about the offal pit?"

"I did not."

"It's done then. We should be rid of it now."

"I think so. I think Lorence will move on to other things after tonight."

"I still don't understand why Nance and MacKenzie let you go," Mary said suddenly. I was surprised. Mary knew everything. It was the only way for us to even have a chance of moving forward. I had spent many nights asking myself the same question, but this was the first time Mary had brought it up. Then I got it. To contemplate closure, she had to understand it all.

"I was probably a threat to Becker and he might have turned on me if he had shot Nance," I began slowly. "Nance was chasing Dylan in the woods. MacKenzie had just killed a man. I was down a ravine. It was a strategic gamble by Nance and especially MacKenzie to let me be. Nance was going to disappear anyway. Start over with a new identity. I don't think he would ever count on Putin keeping his end of the deal. I never actually saw him kill Dylan. All and all, I was no real threat to him. Mackenzie's reasons are harder to follow. The government would never acknowledge Becker's death and Mackenzie was an unknown outlier. His priority was to dispose of Becker's body quickly before some hunter happened by. Time was of the essence and I was down a ravine.

Whether his shove was impulsive or purposeful, I don't know. He might have thought he didn't have time to go down the slope in the dark, finish me, then haul me back up to his Range Rover. He knew Nance thought of me as a friend and he might have been concerned Nance would retaliate if he harmed me." I paused. Mary was listening intently.

I continued. "I believe Mackenzie thought I was just a bumbling doctor and had no skin in the game. If I ended up dead the government cover-up might be blown with too much attention. So that wouldn't work. If I talked, there would be a good chance people wouldn't believe me. I could be easily framed, or at least ruined. In the end, to them I was a little fish and their best play was to throw me back into the water."

"So, the government told Lorence to keep an eye on you to make sure you wouldn't be a problem?" Mary asked.

"That's the way I see it. I don't know how involved Lorence is or even how much he knows. He's a survivor though and he knows who butters his bread."

We both sipped our drinks in silence for a while.

"I've a question for you," I said. "The Sheriff told me Tiger was found in Dylan's jacket pocket when he died. What was Dylan doing with Tiger in his pocket?"

Mary took a deep breath. "Dylan knew Tiger meant a lot to me. He never knew why. I guess he thought it was something from my childhood. I let him believe that little white lie. But one day he surprised me by asking if he could carry it with him when he was away from me. He said it would be like having a part of me with him when we were apart. I was conflicted, but it was so sweet at the time and I said yes."

I let her answer sink in. It was very tender of him and that made me even more melancholy than the act of Mary loaning Tiger to Dylan. Who wouldn't want to feel that important to another person? Mary interrupted my thoughts. She was becoming adept at not letting me spiral down and away.

She got up, came to me and put her hands on my shoulders. Very seriously, she said, "I'm glad they let you go up in the mountains." Her eyes then got misty. "Very glad."

I went to stand and to hug her, but her hands pressed down on my shoulders and she shook her head. Slowly, she composed herself. I wasn't sure if the tears were for me or for Dylan.

"Let's talk about something else," Mary said.

"Okay." She had pulled me out of my dive, but physical interaction wasn't called for. I could go with it. "How were your friends tonight?" I asked, changing gears. "What did you end up doing?"

"We went to the movies," Mary said. She got up and went into the kitchen. She came back with a wine bottle and poured herself a glass of chardonnay. "I'm just going to have a sip," she said, preempting any disapproval I might express at her drinking alcohol for the next few months. "I didn't have any when I was out tonight."

"What movie did you see?" I asked. She raised the bottle to me questioningly. "No thanks," I said.

"An old movie about a woman and an affair," Mary said, turning to go back to the kitchen. She replaced the wine bottle in the refrigerator.

"Maybe I'll have some water, please," I called after her. I pushed aside my empty tumbler. "The Sheriff got me started on scotch." Mary filled an empty glass from the tap. It didn't occur to her to ask where the scotch came from. We usually didn't have scotch around the cabin.

"I'm so glad you accepted the clinic's offer," Mary said.

"So am I," I said. She sat down next to me on the couch. "Tell me about the movie," I asked, as she got settled.

"This housewife is happily married with a child, but then she gets tangled up with a younger man," Mary began. "He helps her out during a bad storm and sparks fly between them. He's French, gorgeous, exotic and a free spirit. He's so unsafe compared to her predictable life that it all seems so exciting and desirable. But it ends badly."

"Did you like it?"

"Well . . . yes, I think so." Then she shivered. "He was . . . dangerous."

We both took sips from our glasses. Both of us thinking of one person in two different ways. She looked wistful and I felt somber. Mary placed her hand on mine and squeezed.

"There was a strange epilogue at the end of the movie," Mary said. "The scene goes back to that first moment when the Frenchman helps the housewife during the storm. Then, when she's okay, instead of getting coffee with him as he suggests, she just thanks him with a smile and a wave. She gets into a cab and goes back to her husband and child." Mary turned and looked directly into my eyes. "The audience realizes when she makes that decision, her path is altered. All that excitement and ugliness never takes place."

*   *   *

The biological purpose of pain is to protect us from injury and avoid harmful situations in the future in order to survive. But chronic pain doesn't protect anyone. It is associated with depression, anxiety, fear and anger. Mary had been a source of pain to me, but I didn't want to be in chronic pain for the rest of my life. Only humans have psychic pain and the brain can be kinder with us in this regard. It can bury the acuity of sorrow under layers of fresh neuronal circuits. We remember, but it doesn't hurt as much. This is also part of our survival mechanism.

It would be difficult to describe my relationship with Mary in the first weeks after Dylan died. We kept our separate residences. When we started to tentatively see each other again, we moved at glacier-like speed.

But I was stuck. There were some things I needed to know if we were ever going to get past Dylan's death.

"Did you know what Dylan was up to Mary?" I
asked one night when we were having dinner at her
apartment.

She looked down at her food for a long moment.
Then she raised her chin and looked me straight in
the eye. "I didn't know, Harper. Maybe I didn't want
to know. I knew he was doing something more than
technical support for the tower project, but when I
probed him on his work he became evasive." Mary
dropped her eyes back down to her plate and picked
at her food with her fork. Without looking up, she
added, "I think...I think he was trying to protect
me."

"That was very honorable of him," I said.
I waited for her to continue, but realized her eyes
were tearing. I waited until she had gathered herself
and decided to push on. I wanted to get this behind
us. I didn't want multiple conversational forays into
this territory. Emotional reaction on both sides was
inevitable and hopefully, healthy and healing.

"What was it about Dylan for you?" I got the
question out, but it was hard to ask. I wasn't sure
I needed to know the answer, but I thought Mary
needed to tell me. In the end, I was wrong. Making
sense of what happened, freed me as well.

"I sensed he was doing something...dark. I
found it...exciting. I've always been the good girl.
Done the right thing. I could see the edge in Dylan
and it was exhilarating. I felt like a moth attracted to
the flame of his danger. I don't know if it – us - would
have lasted, but I felt so alive when I was with him. I
didn't agree with him a lot, but I was intoxicated by

his passion." She hesitated for a moment. Her eyes dropped down and then slowly came up to meet me. "There's something else I'm not proud of at all." I waited. "I was so torn between loving you and being in lust with Dylan ... it was tearing me up inside." She took a deep breath as tears came to her eyes. "When we went to the morgue and the sheriff said Dylan was dead, I was sad, of course." She was pleading with me to understand. "But, I hated myself, because ... I part of me I'm not proud of, also felt relief. What we had was unsustainable. It was too intense for me. If Dylan hadn't died, it would have killed me. Do you understand?"

I hesitated. "I ... think so."

"Do you think I'm an awful person?"

"No. I do not. I think love is a difficult road to travel. Some roads are more treacherous than others." Mary dabbed at her tears. I had not convinced her.

"Did you see him the night he died?" I asked.

"No, I had an appointment with my ob-gyn doctor in Tucson. Dylan called me while I was in Tucson. He wanted to get together, but I told him I wanted to talk to both of you. He said he had a work meeting and suggested the three of us meet at your cabin around 10:00PM."

"You called the meeting?"

Mary was looking right at me now. "Yes." She registered my surprise.

"Dylan didn't know you were pregnant?"

She held her gaze. "No."

I turned this information over in my mind. Mary did not wait for me.

"You see, either of you could be the father."

"Dylan never knew."

"No."

"Do you want to know?" I asked.

"No." Mary looked away. She focused on the picture window, but it was nighttime, the curtains were drawn and there was nothing to see. She turned back to me.

"Do you?" she asked.

"I don't need to know."

*   *   *

After a while it became sensible to not drive home late at night. When we did stay the night together we slept in different bedrooms. We shared meals and went through the polite ceremonies of a new courtship. Mary was often lost in her thoughts and I was careful not to intrude on that voyage she had unto herself. Then one night during an early seasonal monsoon storm that was raging outside the cabin, she came to me in my room where I had fallen asleep reading a book. With a mystical combination of lightning, wind and torrential rain engulfing the outside of the cabin I felt the covers pull back and Mary joined me in bed. She spooned beside me and placed her left arm over my side. I could feel the warm heat and silky skin of her body against mine. Lightning flashes from the bedside window silhouetted our bodies against the far bedroom wall. The shadowy lines were distinct yet appeared to be one figure. A searing tear fell on my upper back, but I did not move. In time, we both fell asleep.

The light of morning woke me and I rolled over to face Mary. The storm outside had passed and all was very still. I could feel the energy of nature surrounding the cabin. It had been restored and rejuvenated by the rain. Mary's eyes slowly opened and consciousness seeped through her brain. She leaned slowly into me and ever-so-softly placed her mouth onto mine. I savored the sweetness and her weight shifting onto me. I tenderly caressed her expanding belly and felt a tiny kick. The fullness of her breasts began to push against me and with exquisite gentleness I placed my arms around her and dared to hold her. Her breath began to quicken and mine caught in my throat. For how often in life can pain and love merge successfully with acceptance, tenderness and reaffirmation? I didn't deserve Mary; perhaps she didn't deserve me. However, if people only coupled because they were worthy of each other, the world would be an even more sorrowful and lonely place.

After Dylan died and Mary came back to me, I noticed a feeling apace with my love. Initially, I couldn't put my finger on it. It was a good feeling but I couldn't quite crystallize it. Eventually it came back to me: this is what hope feels like. I thought of Dylan and how relieved he looked when I came out of surgery. I put my arm around Mary and she nestled into me easily, naturally. We kissed. Each act of love is a form of dying. Not just the sperm or the egg, but rather a step closer to the end. One less time you will make love in your lifetime. The act that gives us life, whittling yet another notch on one's timeline. Perhaps in our future, we could have this child together.

END

About the Author

Derrik F. Woodbury has been a licensed physician for 42 years. His writing has contributed to scientific medical journals as well as his favorite topic of medical education. In the early 1980's he was asked to do educational topics on television and became one of the first health reporters in the United States. For his reporting, he won an Associated Press award and was nominated for New England Emmys. His article - "An Untimely Frost" - on the death of his young wife to ovarian cancer won second place in the Sunday Newspaper Supplement national competition for the year 1995.

Dr. Woodbury has climbed the highest mountains on five continents and his documentaries have appeared on CBS and ESPN. He wrote, directed and produced a feature 35mm film which was shown at Sundance, Cannes and the New York Film Festival.

He received his M.D. from Dartmouth Medical School and his surgical training from Georgetown, Dartmouth and the University of Pennsylvania. He has two children and lives in Arizona and Connecticut.